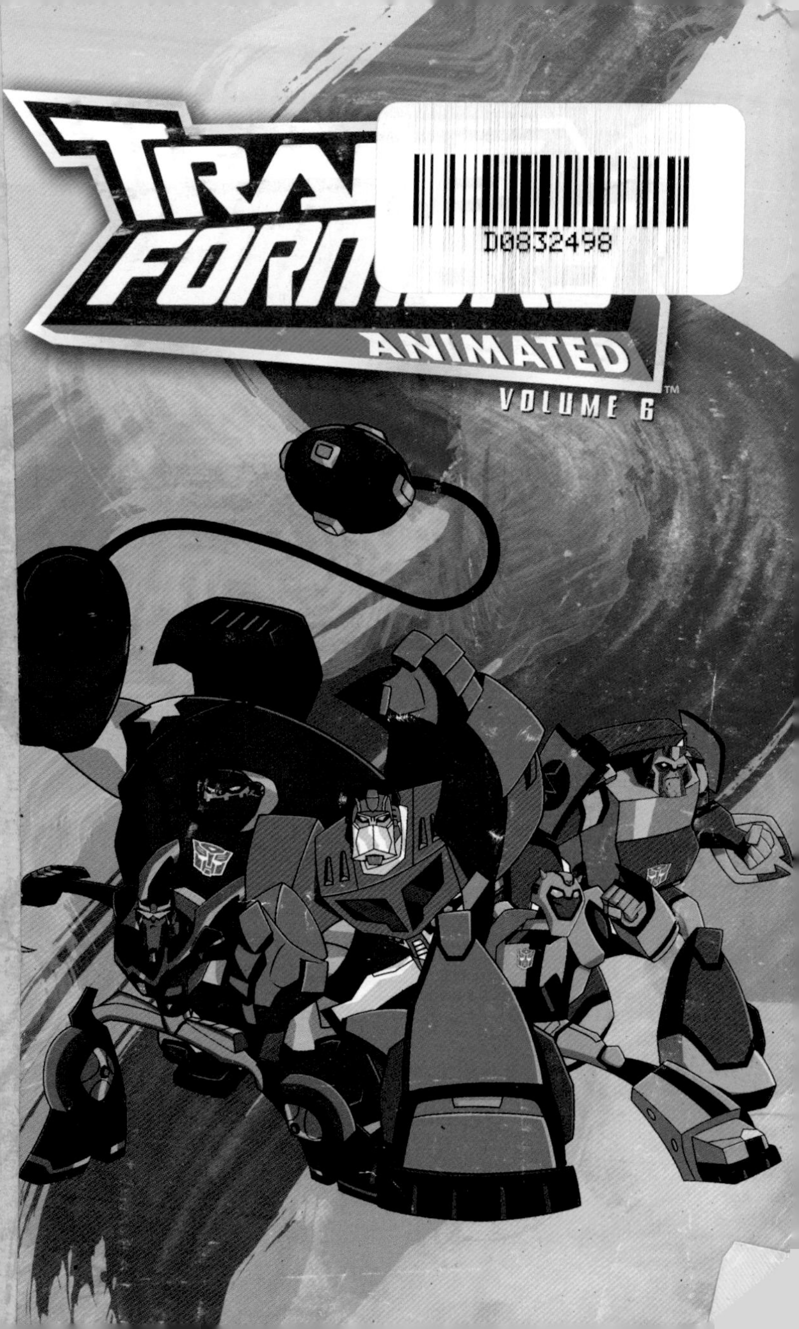
ANIMATED
VOLUME 6

HEADMASTER

WRITTEN BY:
MICHAEL RYAN

WHEN NATURE CALLS

WRITTEN BY:
TODD CASEY

ADAPTATION BY:
ZACHARY RAU

EDITS BY:
JUSTIN EISINGER

LETTERS AND DESIGN BY:
TOM B. LONG

ISBN: 978-1-60010-281-3
11 10 9 8 1 2 3 4 5

Licensed by:

Special thanks to Hasbro's Aaron Archer, Michael Kelly, Amie Lozanski, Val Roca, Ed Lane, Michael Provost, Erin Hillman, Samantha Lomow, and Michael Verrecchia for their invaluable assistance.

IDW Publishing is:
Operations:
Moshe Berger, Chairman
Ted Adams, Chief Executive Officer
Greg Goldstein, Chief Operating Officer
Matthew Ruzicka, CPA, Chief Financial Officer
Editorial:
Chris Ryall, Publisher/Editor-in-Chief
Scott Dunbier, Editor, Special Projects
Andy Schmidt, Senior Editor
Justin Eisinger, Editor
Design:
Robbie Robbins, EVP/Sr. Graphic Artist
Ben Templesmith, Artist/Designer
Neil Uyetake, Art Director

Alan Payne, VP of Sales
Lorelei Bunjes, Dir. of Digital Services
Marci Hubbard, Executive Assistant
Alonzo Simon, Shipping Manager

Kris Oprisko, Editor/Foreign Lic.
Denton J. Tipton, Editor
Tom Waltz, Editor
Mariah Huehner, Assistant Editor

Chris Mowry, Graphic Artist
Amauri Osorio, Graphic Artist

To discuss this issue of *Transformers*, or join the IDW Insiders, or to check out exclusive Web offers, check out our site:

www.IDWPUBLISHING.com

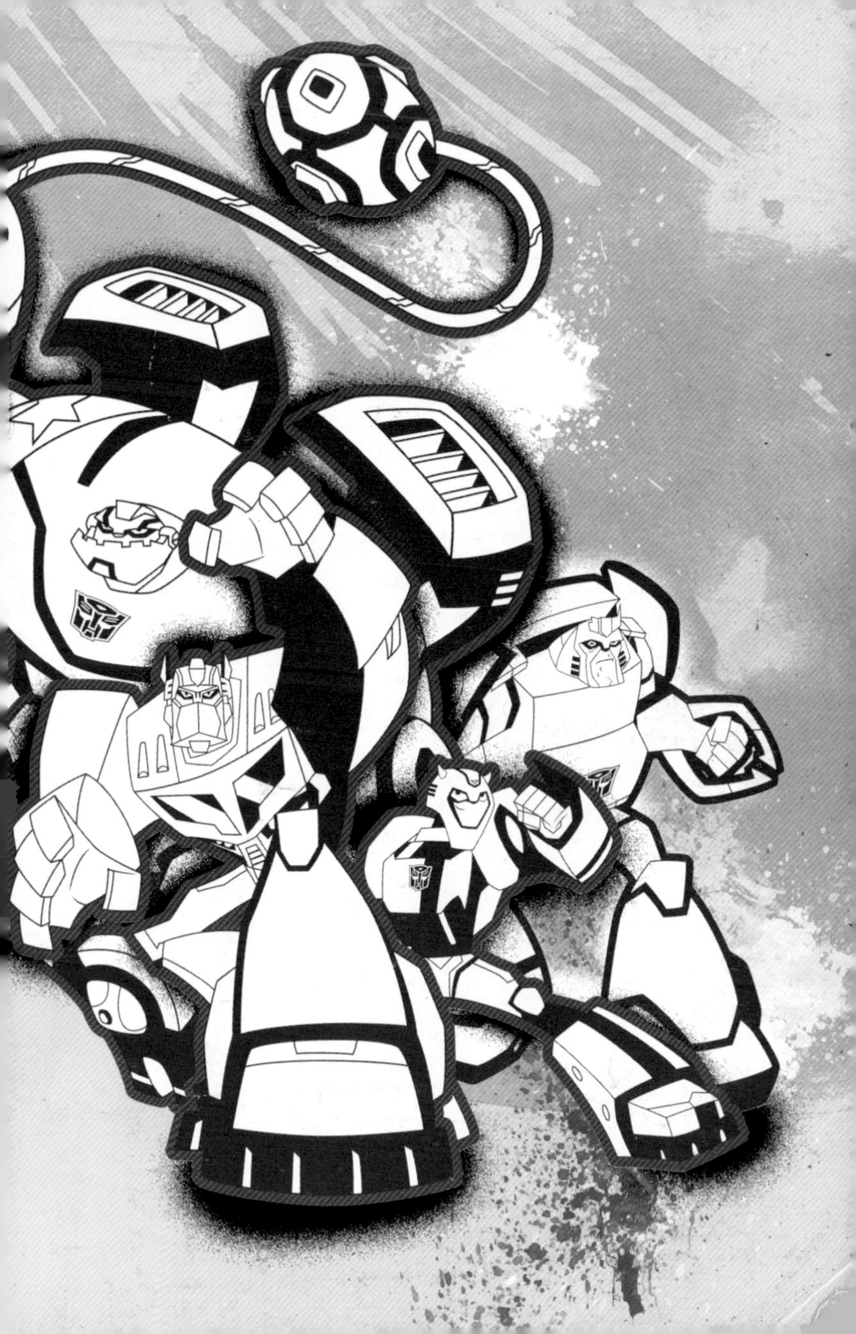

Roll Call

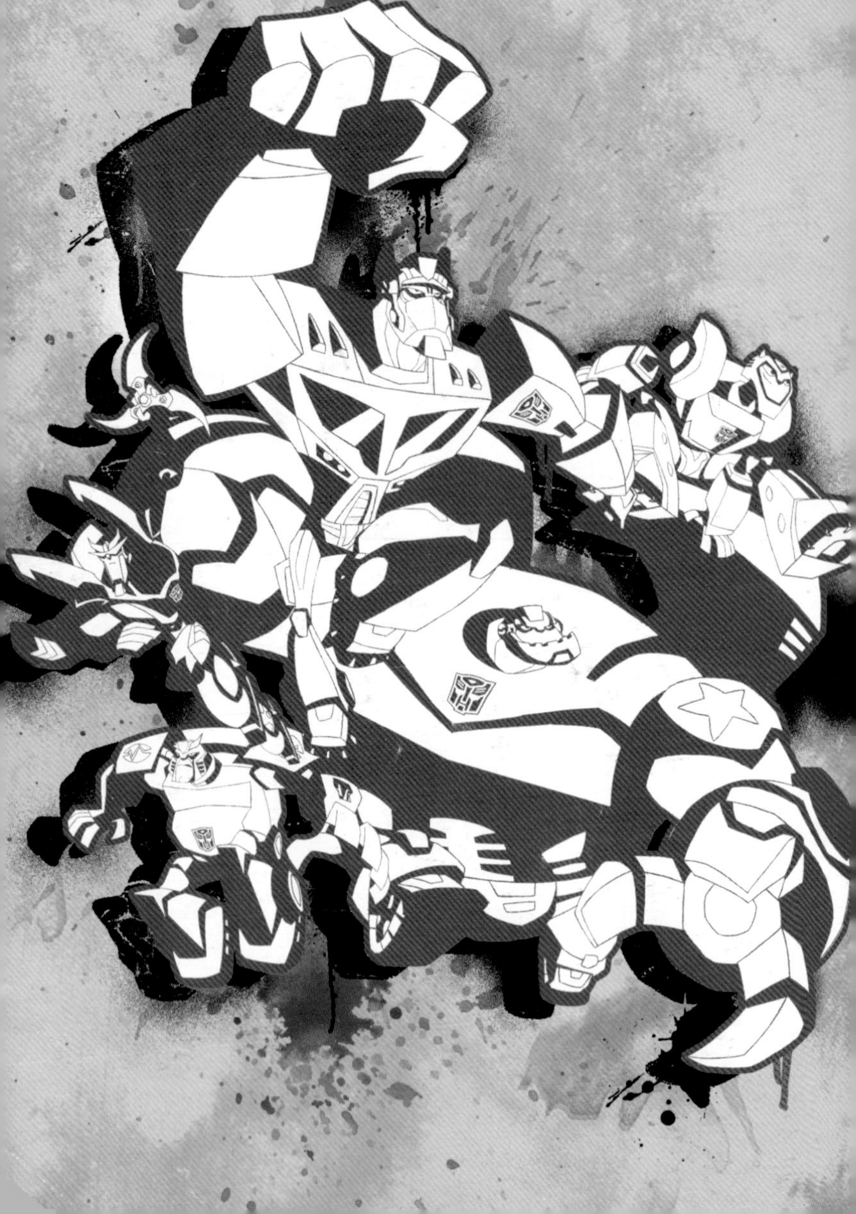

Optimus Prime

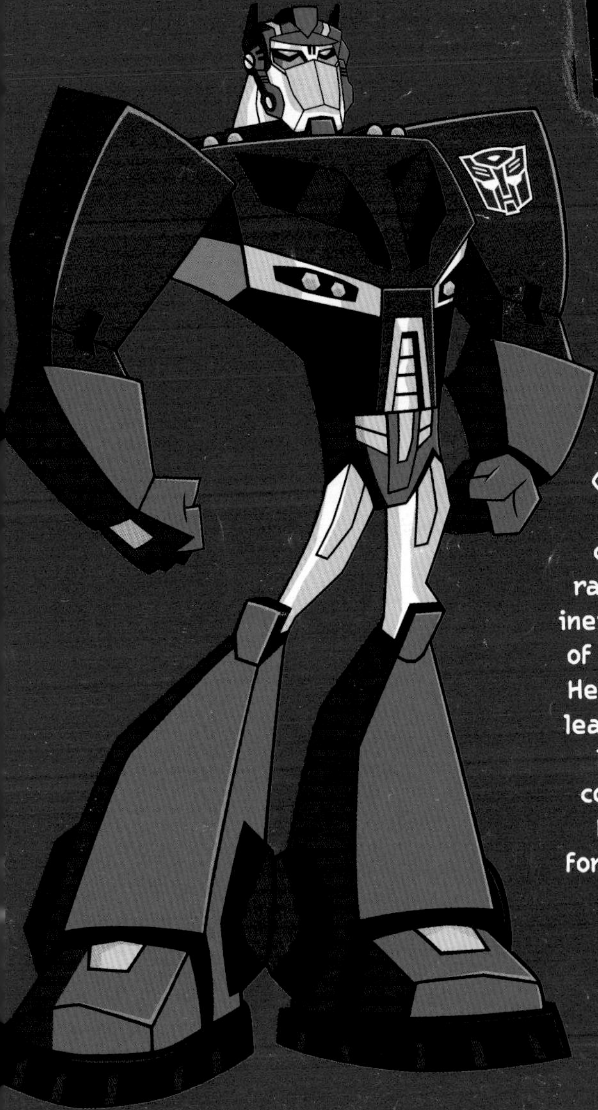

OPTIMUS PRIME is the young commander of a ragtag and largely inexperienced group of misfit AUTOBOTS. He's not the kind of leader who needs to bark orders to command respect. His mechanized form is a fire truck.

Ratchet

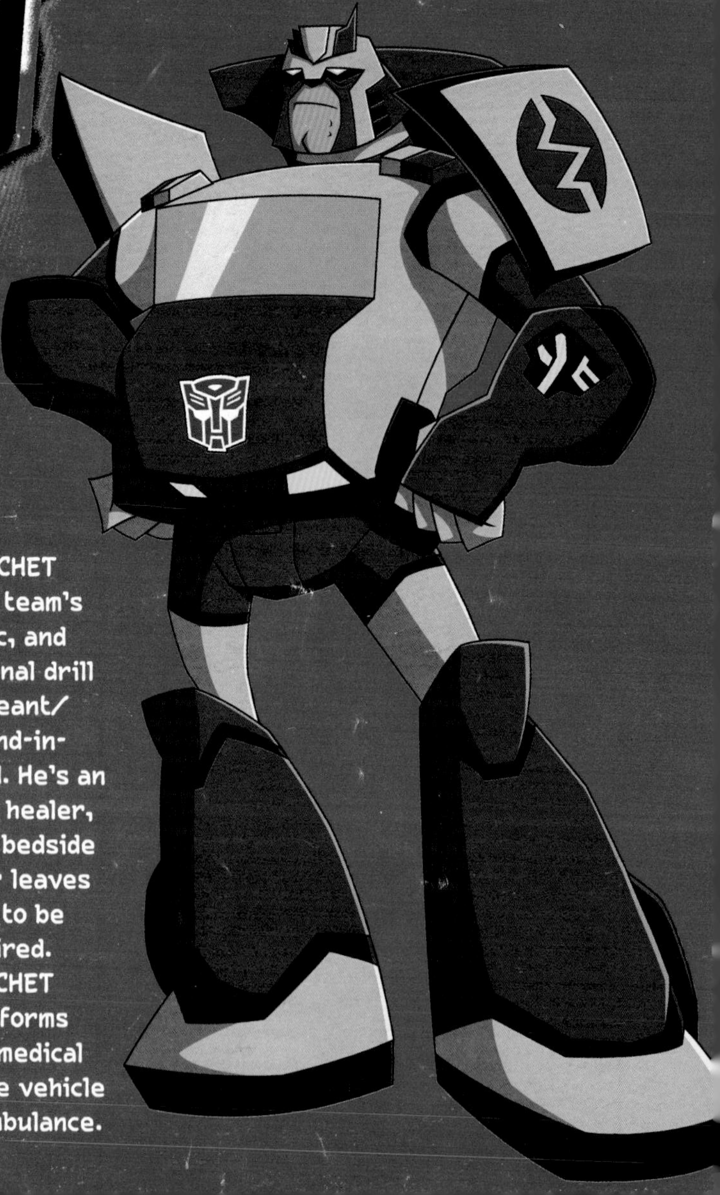

RATCHET is the team's medic, and occasional drill sergeant/second-in-command. He's an expert healer, but his bedside manner leaves a lot to be desired. RATCHET transforms into a medical response vehicle or an ambulance.

Bulkhead

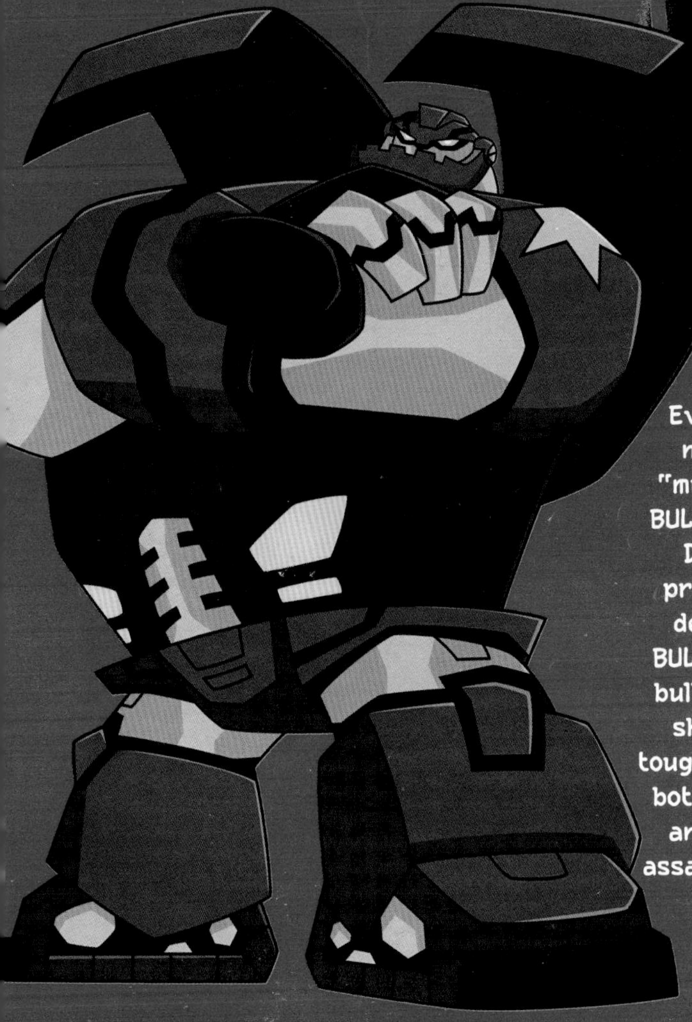

Every team needs its "muscle" and BULKHEAD is it. Designed primarily for demolition, BULKHEAD is a bull in a china shop. He is tough as nails in both his robot and S.W.A.T. assault cruiser forms.

Bumblebee

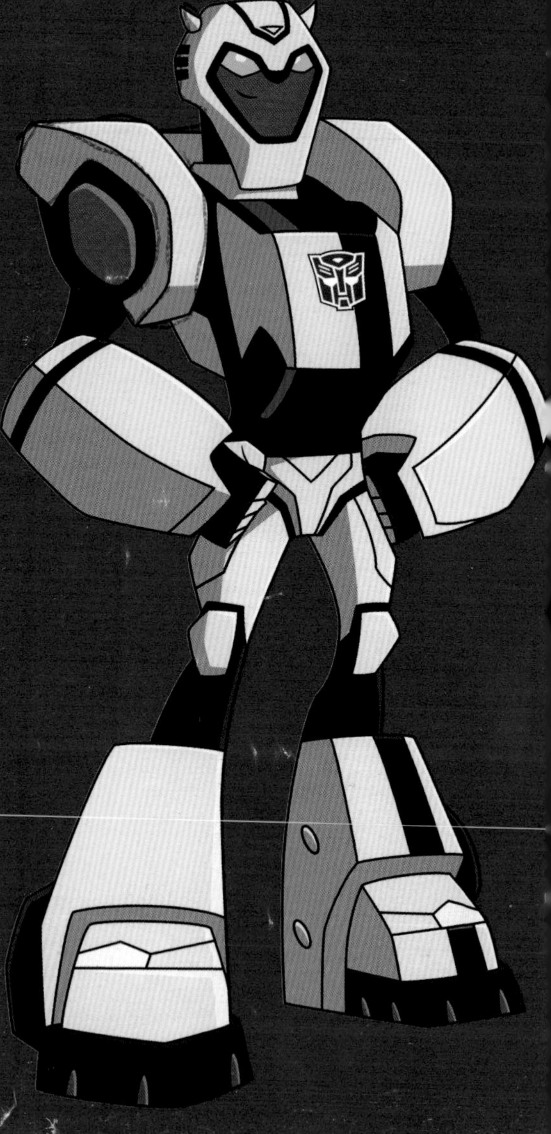

BUMBLEBEE is the "kid" of the team, easily the youngest and least mature of the AUTOBOTS. He's a bit of a showoff, always acting on impulse and rarely considering the consequences. But he looks awesome in his undercover police cruiser form.

Prowl

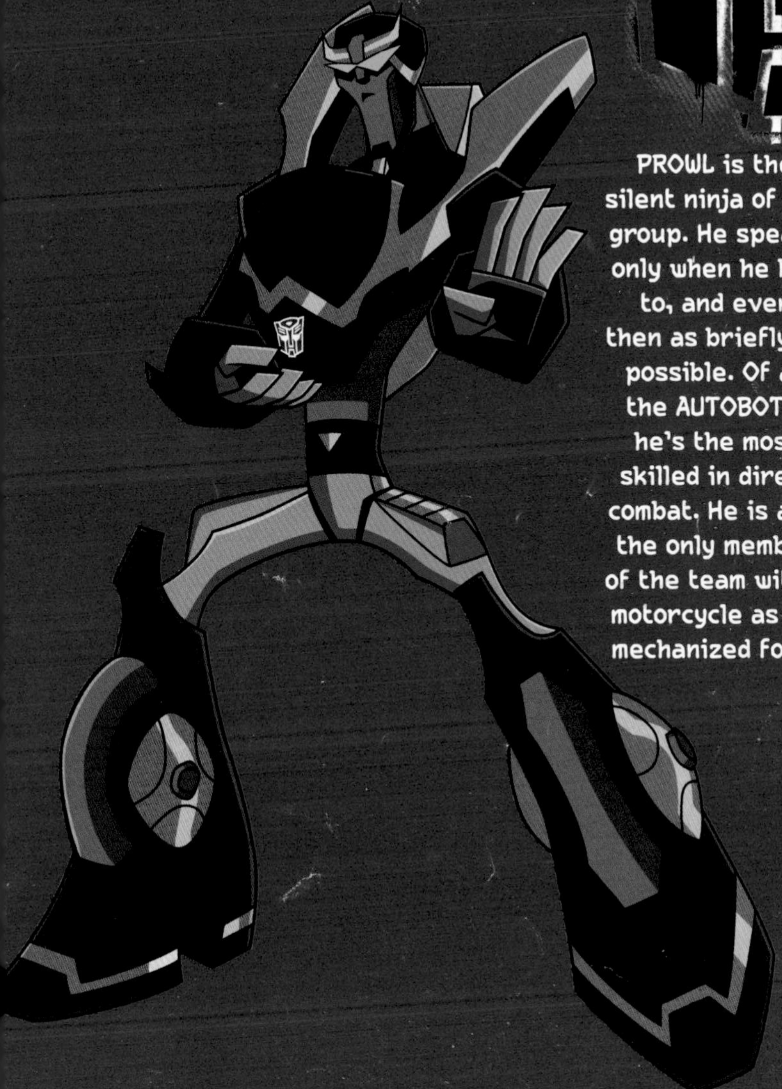

PROWL is the silent ninja of the group. He speaks only when he has to, and even then as briefly as possible. Of all the AUTOBOTS, he's the most skilled in direct combat. He is also the only member of the team with a motorcycle as his mechanized form.

Sari

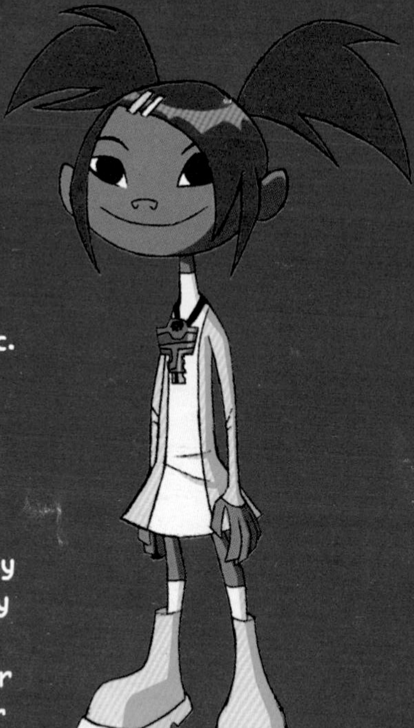

SARI is the adopted daughter of Professor Sumdac. Call it an accident or call it destiny, but the AllSpark projected part of itself onto her in the form of a key. Wearing it on a chain around her neck, SARI can use the key to absorb the AllSpark energy and store it like a battery, providing an emergency power supply and healing source for the AUTOBOTS in battle. It also provides her with an almost psychic connection to the AUTOBOTS.

Professor Sumdac

One night in the late
21st Century, the young
SUMDAC thought he saw
a falling star cascade into
his back field, but it was
something much better.
It was the smoldering,
non-functioning remains
of the head of an alien robot,
MEGATRON. In the decades
that passed while the
AUTOBOTS slumbered in
stasis at the bottom of Lake
Erie, SUMDAC was able
to reverse engineer the
Cybertronian technology
within MEGATRON and usher
in the Automatronic
Revolution of the
22nd Century.

Captain Fanzone

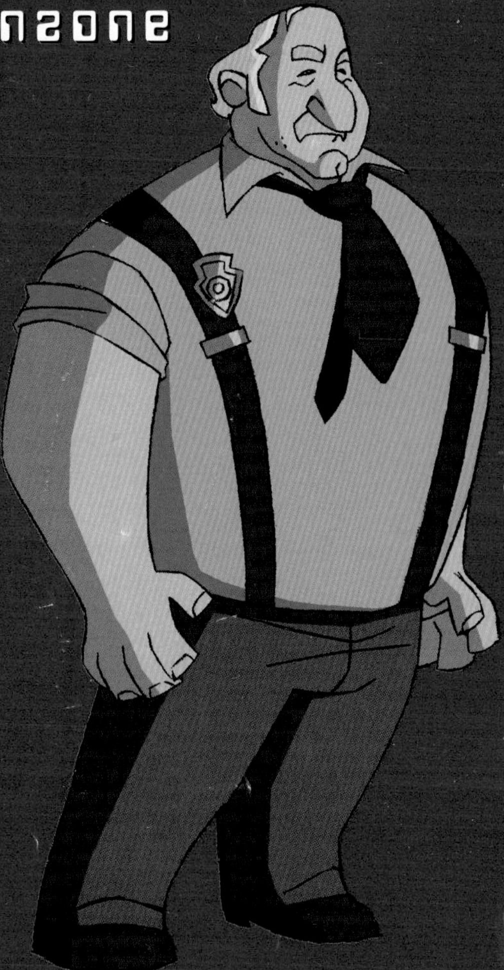

CAPTAIN FANZONE is not an AUTOBOT, but a police detective whose car was scanned to become the vehicle mode for BUMBLEBEE. He's a harried, overworked, but basically good and honest cop, albeit one whose day is perpetually ruined by one of those "giant walking toasters."

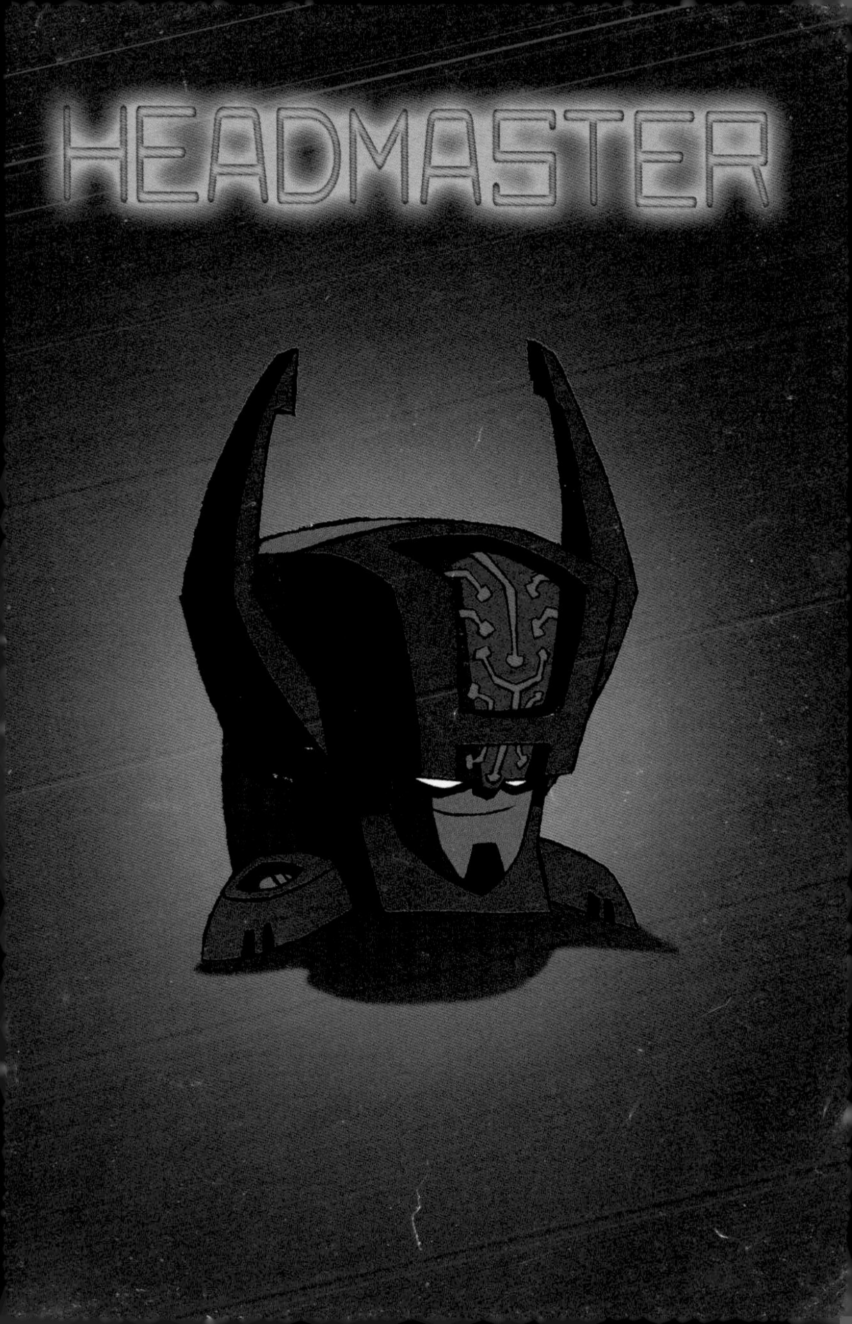
HEADMASTER

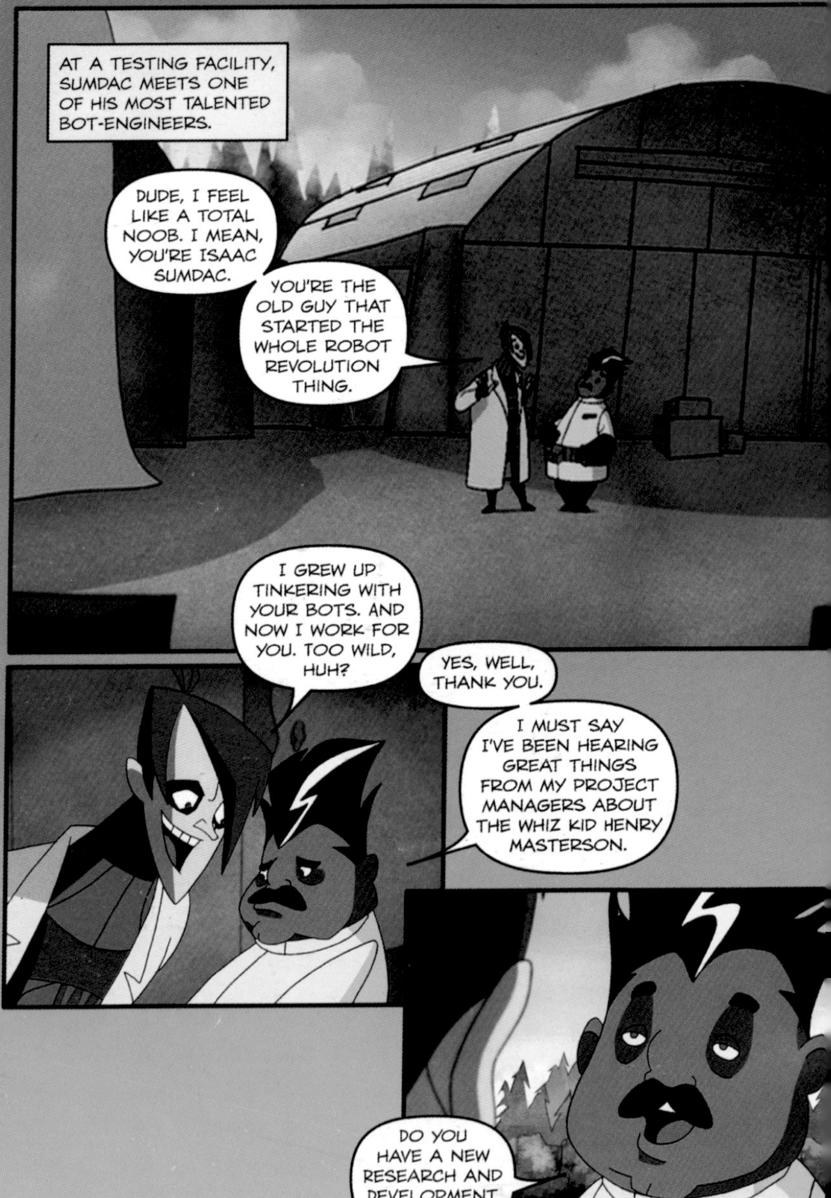
AT A TESTING FACILITY, SUMDAC MEETS ONE OF HIS MOST TALENTED BOT-ENGINEERS.
DUDE, I FEEL LIKE A TOTAL NOOB. I MEAN, YOU'RE ISAAC SUMDAC.
YOU'RE THE OLD GUY THAT STARTED THE WHOLE ROBOT REVOLUTION THING.
I GREW UP TINKERING WITH YOUR BOTS. AND NOW I WORK FOR YOU. TOO WILD, HUH?
YES, WELL, THANK YOU.
I MUST SAY I'VE BEEN HEARING GREAT THINGS FROM MY PROJECT MANAGERS ABOUT THE WHIZ KID HENRY MASTERSON.
DO YOU HAVE A NEW RESEARCH AND DEVELOPMENT IDEA?

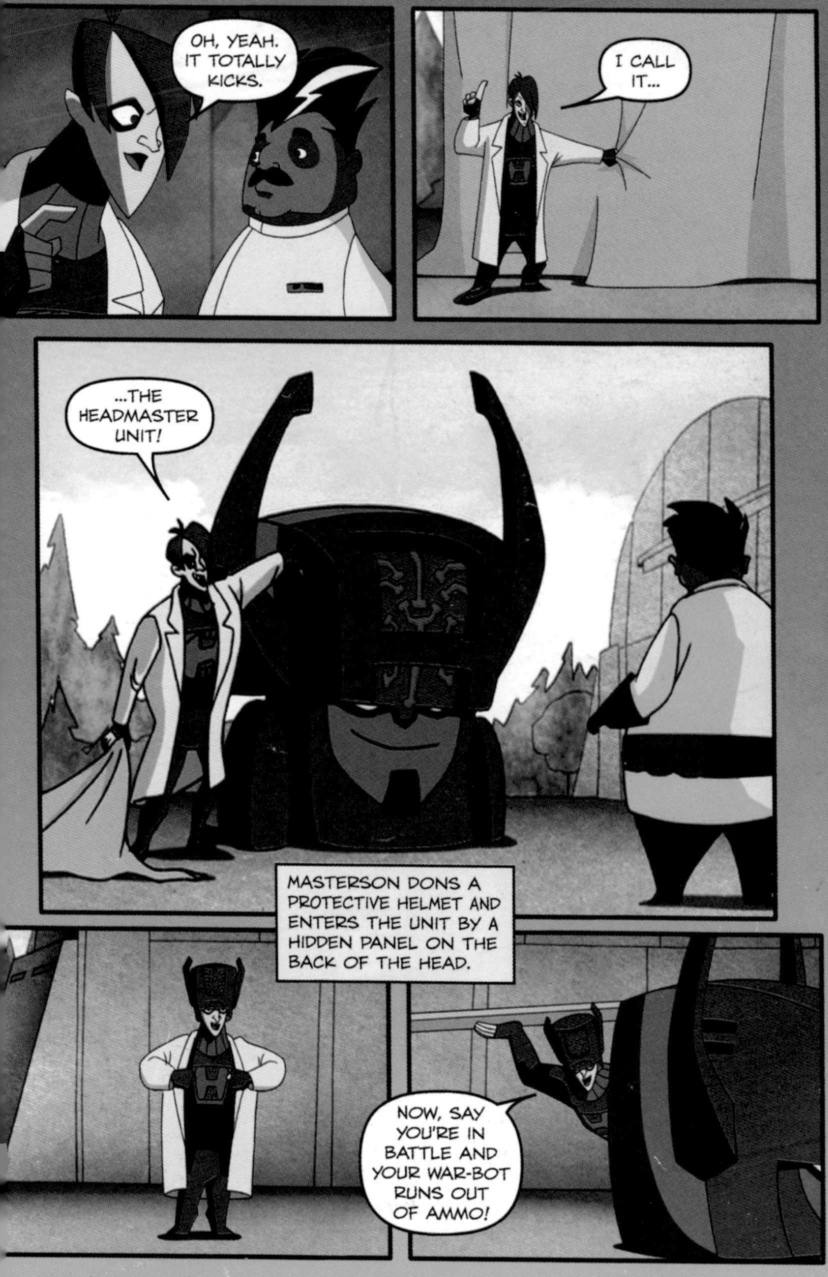
OH, YEAH. IT TOTALLY KICKS.
I CALL IT...
...THE HEADMASTER UNIT!
MASTERSON DONS A PROTECTIVE HELMET AND ENTERS THE UNIT BY A HIDDEN PANEL ON THE BACK OF THE HEAD.
NOW, SAY YOU'RE IN BATTLE AND YOUR WAR-BOT RUNS OUT OF AMMO!

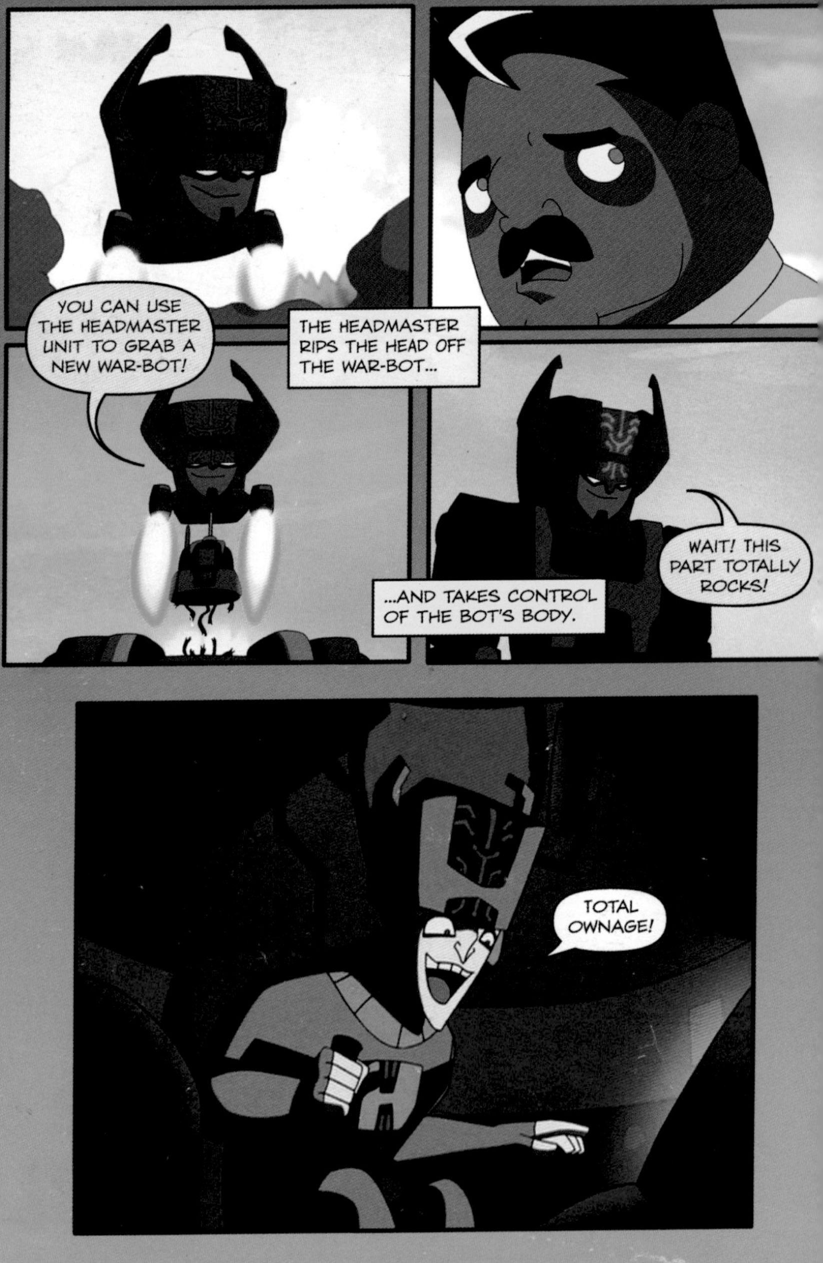
YOU CAN USE THE HEADMASTER UNIT TO GRAB A NEW WAR-BOT!
THE HEADMASTER RIPS THE HEAD OFF THE WAR-BOT...
...AND TAKES CONTROL OF THE BOT'S BODY.
WAIT! THIS PART TOTALLY ROCKS!
TOTAL OWNAGE!

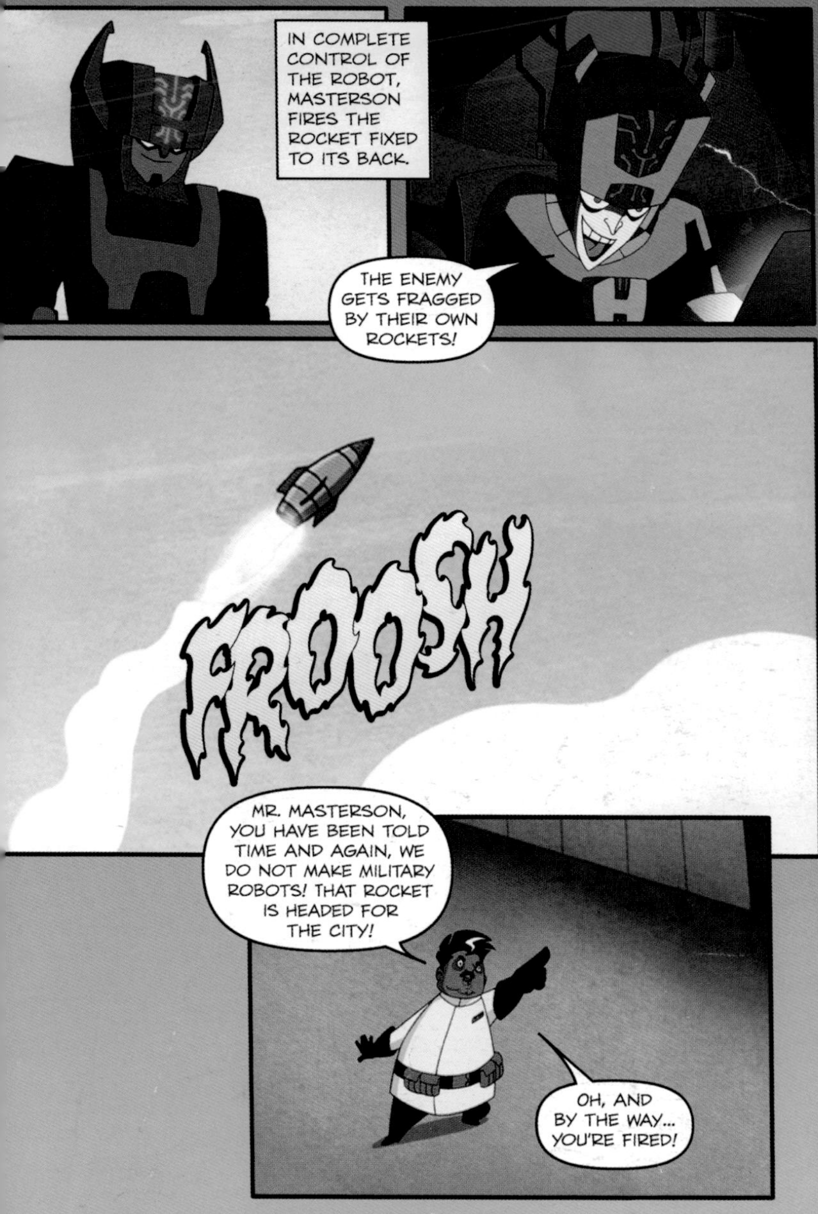
IN COMPLETE CONTROL OF THE ROBOT, MASTERSON FIRES THE ROCKET FIXED TO ITS BACK.
THE ENEMY GETS FRAGGED BY THEIR OWN ROCKETS!
FROOSH
MR. MASTERSON, YOU HAVE BEEN TOLD TIME AND AGAIN, WE DO NOT MAKE MILITARY ROBOTS! THAT ROCKET IS HEADED FOR THE CITY!
OH, AND BY THE WAY... YOU'RE FIRED!

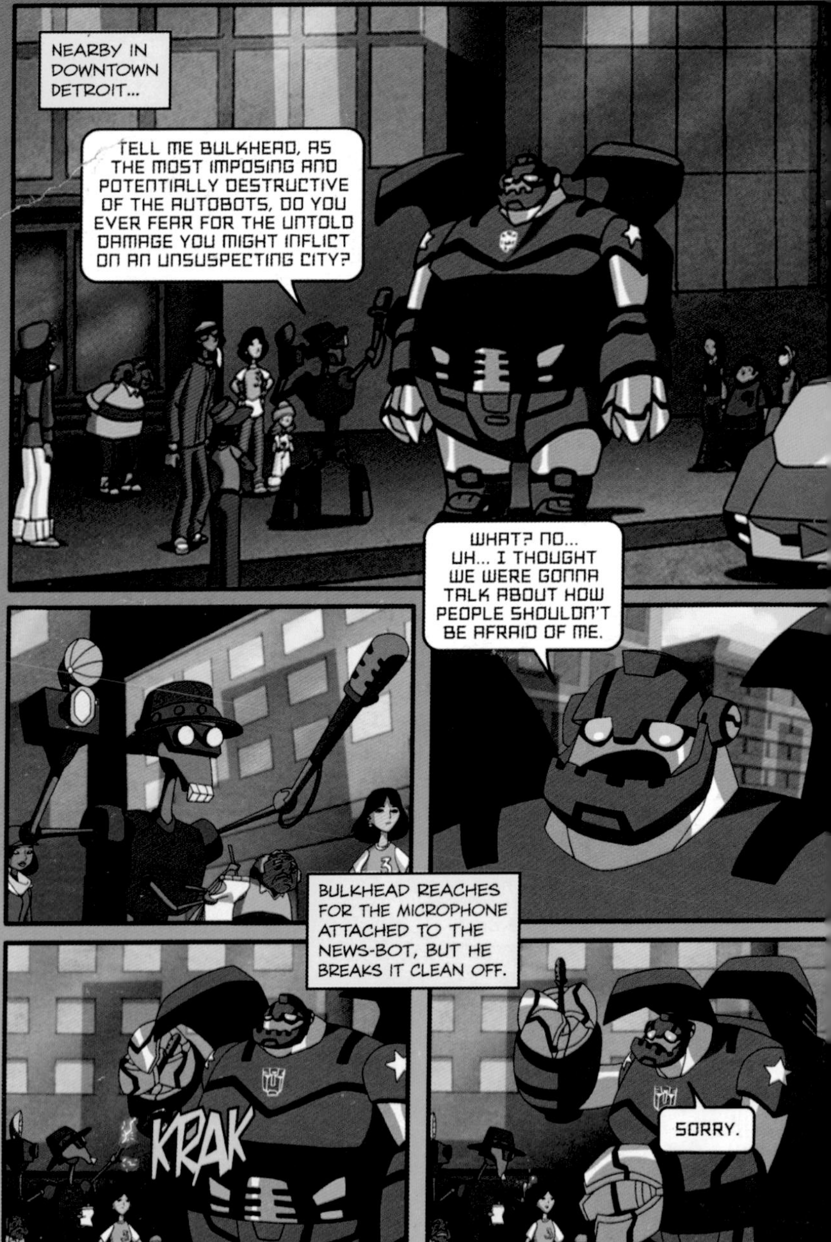
NEARBY IN DOWNTOWN DETROIT...
TELL ME BULKHEAD, AS THE MOST IMPOSING AND POTENTIALLY DESTRUCTIVE OF THE AUTOBOTS, DO YOU EVER FEAR FOR THE UNTOLD DAMAGE YOU MIGHT INFLICT ON AN UNSUSPECTING CITY?
WHAT? NO... UH... I THOUGHT WE WERE GONNA TALK ABOUT HOW PEOPLE SHOULDN'T BE AFRAID OF ME.
BULKHEAD REACHES FOR THE MICROPHONE ATTACHED TO THE NEWS-BOT, BUT HE BREAKS IT CLEAN OFF.
KRAK
SORRY.

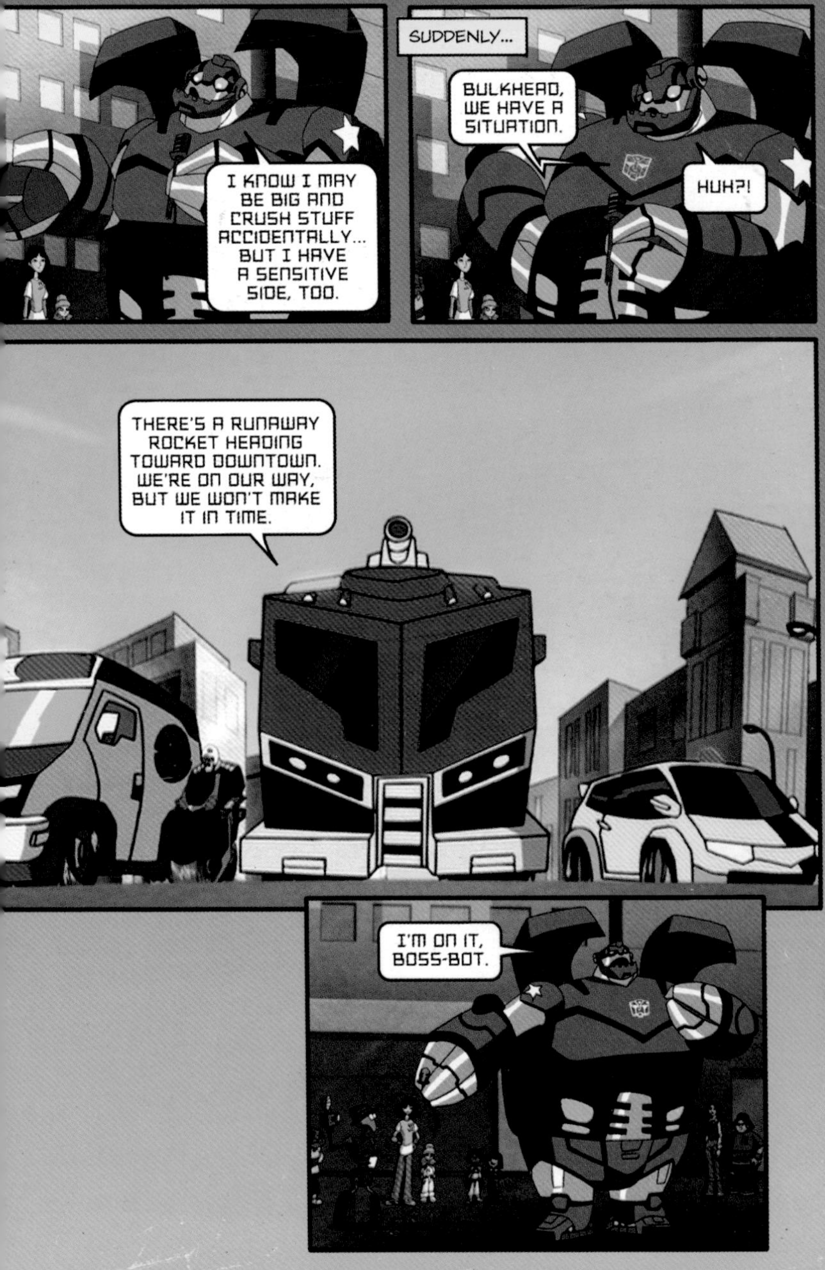
I KNOW I MAY BE BIG AND CRUSH STUFF ACCIDENTALLY... BUT I HAVE A SENSITIVE SIDE, TOO.
SUDDENLY...
BULKHEAD, WE HAVE A SITUATION.
HUH?!
THERE'S A RUNAWAY ROCKET HEADING TOWARD DOWNTOWN. WE'RE ON OUR WAY, BUT WE WON'T MAKE IT IN TIME.
I'M ON IT, BOSS-BOT.

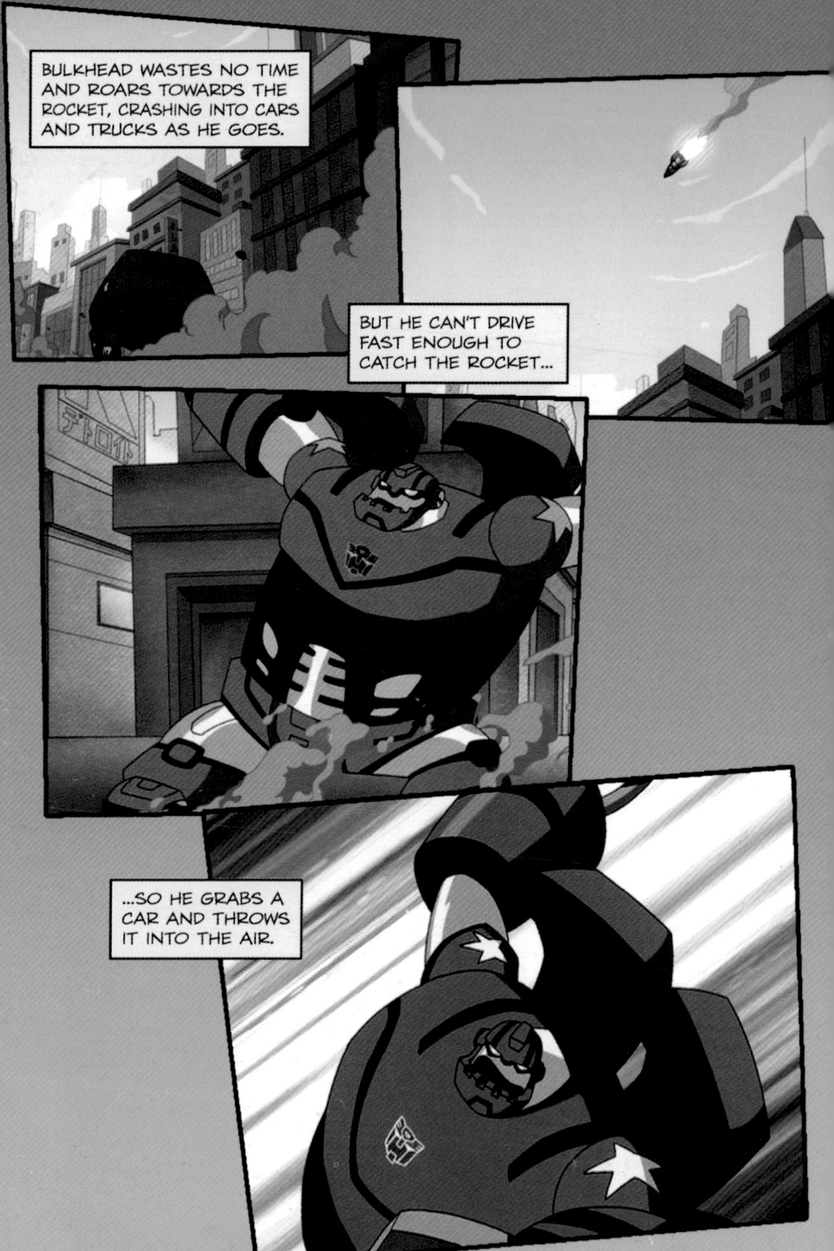
BULKHEAD WASTES NO TIME AND ROARS TOWARDS THE ROCKET, CRASHING INTO CARS AND TRUCKS AS HE GOES.
BUT HE CAN'T DRIVE FAST ENOUGH TO CATCH THE ROCKET...
...SO HE GRABS A CAR AND THROWS IT INTO THE AIR.

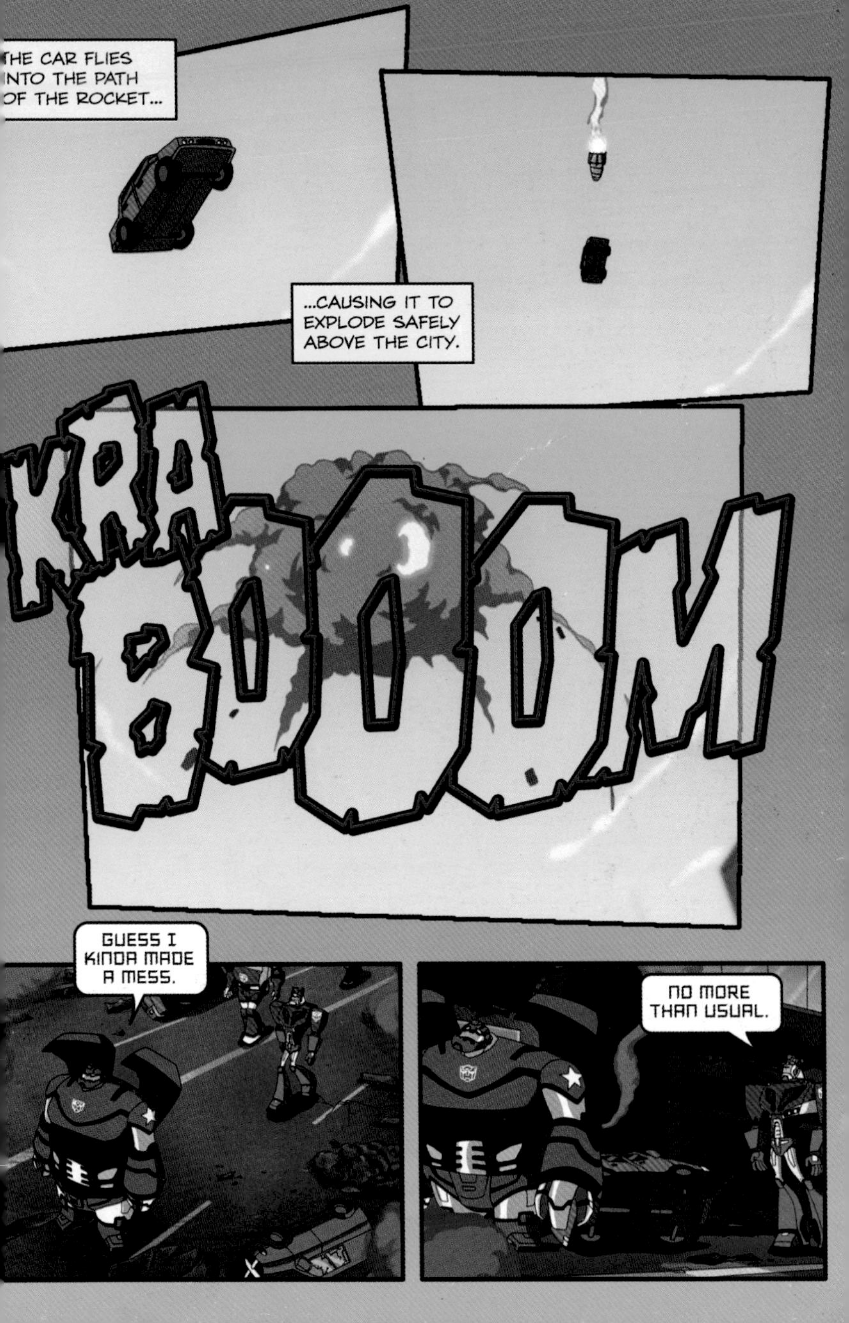
THE CAR FLIES INTO THE PATH OF THE ROCKET...
...CAUSING IT TO EXPLODE SAFELY ABOVE THE CITY.
KRA BOOOM
GUESS I KINDA MADE A MESS.
NO MORE THAN USUAL.

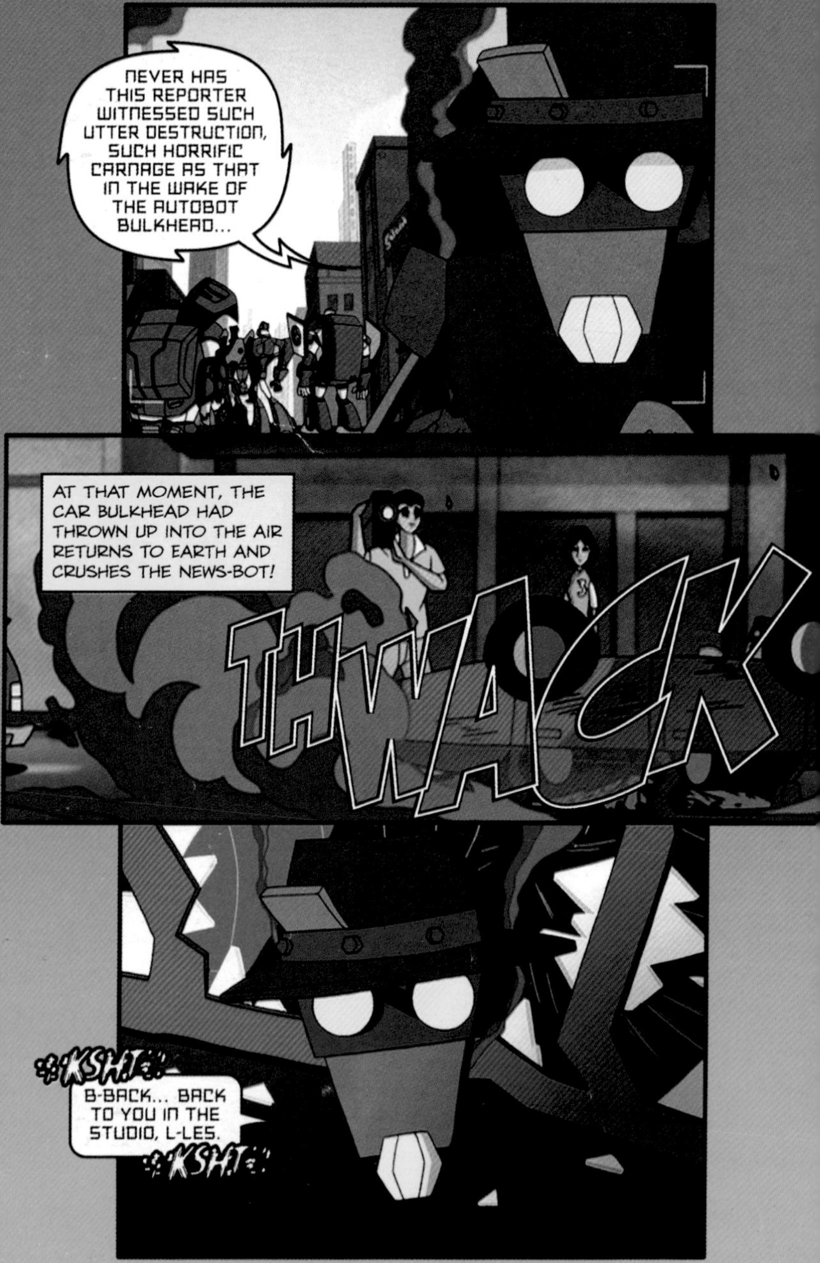
NEVER HAS THIS REPORTER WITNESSED SUCH UTTER DESTRUCTION, SUCH HORRIFIC CARNAGE AS THAT IN THE WAKE OF THE AUTOBOT BULKHEAD...
AT THAT MOMENT, THE CAR BULKHEAD HAD THROWN UP INTO THE AIR RETURNS TO EARTH AND CRUSHES THE NEWS-BOT!
THWACK
KSHT
B-BACK... BACK TO YOU IN THE STUDIO, L-LES.
KSHT

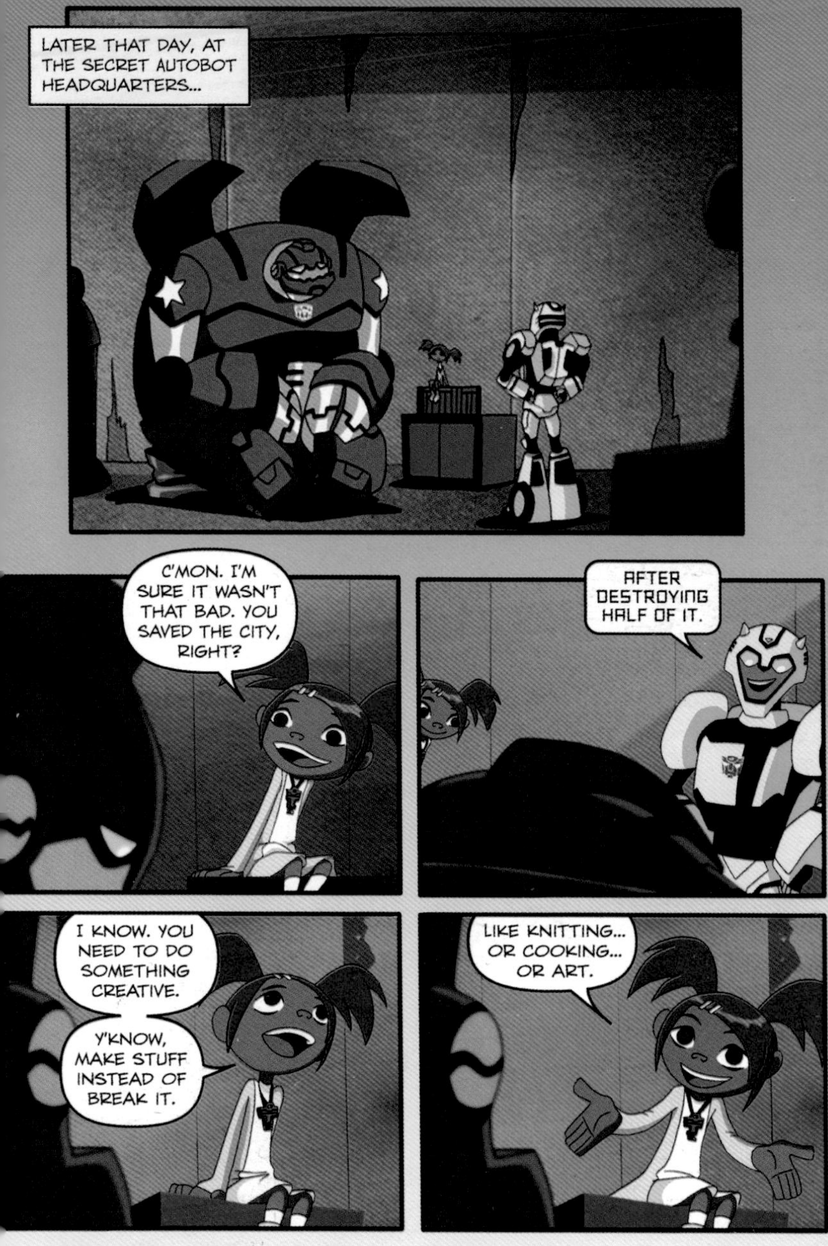
LATER THAT DAY, AT THE SECRET AUTOBOT HEADQUARTERS...
C'MON. I'M SURE IT WASN'T THAT BAD. YOU SAVED THE CITY, RIGHT?
AFTER DESTROYING HALF OF IT.
I KNOW. YOU NEED TO DO SOMETHING CREATIVE.
Y'KNOW, MAKE STUFF INSTEAD OF BREAK IT.
LIKE KNITTING... OR COOKING... OR ART.

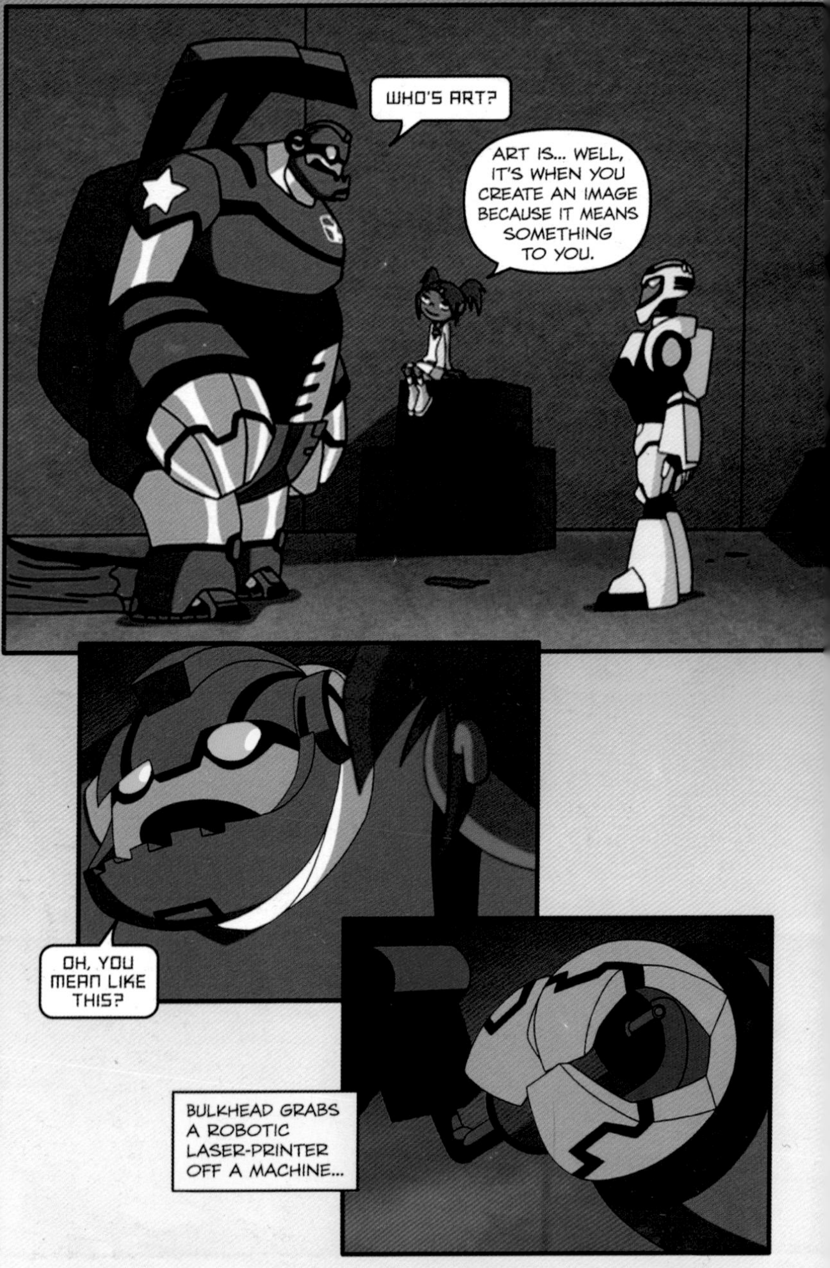
WHO'S ART?
ART IS... WELL, IT'S WHEN YOU CREATE AN IMAGE BECAUSE IT MEANS SOMETHING TO YOU.
OH, YOU MEAN LIKE THIS?
BULKHEAD GRABS A ROBOTIC LASER-PRINTER OFF A MACHINE...

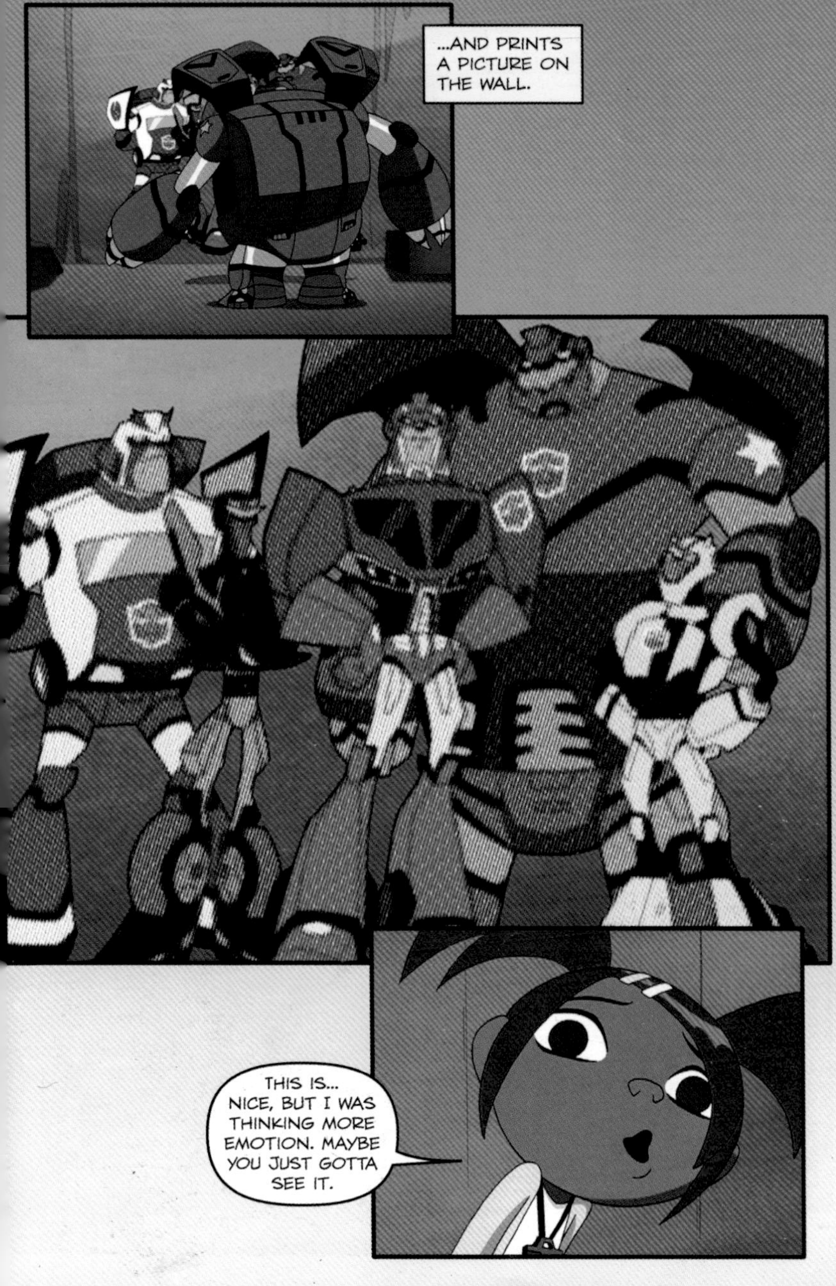
...AND PRINTS A PICTURE ON THE WALL.
THIS IS... NICE, BUT I WAS THINKING MORE EMOTION. MAYBE YOU JUST GOTTA SEE IT.

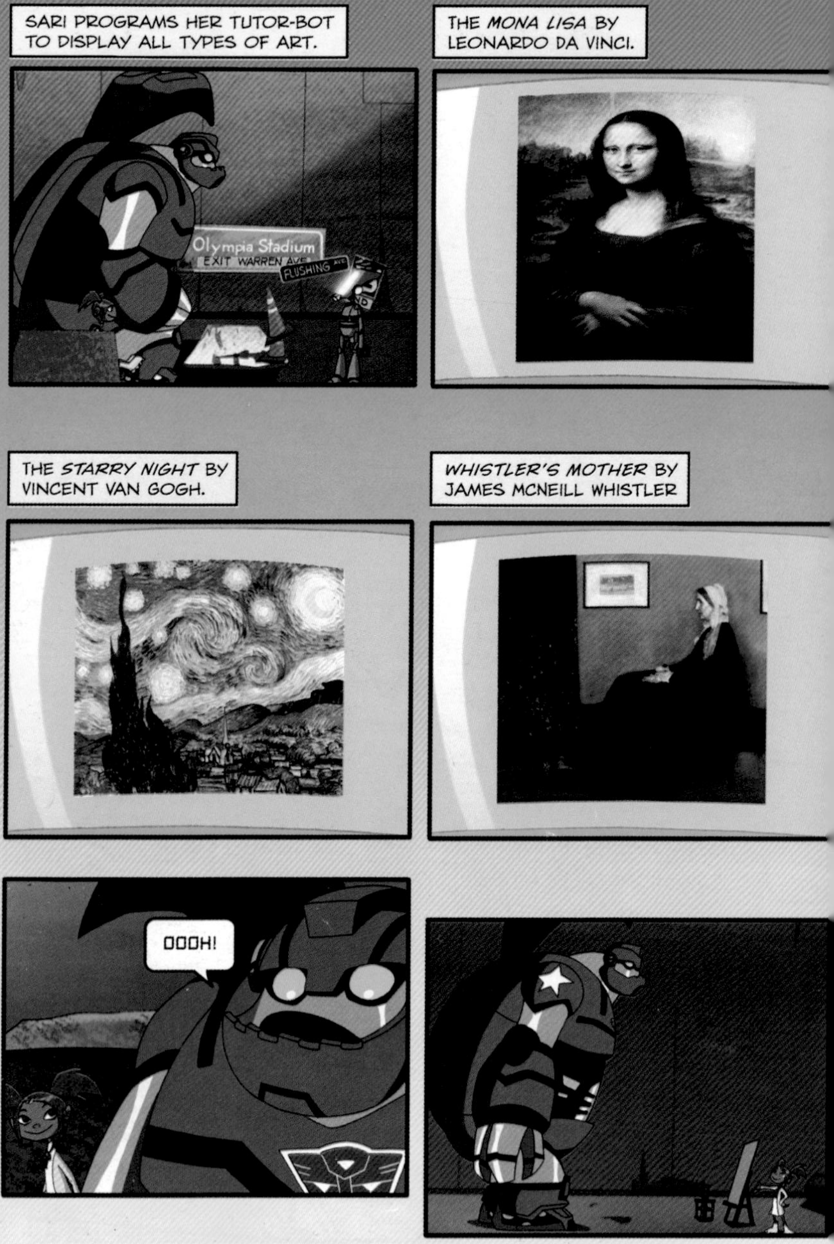
SARI PROGRAMS HER TUTOR-BOT TO DISPLAY ALL TYPES OF ART.
Olympia Stadium
EXIT WARREN AVE
FLUSHING AVE
THE *MONA LISA* BY LEONARDO DA VINCI.
THE *STARRY NIGHT* BY VINCENT VAN GOGH.
WHISTLER'S MOTHER BY JAMES MCNEILL WHISTLER
OOOH!

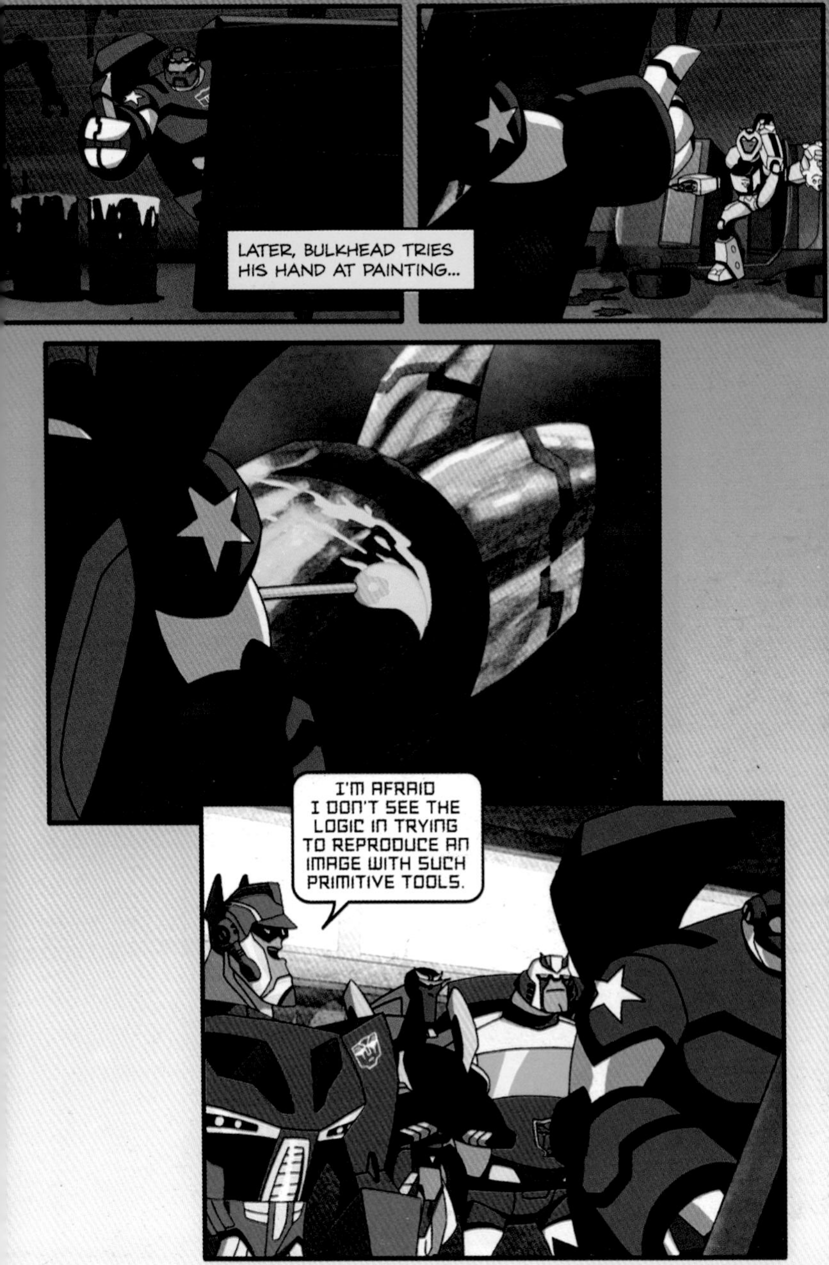
LATER, BULKHEAD TRIES HIS HAND AT PAINTING...
I'M AFRAID I DON'T SEE THE LOGIC IN TRYING TO REPRODUCE AN IMAGE WITH SUCH PRIMITIVE TOOLS.

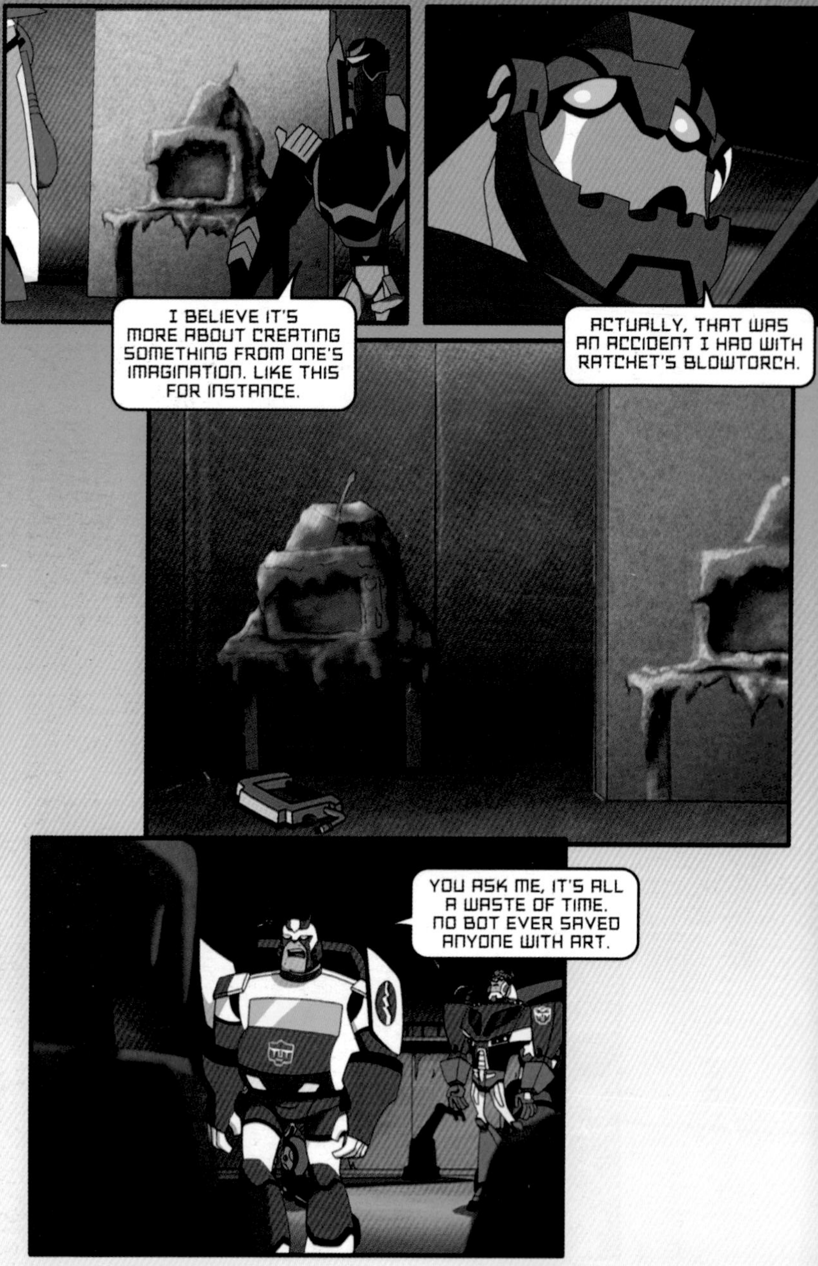
I BELIEVE IT'S MORE ABOUT CREATING SOMETHING FROM ONE'S IMAGINATION. LIKE THIS FOR INSTANCE.
ACTUALLY, THAT WAS AN ACCIDENT I HAD WITH RATCHET'S BLOWTORCH.
YOU ASK ME, IT'S ALL A WASTE OF TIME. NO BOT EVER SAVED ANYONE WITH ART.

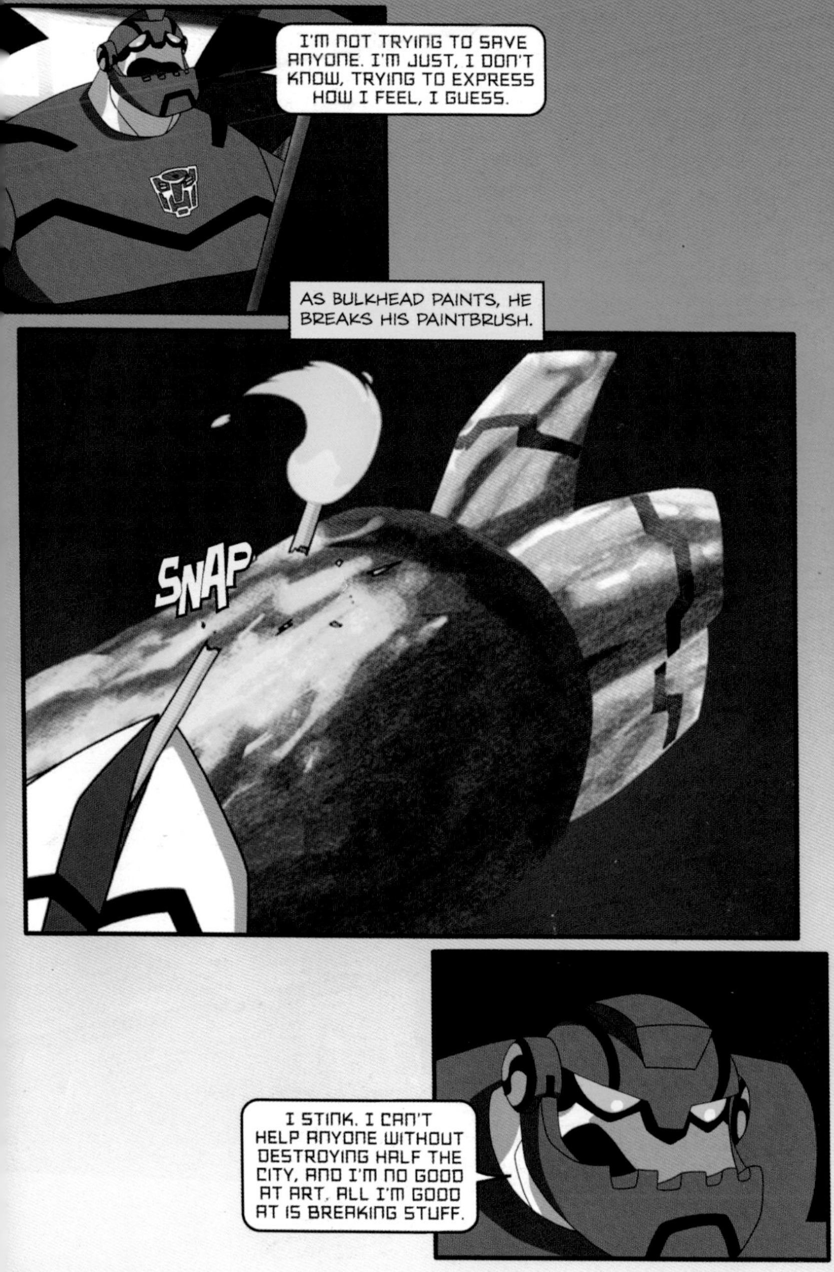
I'M NOT TRYING TO SAVE ANYONE. I'M JUST, I DON'T KNOW, TRYING TO EXPRESS HOW I FEEL, I GUESS.
AS BULKHEAD PAINTS, HE BREAKS HIS PAINTBRUSH.
SNAP
I STINK. I CAN'T HELP ANYONE WITHOUT DESTROYING HALF THE CITY, AND I'M NO GOOD AT ART. ALL I'M GOOD AT IS BREAKING STUFF.

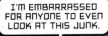

I'M EMBARRASSED FOR ANYONE TO EVEN LOOK AT THIS JUNK.

HEY BULKHEAD, GUESS WHAT?! I JUST BOOKED YOU AN EXHIBITION AT A REAL ART GALLERY. ISN'T THAT EXCITING?!

BULKHEAD TURNS AND RUNS STRAIGHT THROUGH A BRICK WALL, TOO ASHAMED TO FACE HIS FRIENDS ANY LONGER.

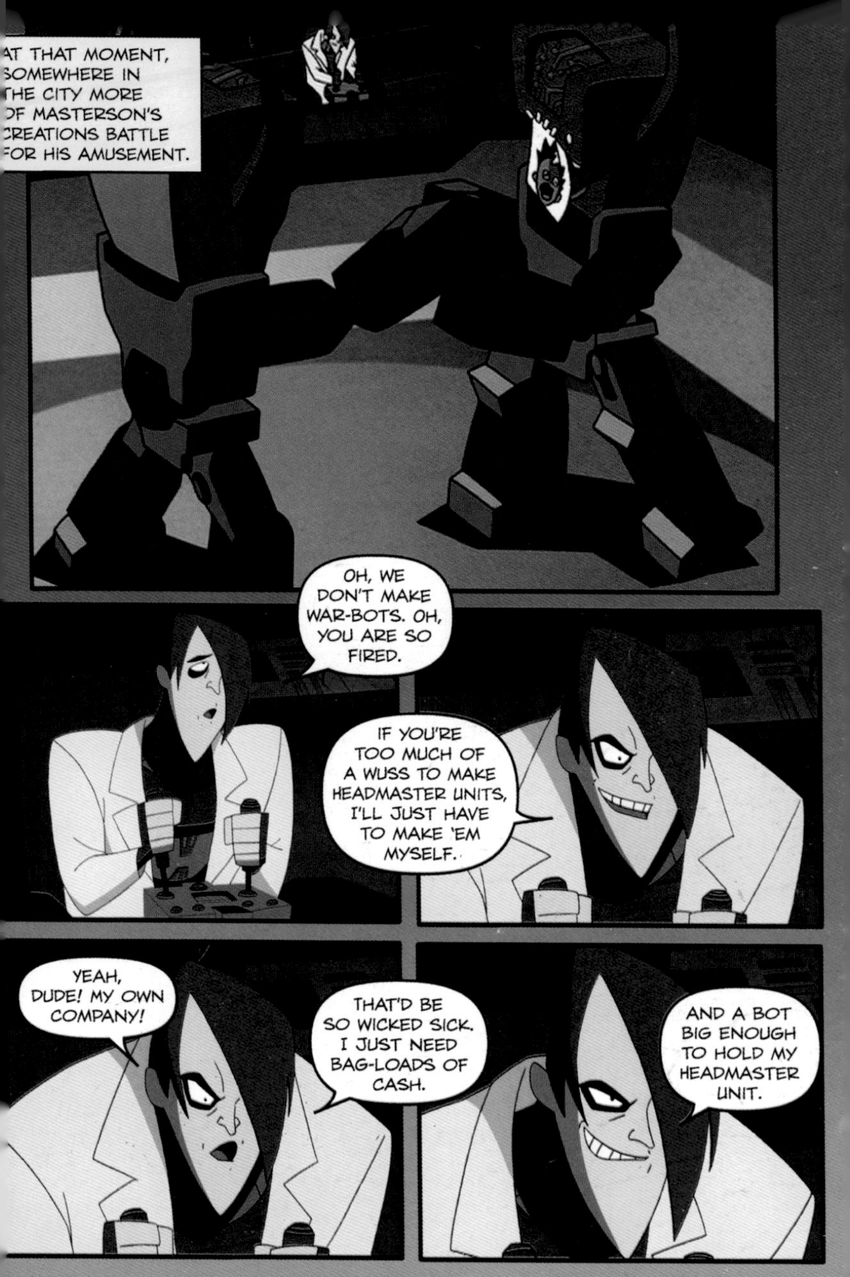
AT THAT MOMENT, SOMEWHERE IN THE CITY MORE OF MASTERSON'S CREATIONS BATTLE FOR HIS AMUSEMENT.
OH, WE DON'T MAKE WAR-BOTS. OH, YOU ARE SO FIRED.
IF YOU'RE TOO MUCH OF A WUSS TO MAKE HEADMASTER UNITS, I'LL JUST HAVE TO MAKE 'EM MYSELF.
YEAH, DUDE! MY OWN COMPANY!
THAT'D BE SO WICKED SICK. I JUST NEED BAG-LOADS OF CASH.
AND A BOT BIG ENOUGH TO HOLD MY HEADMASTER UNIT.

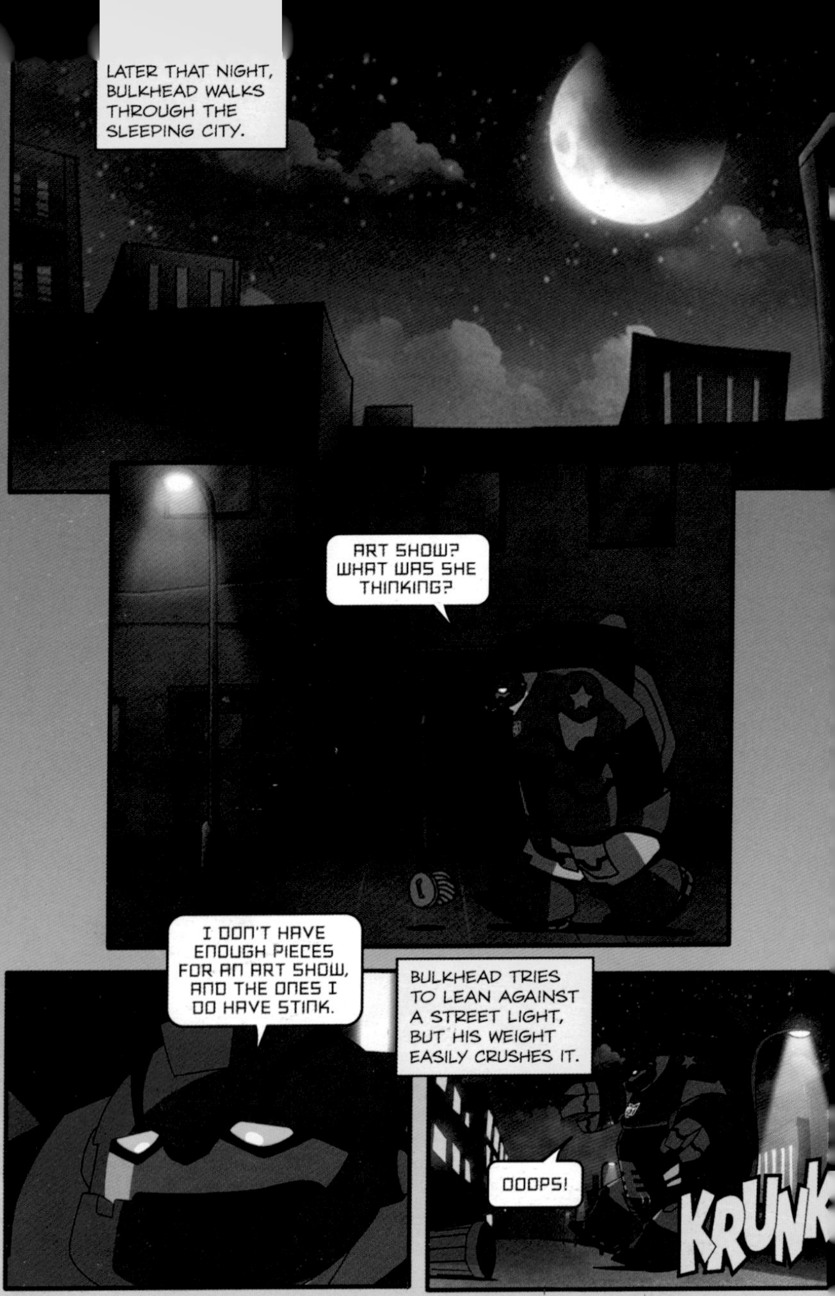
LATER THAT NIGHT, BULKHEAD WALKS THROUGH THE SLEEPING CITY.
ART SHOW? WHAT WAS SHE THINKING?
I DON'T HAVE ENOUGH PIECES FOR AN ART SHOW, AND THE ONES I DO HAVE STINK.
BULKHEAD TRIES TO LEAN AGAINST A STREET LIGHT, BUT HIS WEIGHT EASILY CRUSHES IT.
OOOPS!
KRUNK

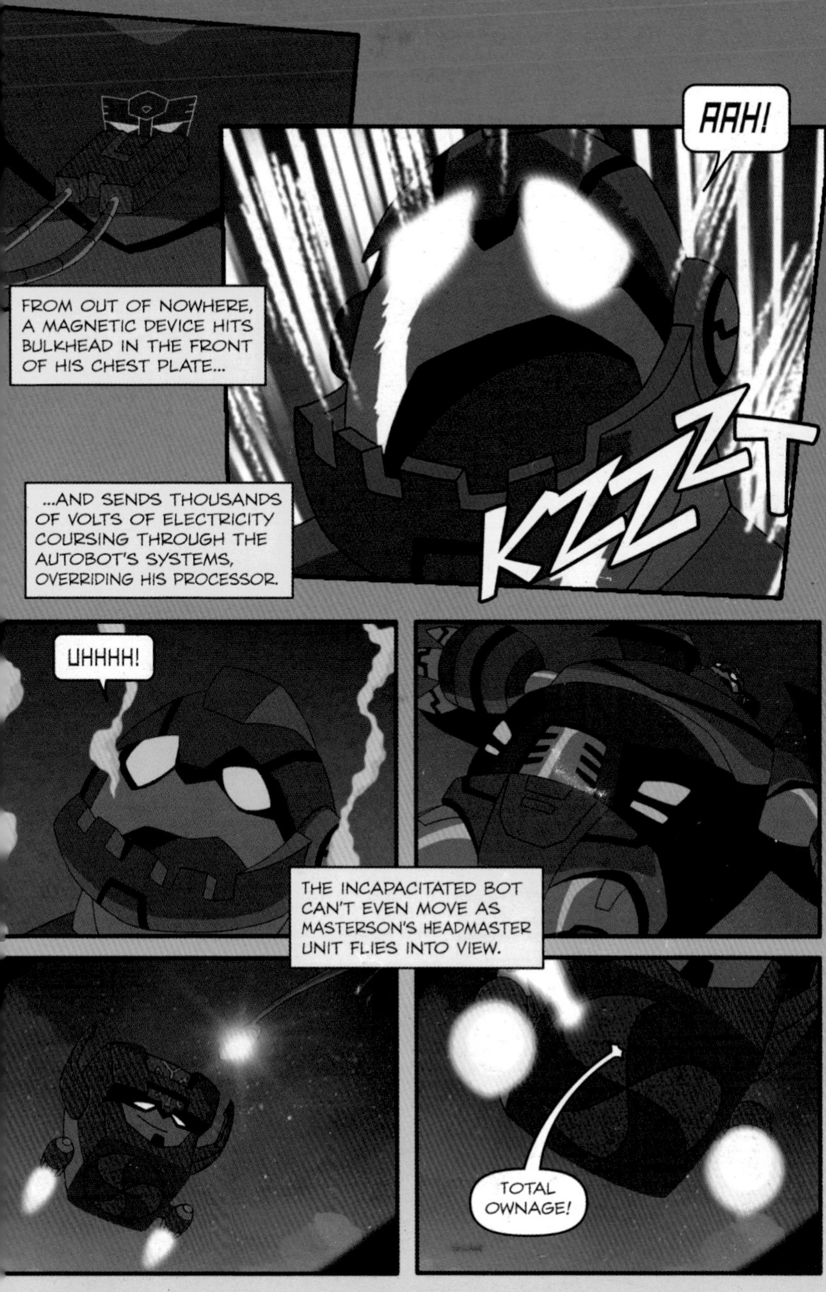
AAH!
FROM OUT OF NOWHERE, A MAGNETIC DEVICE HITS BULKHEAD IN THE FRONT OF HIS CHEST PLATE...
...AND SENDS THOUSANDS OF VOLTS OF ELECTRICITY COURSING THROUGH THE AUTOBOT'S SYSTEMS, OVERRIDING HIS PROCESSOR.
KZZZZT
UHHHH!
THE INCAPACITATED BOT CAN'T EVEN MOVE AS MASTERSON'S HEADMASTER UNIT FLIES INTO VIEW.
TOTAL OWNAGE!

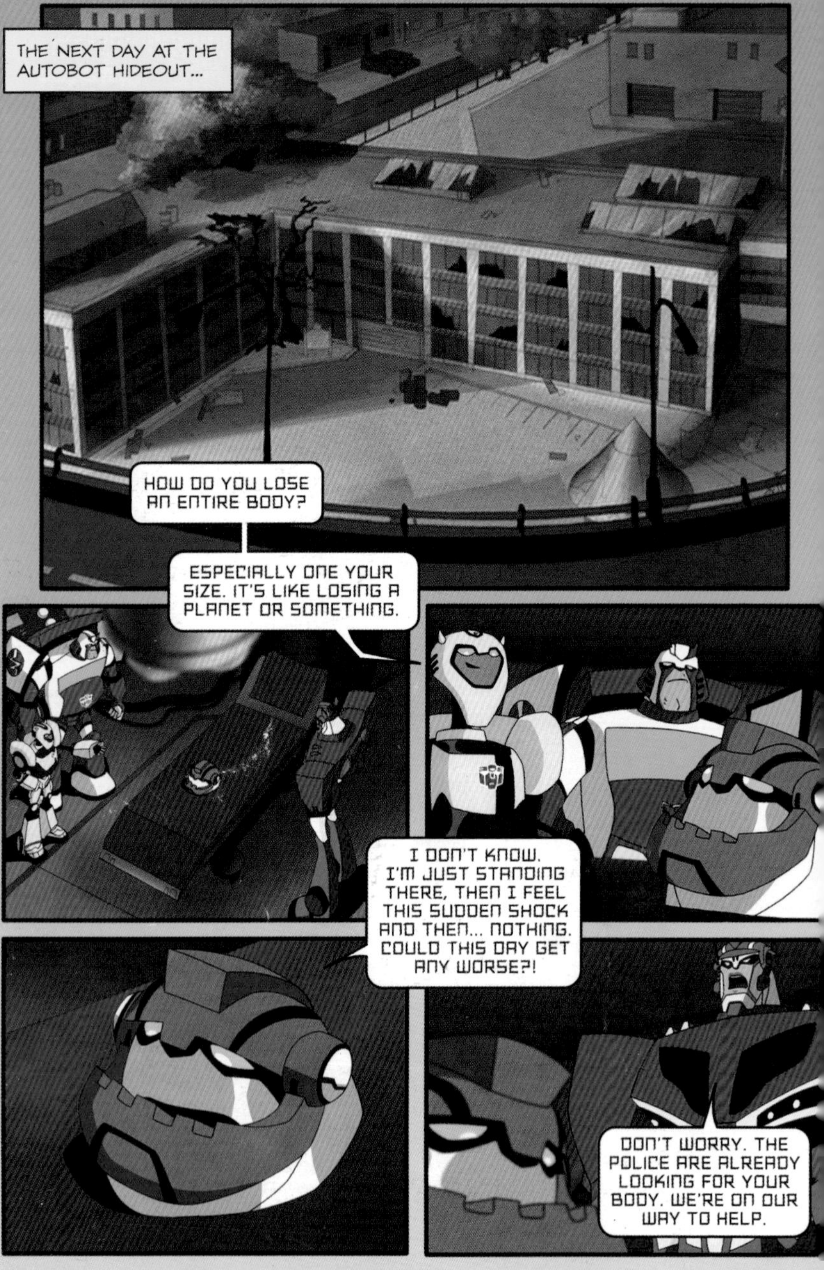
THE NEXT DAY AT THE AUTOBOT HIDEOUT...
HOW DO YOU LOSE AN ENTIRE BODY?
ESPECIALLY ONE YOUR SIZE. IT'S LIKE LOSING A PLANET OR SOMETHING.
I DON'T KNOW. I'M JUST STANDING THERE, THEN I FEEL THIS SUDDEN SHOCK AND THEN... NOTHING. COULD THIS DAY GET ANY WORSE?!
DON'T WORRY. THE POLICE ARE ALREADY LOOKING FOR YOUR BODY. WE'RE ON OUR WAY TO HELP.

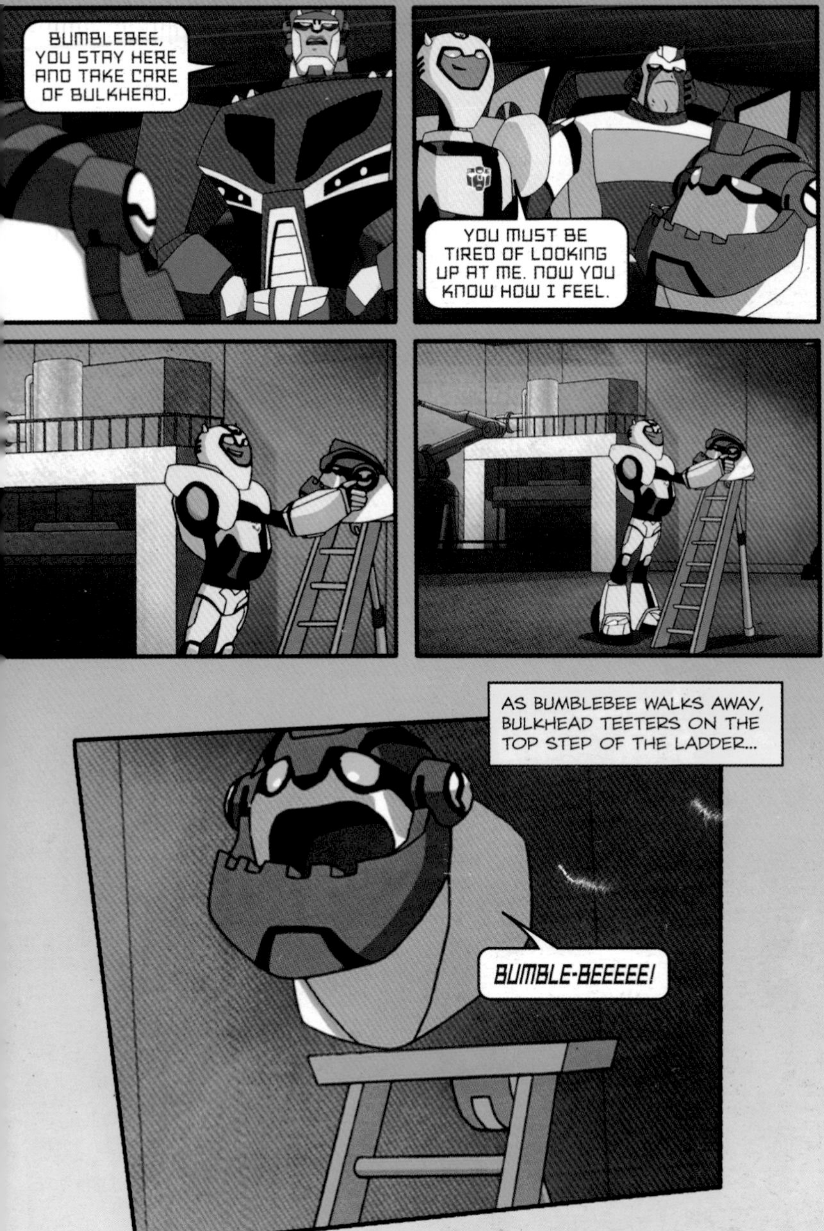
BUMBLEBEE, YOU STAY HERE AND TAKE CARE OF BULKHEAD.
YOU MUST BE TIRED OF LOOKING UP AT ME. NOW YOU KNOW HOW I FEEL.
AS BUMBLEBEE WALKS AWAY, BULKHEAD TEETERS ON THE TOP STEP OF THE LADDER...
BUMBLE-BEEEEEE!

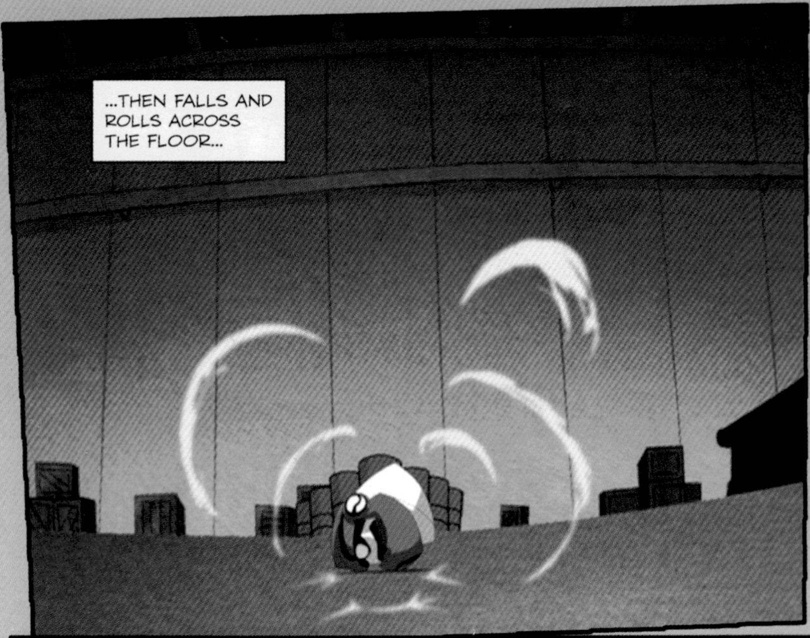
...THEN FALLS AND ROLLS ACROSS THE FLOOR...

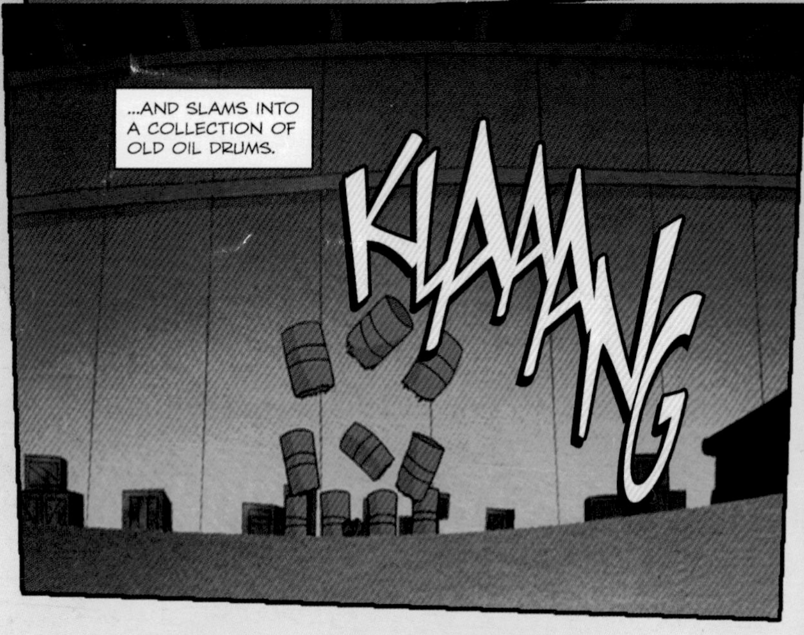
...AND SLAMS INTO A COLLECTION OF OLD OIL DRUMS.
KLAAAANG

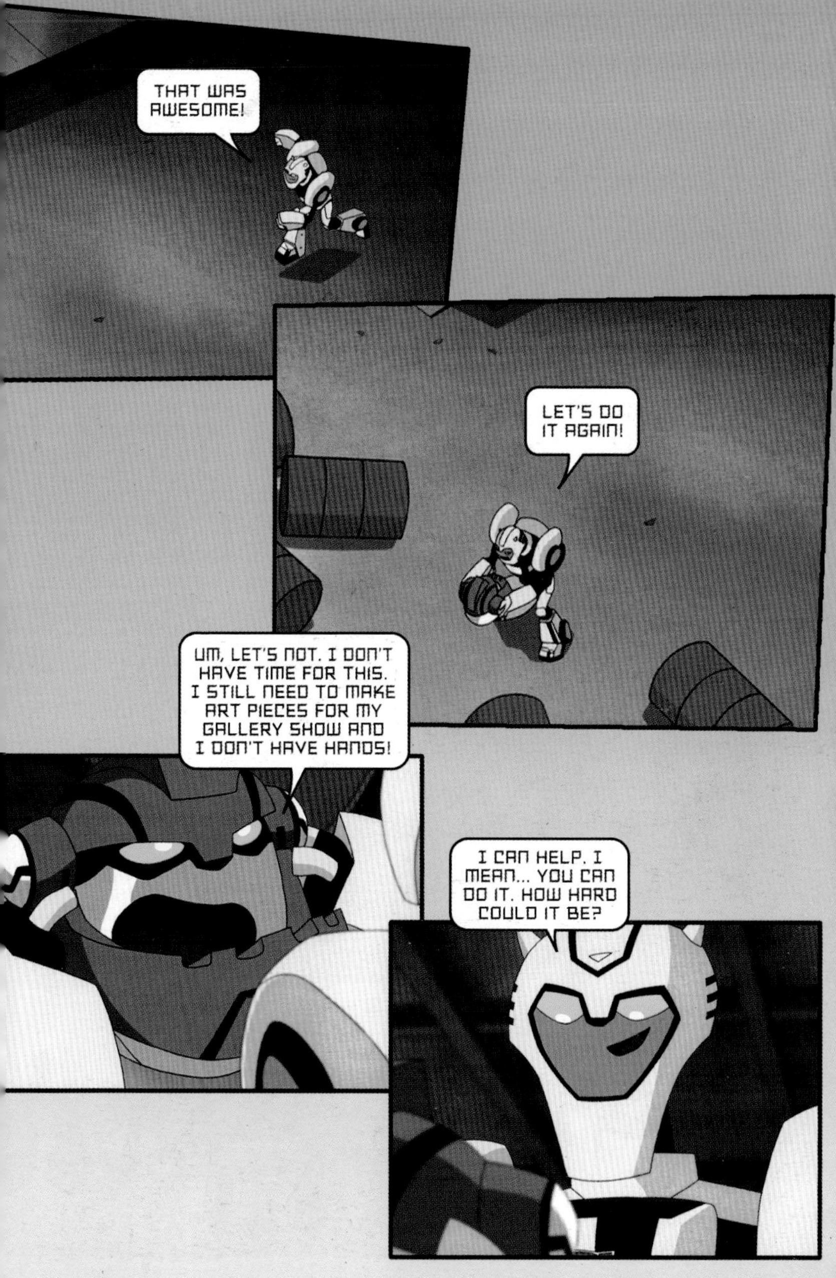
THAT WAS AWESOME!
LET'S DO IT AGAIN!
UM, LET'S NOT. I DON'T HAVE TIME FOR THIS. I STILL NEED TO MAKE ART PIECES FOR MY GALLERY SHOW AND I DON'T HAVE HANDS!
I CAN HELP. I MEAN... YOU CAN DO IT. HOW HARD COULD IT BE?

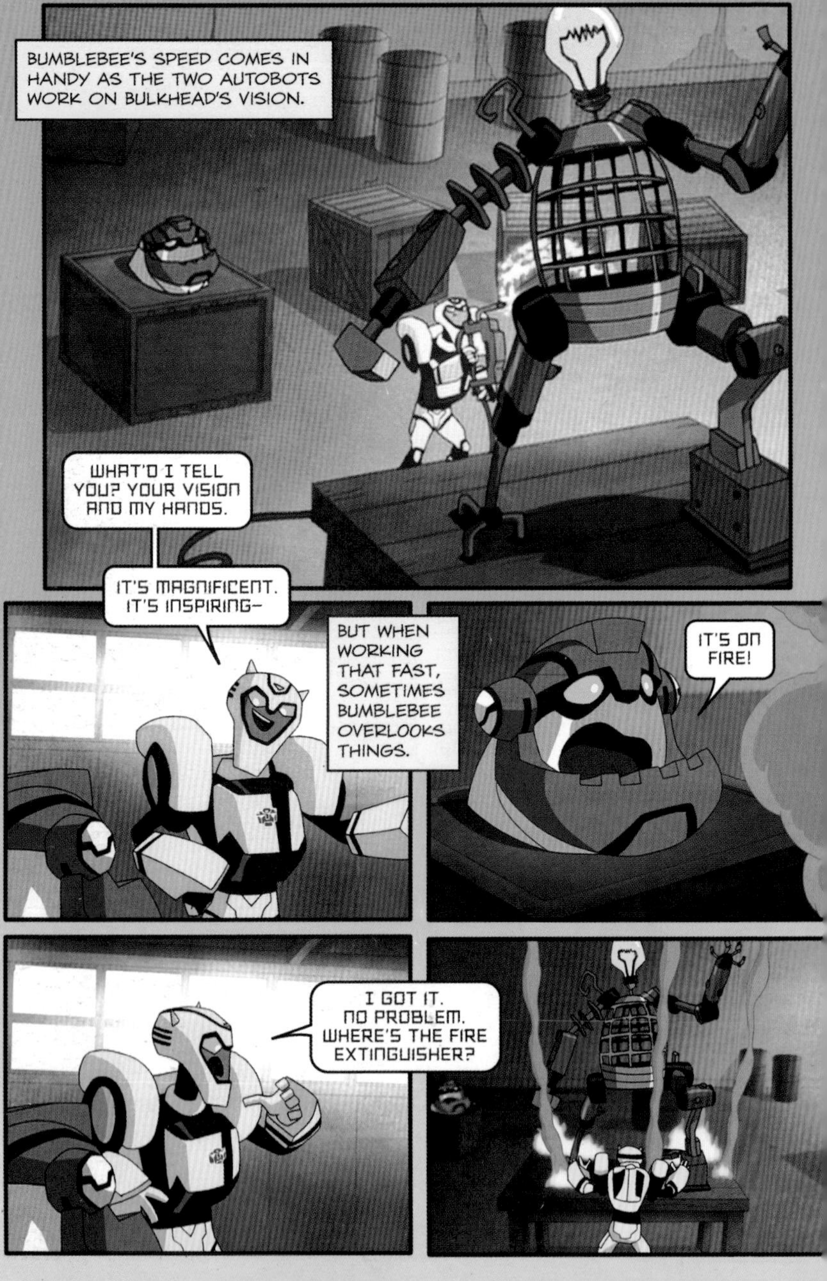
BUMBLEBEE'S SPEED COMES IN HANDY AS THE TWO AUTOBOTS WORK ON BULKHEAD'S VISION.
WHAT'D I TELL YOU? YOUR VISION AND MY HANDS.
IT'S MAGNIFICENT. IT'S INSPIRING–
BUT WHEN WORKING THAT FAST, SOMETIMES BUMBLEBEE OVERLOOKS THINGS.
IT'S ON FIRE!
I GOT IT. NO PROBLEM. WHERE'S THE FIRE EXTINGUISHER?

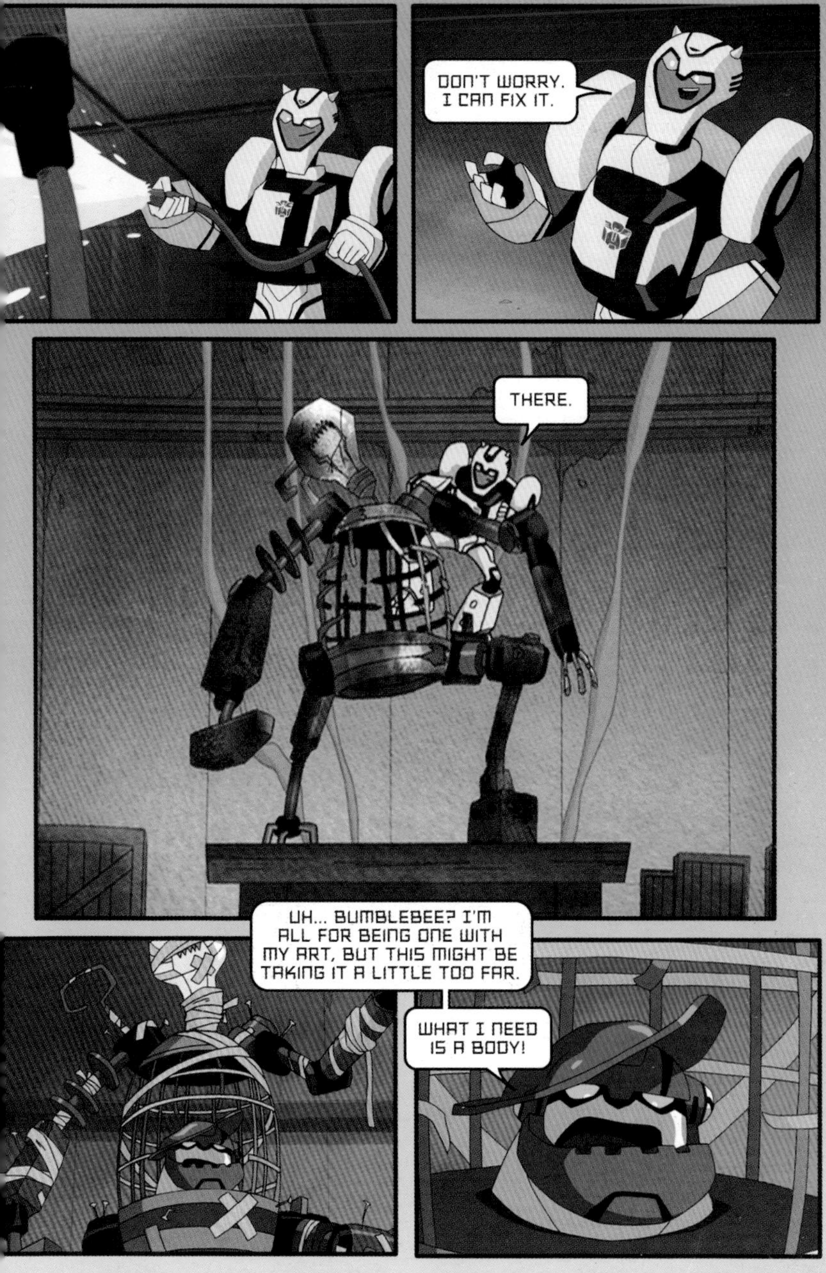
DON'T WORRY. I CAN FIX IT.
THERE.
UH... BUMBLEBEE? I'M ALL FOR BEING ONE WITH MY ART, BUT THIS MIGHT BE TAKING IT A LITTLE TOO FAR.
WHAT I NEED IS A BODY!

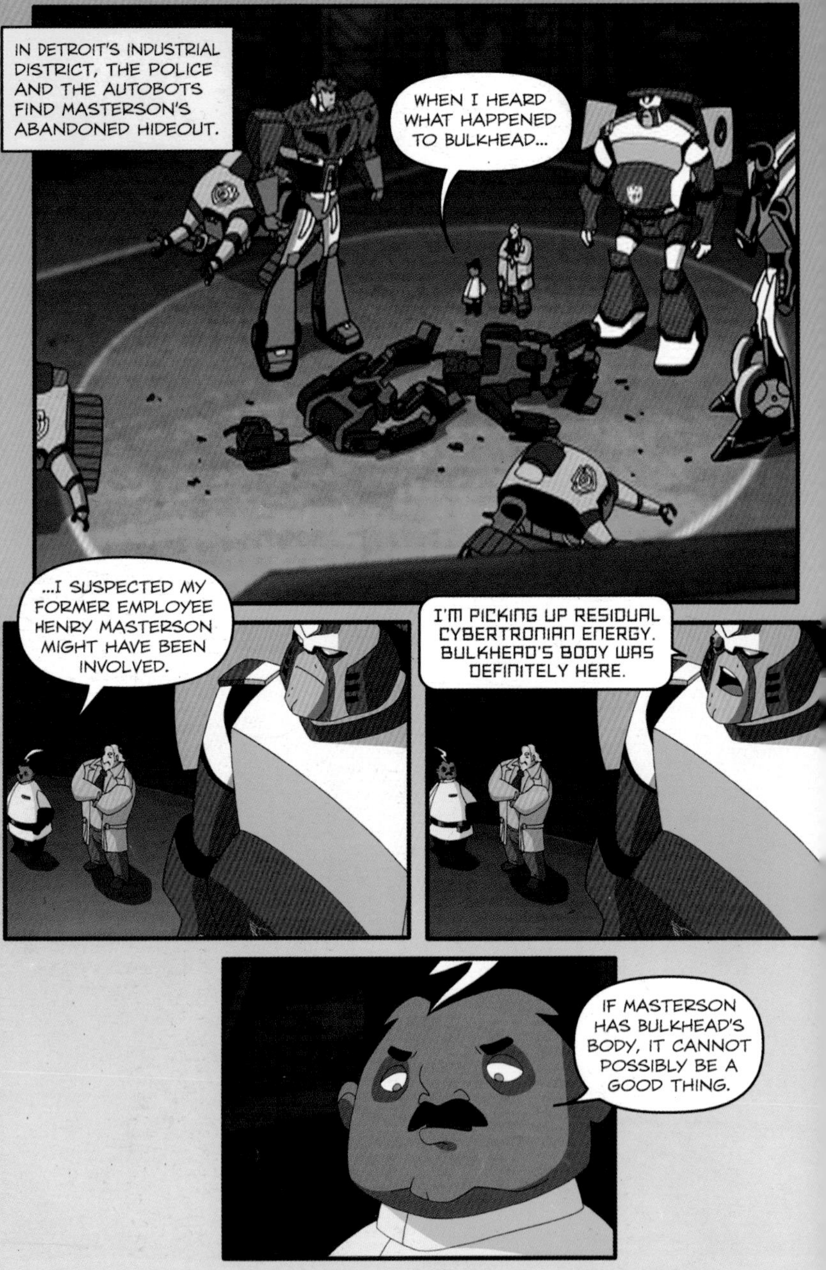
IN DETROIT'S INDUSTRIAL DISTRICT, THE POLICE AND THE AUTOBOTS FIND MASTERSON'S ABANDONED HIDEOUT.
WHEN I HEARD WHAT HAPPENED TO BULKHEAD...
...I SUSPECTED MY FORMER EMPLOYEE HENRY MASTERSON MIGHT HAVE BEEN INVOLVED.
I'M PICKING UP RESIDUAL CYBERTRONIAN ENERGY. BULKHEAD'S BODY WAS DEFINITELY HERE.
IF MASTERSON HAS BULKHEAD'S BODY, IT CANNOT POSSIBLY BE A GOOD THING.

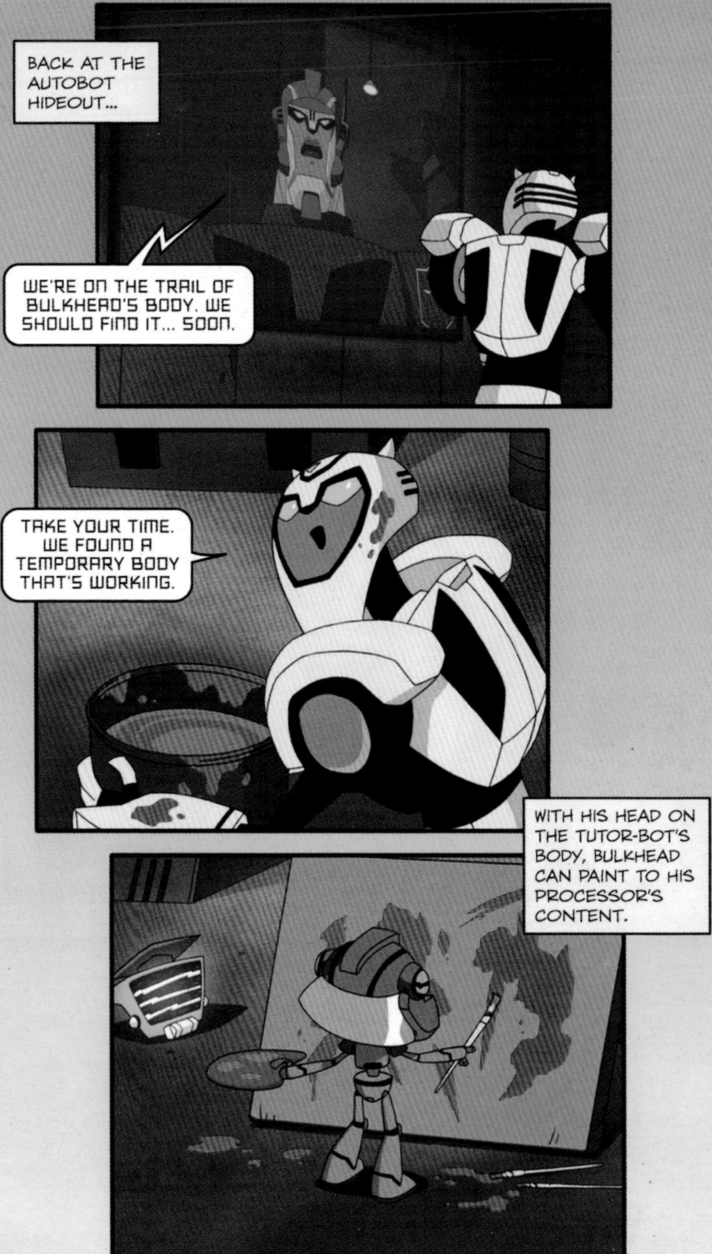

BACK AT THE AUTOBOT HIDEOUT...
WE'RE ON THE TRAIL OF BULKHEAD'S BODY. WE SHOULD FIND IT... SOON.
TAKE YOUR TIME. WE FOUND A TEMPORARY BODY THAT'S WORKING.
WITH HIS HEAD ON THE TUTOR-BOT'S BODY, BULKHEAD CAN PAINT TO HIS PROCESSOR'S CONTENT.

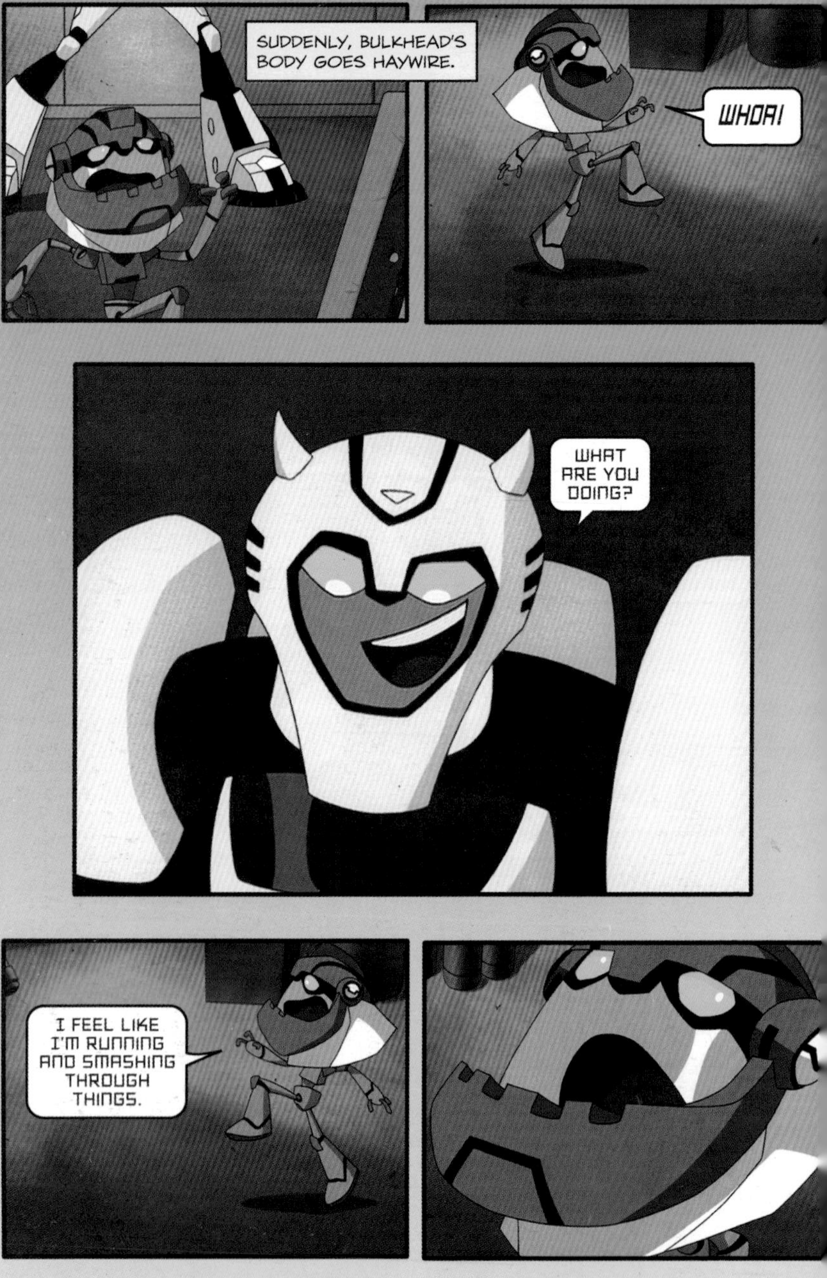
SUDDENLY, BULKHEAD'S BODY GOES HAYWIRE.
WHOA!
WHAT ARE YOU DOING?
I FEEL LIKE I'M RUNNING AND SMASHING THROUGH THINGS.

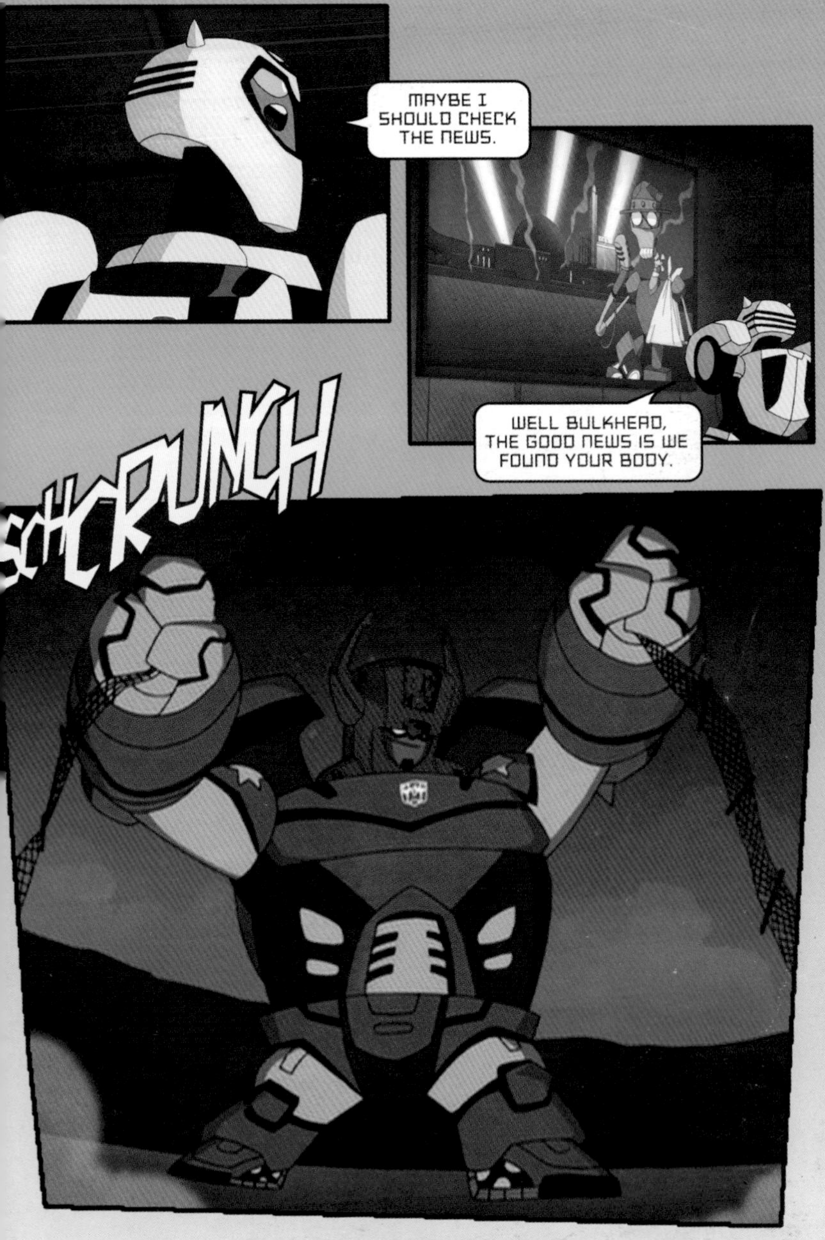
MAYBE I SHOULD CHECK THE NEWS.
WELL BULKHEAD, THE GOOD NEWS IS WE FOUND YOUR BODY.
SCHCRUNCH

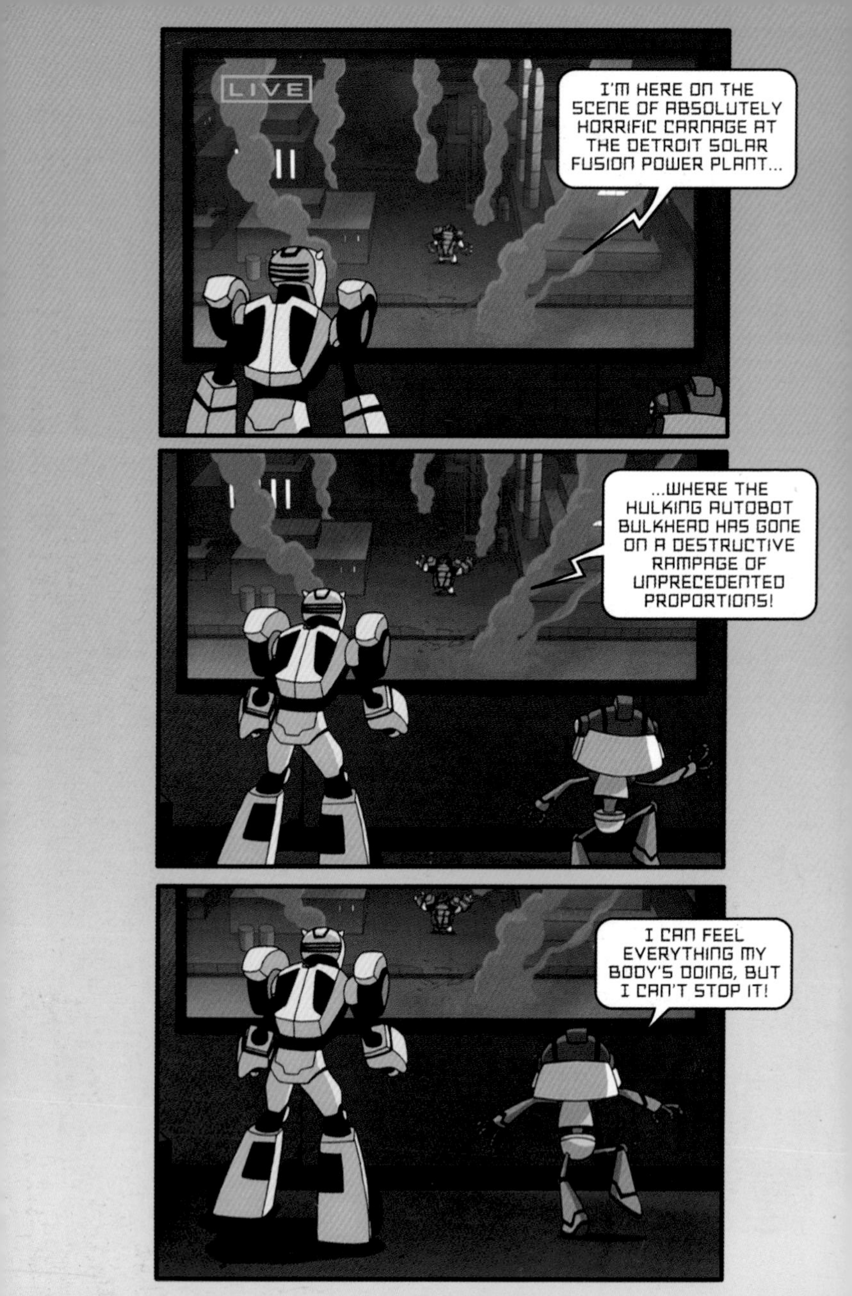
LIVE
I'M HERE ON THE SCENE OF ABSOLUTELY HORRIFIC CARNAGE AT THE DETROIT SOLAR FUSION POWER PLANT...
...WHERE THE HULKING AUTOBOT BULKHEAD HAS GONE ON A DESTRUCTIVE RAMPAGE OF UNPRECEDENTED PROPORTIONS!
I CAN FEEL EVERYTHING MY BODY'S DOING, BUT I CAN'T STOP IT!

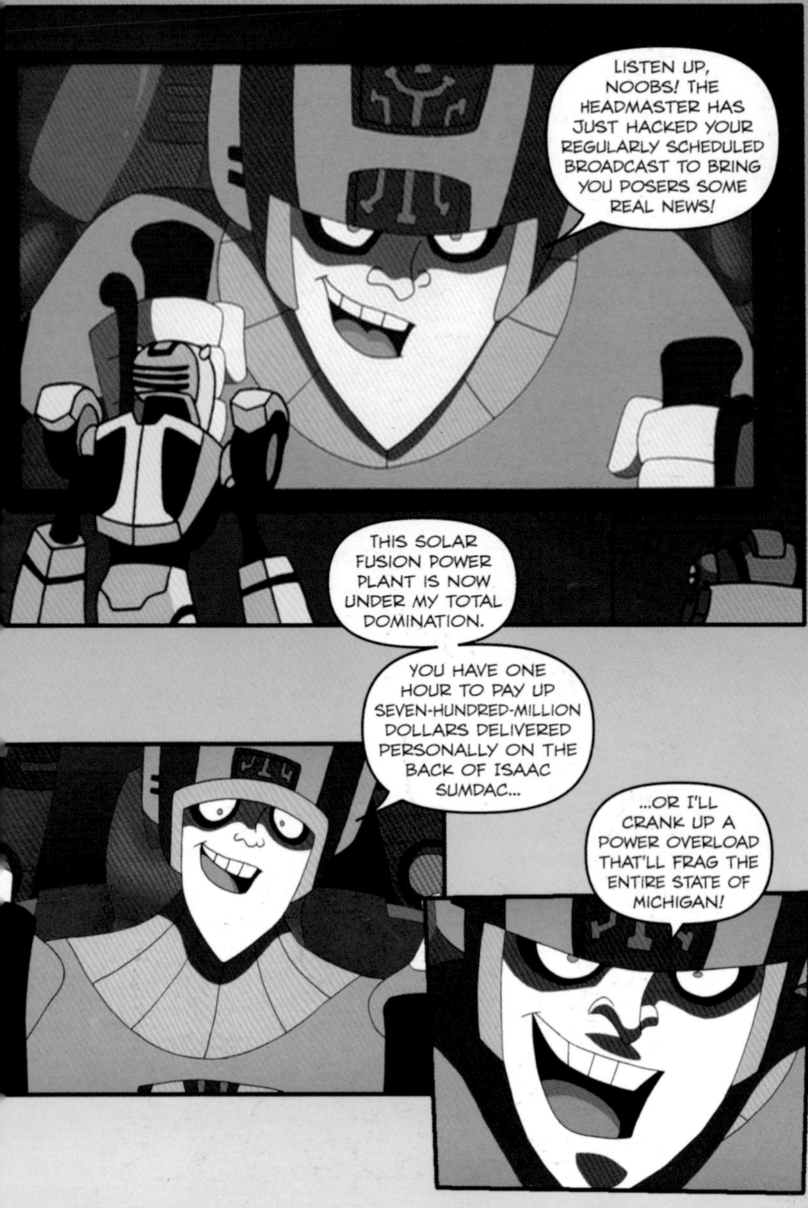
LISTEN UP, NOOBS! THE HEADMASTER HAS JUST HACKED YOUR REGULARLY SCHEDULED BROADCAST TO BRING YOU POSERS SOME REAL NEWS!
THIS SOLAR FUSION POWER PLANT IS NOW UNDER MY TOTAL DOMINATION.
YOU HAVE ONE HOUR TO PAY UP SEVEN-HUNDRED-MILLION DOLLARS DELIVERED PERSONALLY ON THE BACK OF ISAAC SUMDAC...
...OR I'LL CRANK UP A POWER OVERLOAD THAT'LL FRAG THE ENTIRE STATE OF MICHIGAN!

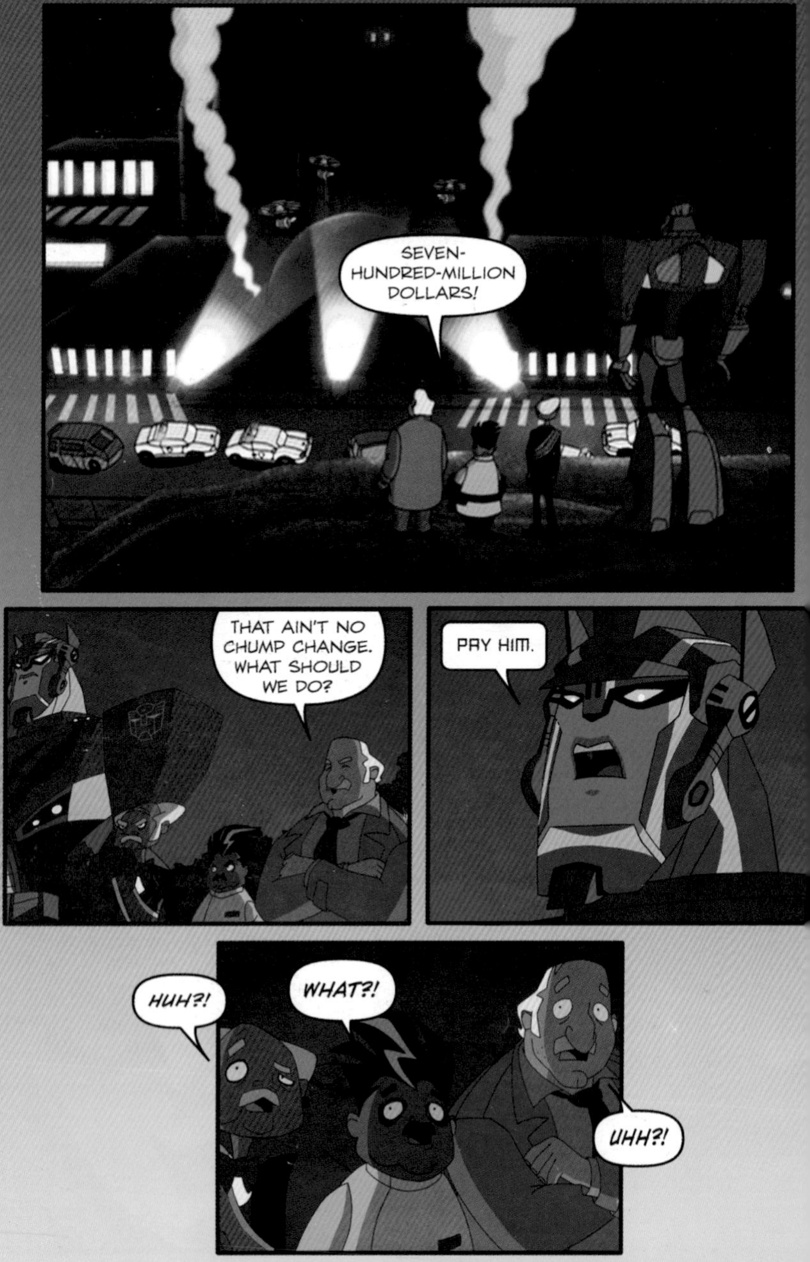
SEVEN-HUNDRED-MILLION DOLLARS!
THAT AIN'T NO CHUMP CHANGE. WHAT SHOULD WE DO?
PAY HIM.
HUH?!
WHAT?!
UHH?!

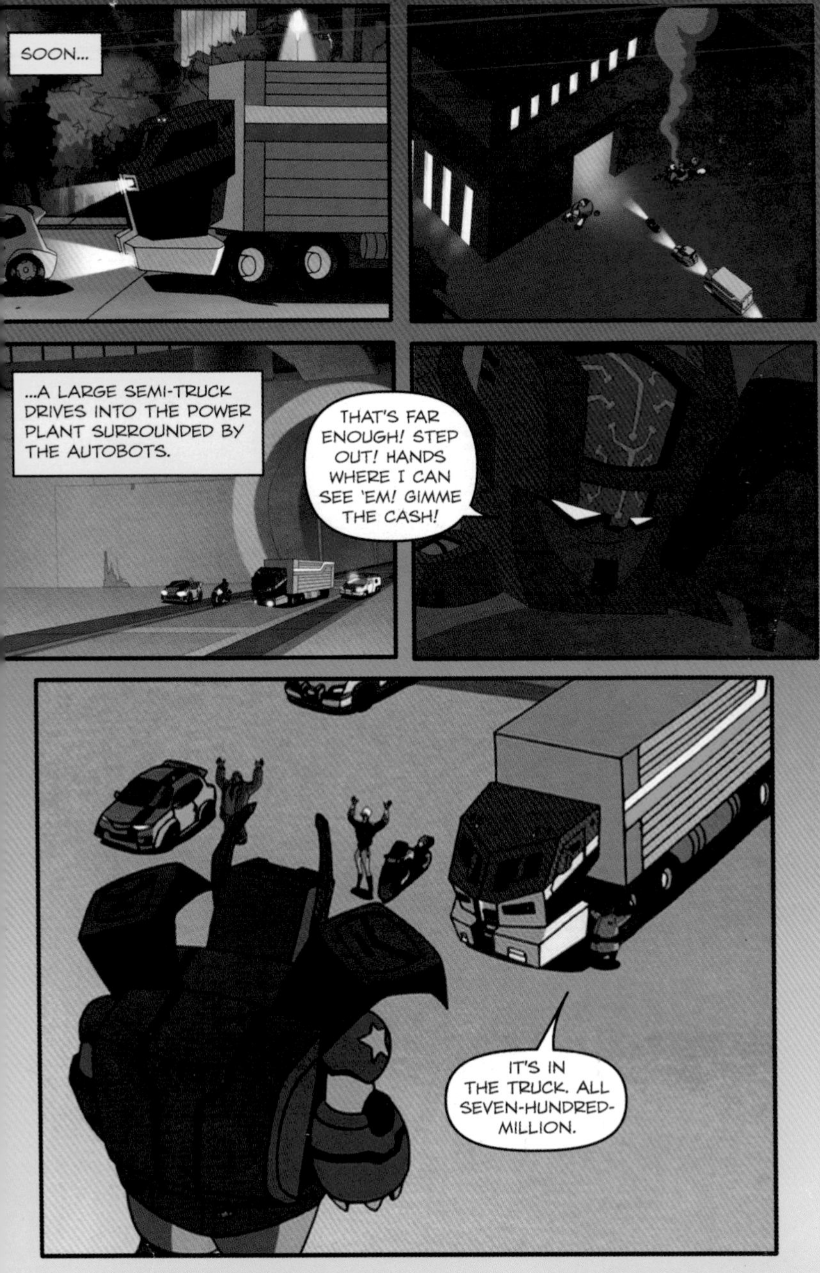
SOON...
...A LARGE SEMI-TRUCK DRIVES INTO THE POWER PLANT SURROUNDED BY THE AUTOBOTS.
THAT'S FAR ENOUGH! STEP OUT! HANDS WHERE I CAN SEE 'EM! GIMME THE CASH!
IT'S IN THE TRUCK. ALL SEVEN-HUNDRED-MILLION.

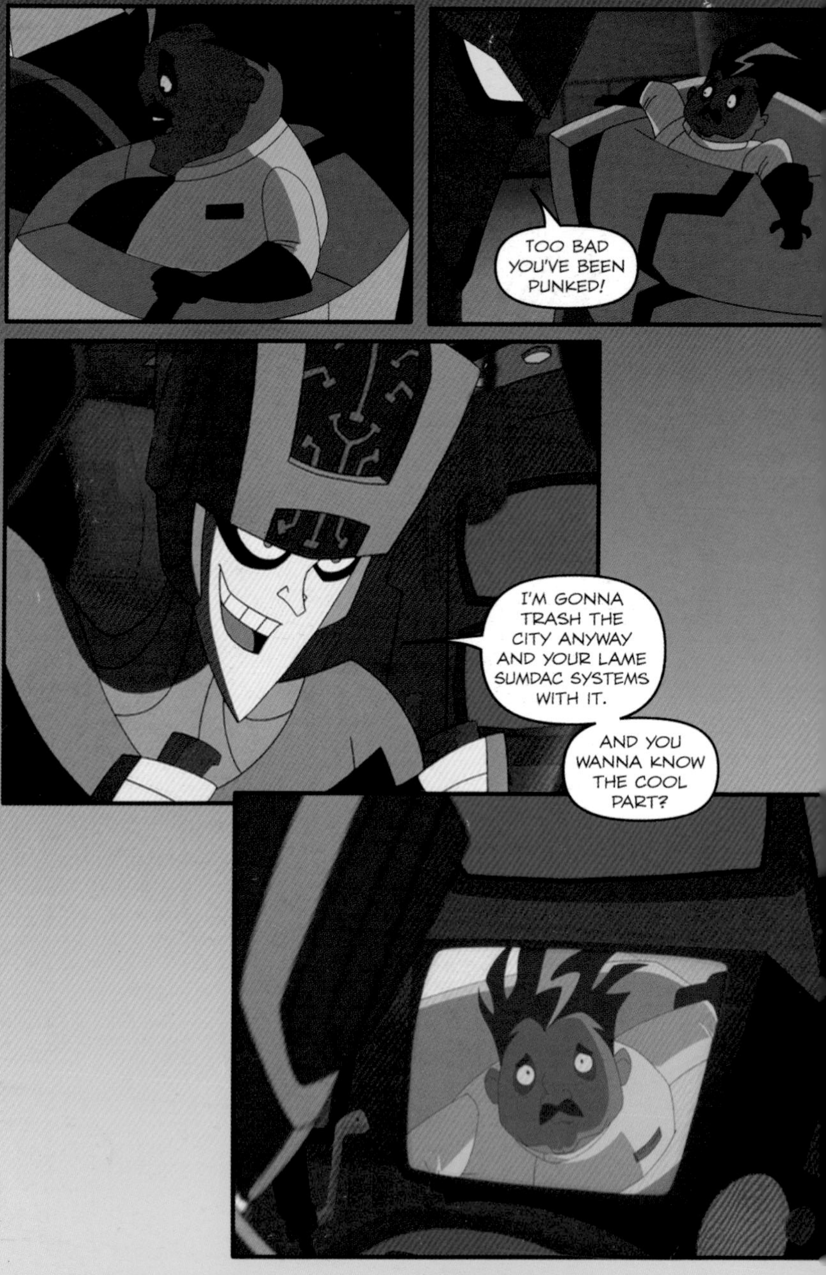
TOO BAD YOU'VE BEEN PUNKED!
I'M GONNA TRASH THE CITY ANYWAY AND YOUR LAME SUMDAC SYSTEMS WITH IT.
AND YOU WANNA KNOW THE COOL PART?

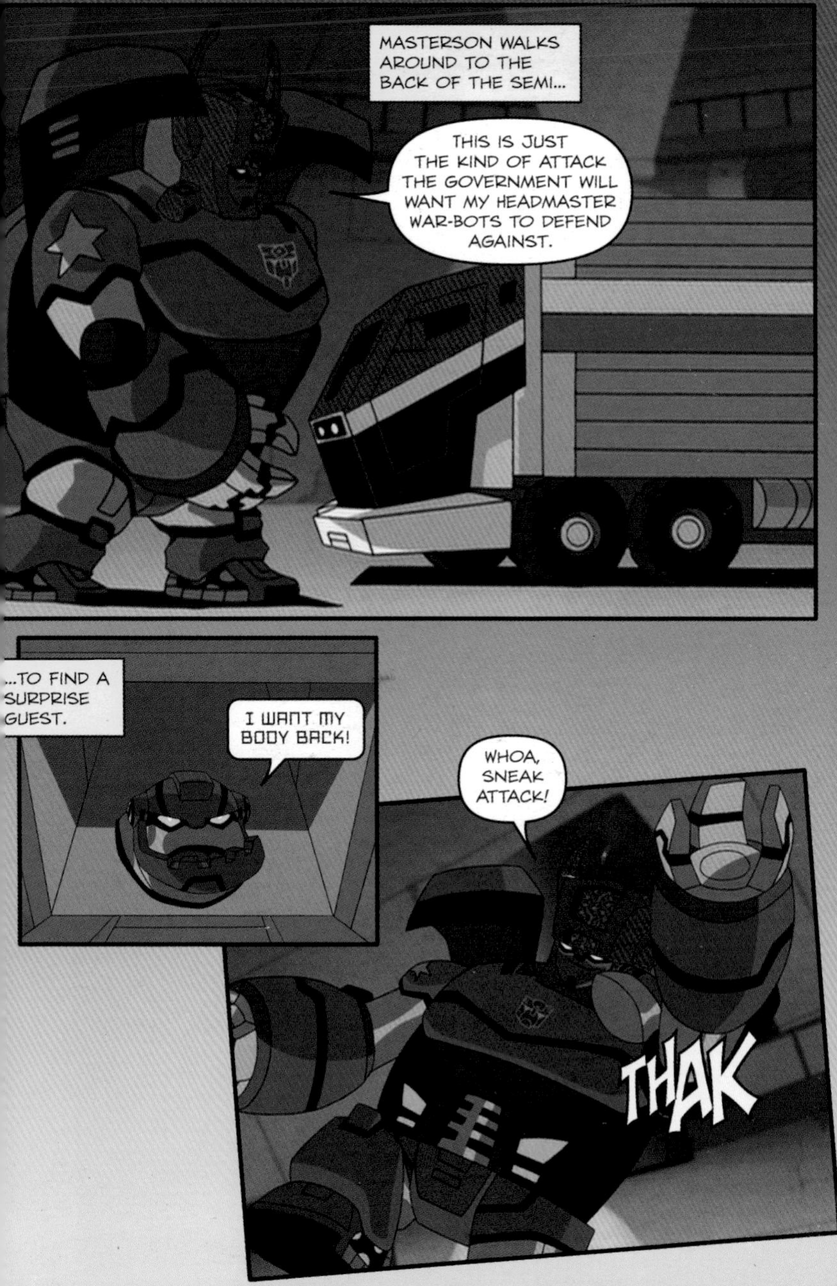
MASTERSON WALKS AROUND TO THE BACK OF THE SEMI...
THIS IS JUST THE KIND OF ATTACK THE GOVERNMENT WILL WANT MY HEADMASTER WAR-BOTS TO DEFEND AGAINST.
...TO FIND A SURPRISE GUEST.
I WANT MY BODY BACK!
WHOA, SNEAK ATTACK!
THAK

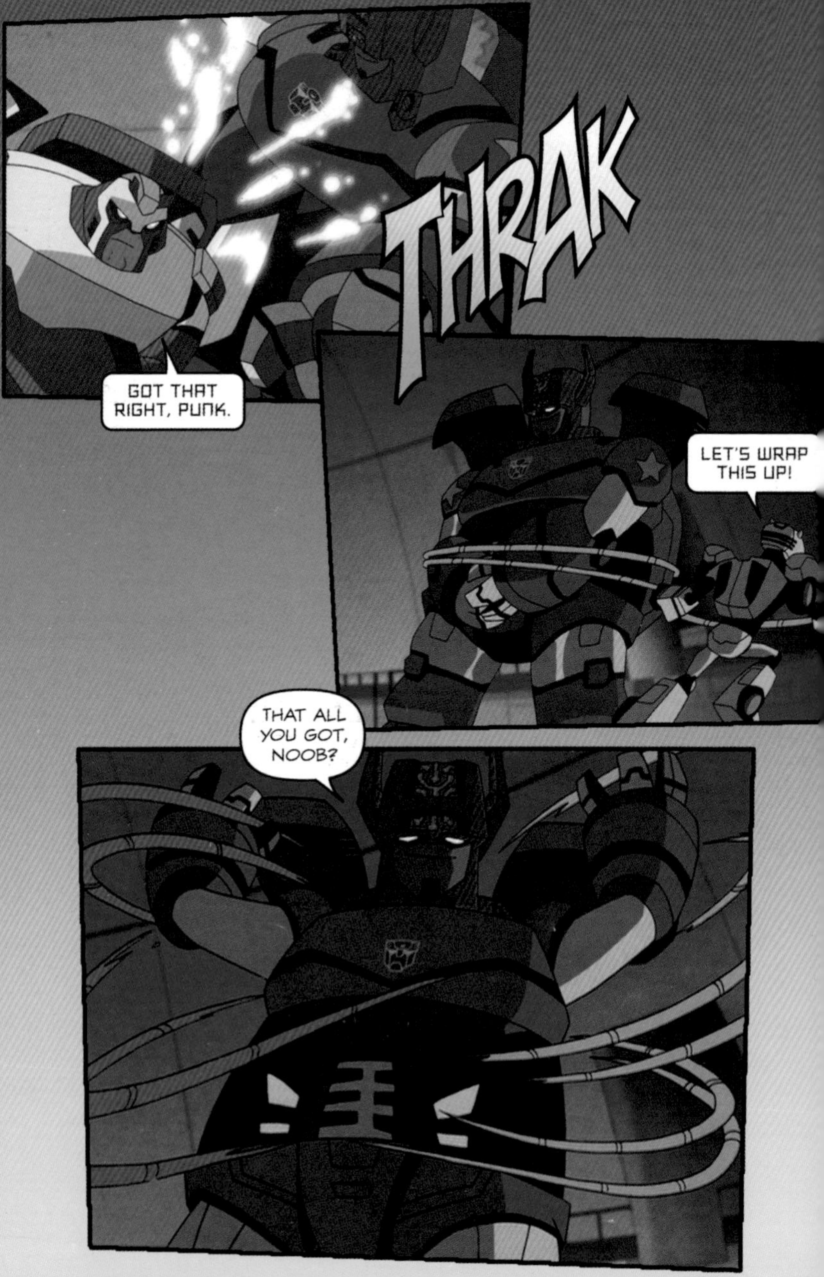
THRAK
GOT THAT RIGHT, PUNK.
LET'S WRAP THIS UP!
THAT ALL YOU GOT, NOOB?

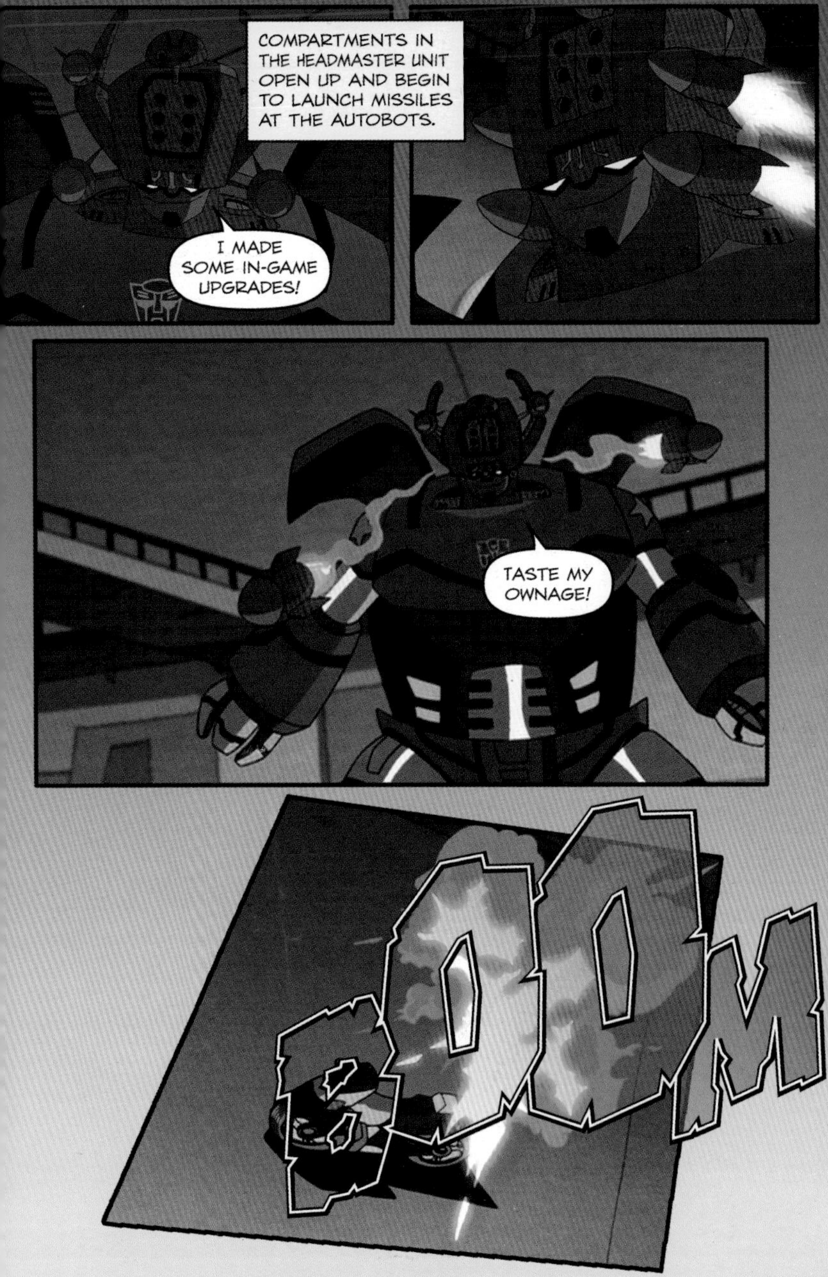
COMPARTMENTS IN THE HEADMASTER UNIT OPEN UP AND BEGIN TO LAUNCH MISSILES AT THE AUTOBOTS.
I MADE SOME IN-GAME UPGRADES!
TASTE MY OWNAGE!
BOOM

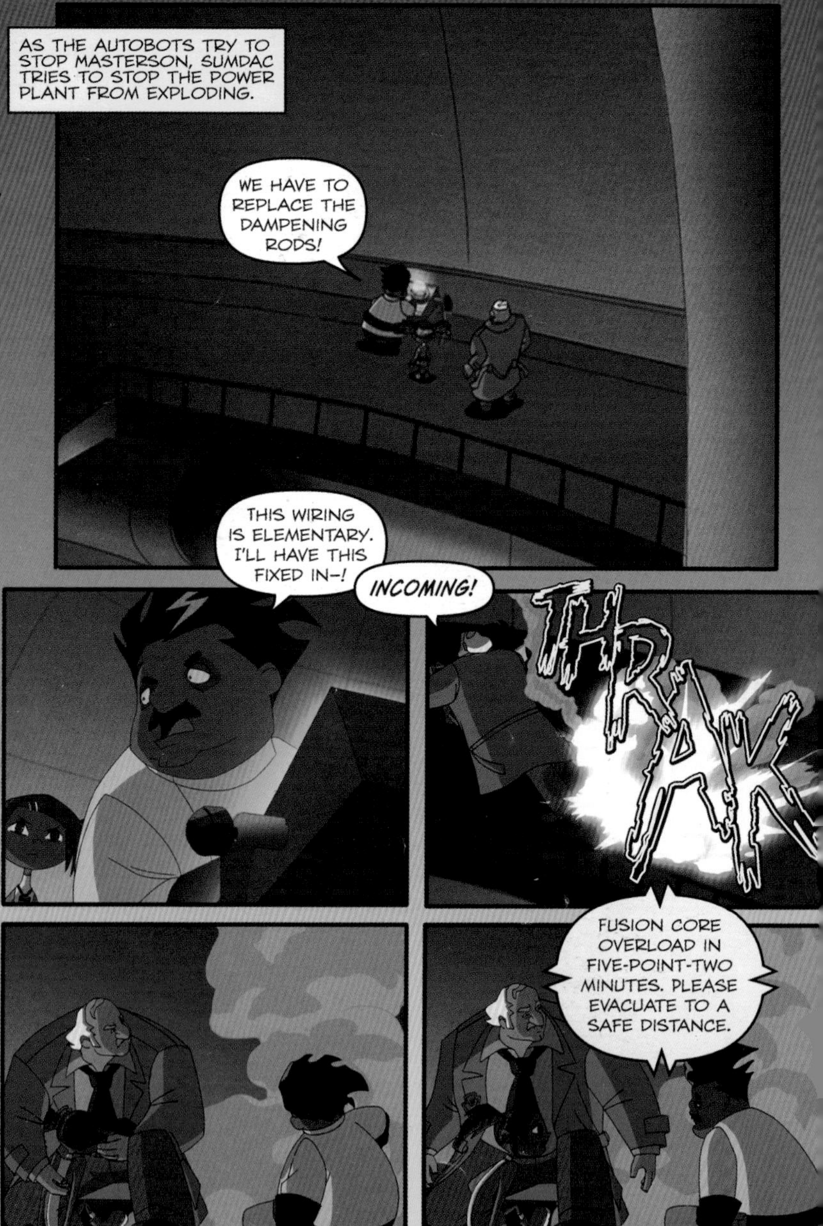
AS THE AUTOBOTS TRY TO STOP MASTERSON, SUMDAC TRIES TO STOP THE POWER PLANT FROM EXPLODING.
WE HAVE TO REPLACE THE DAMPENING RODS!
THIS WIRING IS ELEMENTARY. I'LL HAVE THIS FIXED IN–!
INCOMING!
THRAK
FUSION CORE OVERLOAD IN FIVE-POINT-TWO MINUTES. PLEASE EVACUATE TO A SAFE DISTANCE.

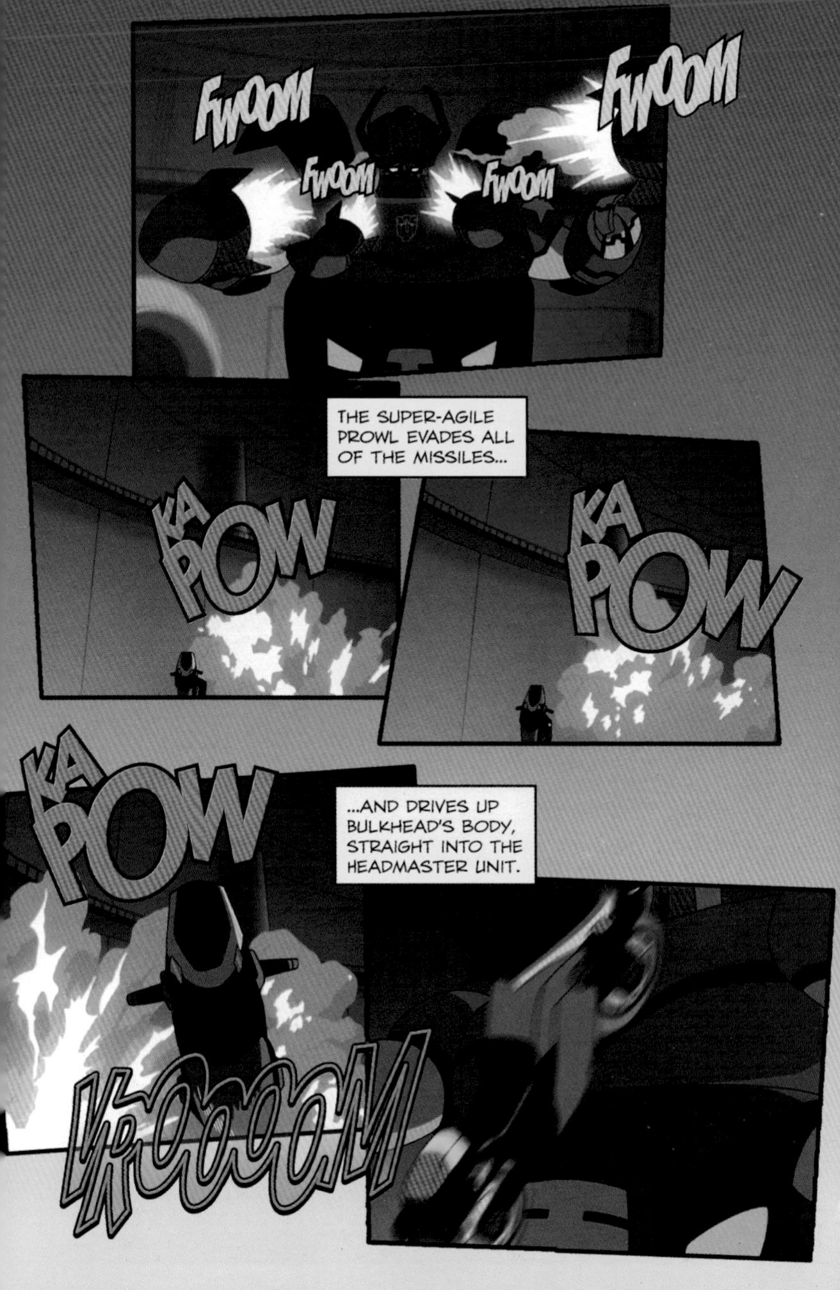
FWOOM
FWOOM
FWOOM
FWOOM
THE SUPER-AGILE PROWL EVADES ALL OF THE MISSILES...
KA POW
KA POW
KA POW
...AND DRIVES UP BULKHEAD'S BODY, STRAIGHT INTO THE HEADMASTER UNIT.
VROOOOOM

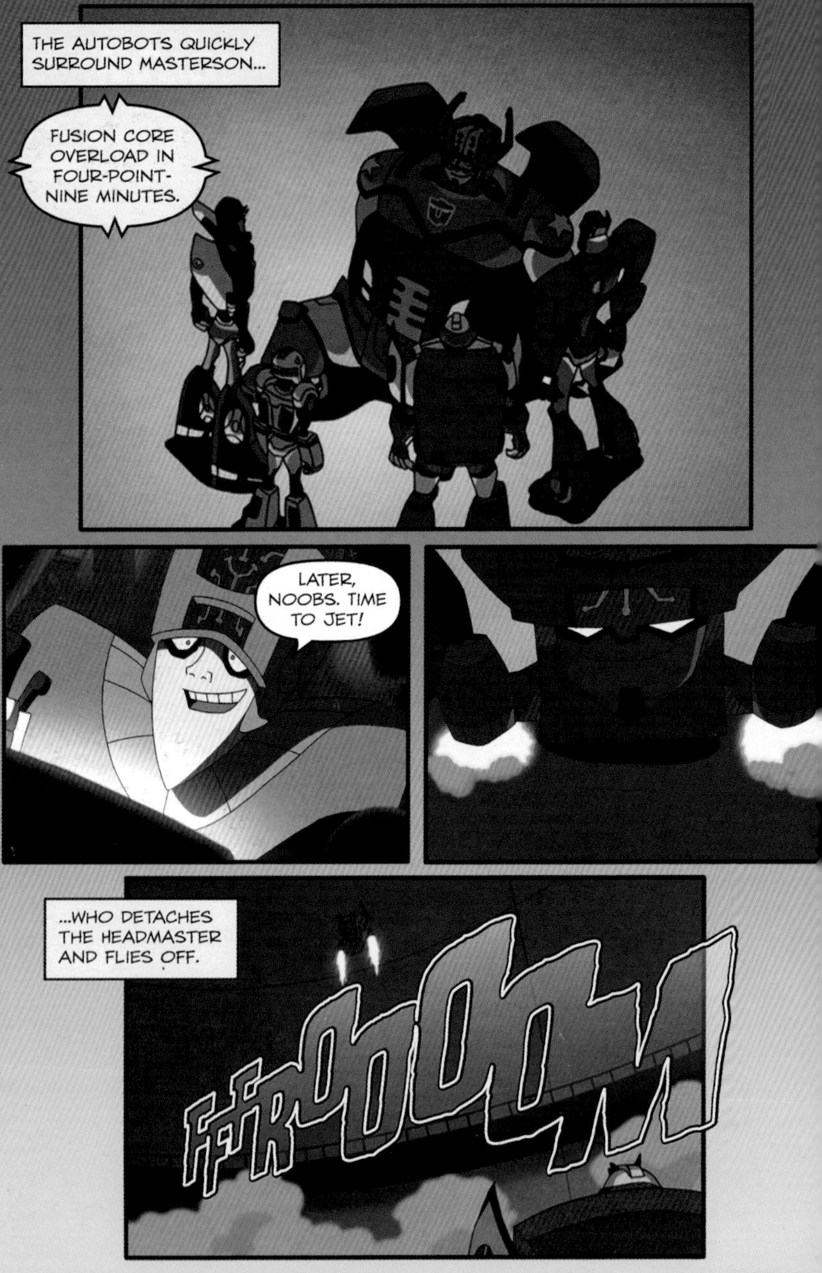
THE AUTOBOTS QUICKLY SURROUND MASTERSON...
FUSION CORE OVERLOAD IN FOUR-POINT-NINE MINUTES.
LATER, NOOBS. TIME TO JET!
...WHO DETACHES THE HEADMASTER AND FLIES OFF.
FFROOOOM

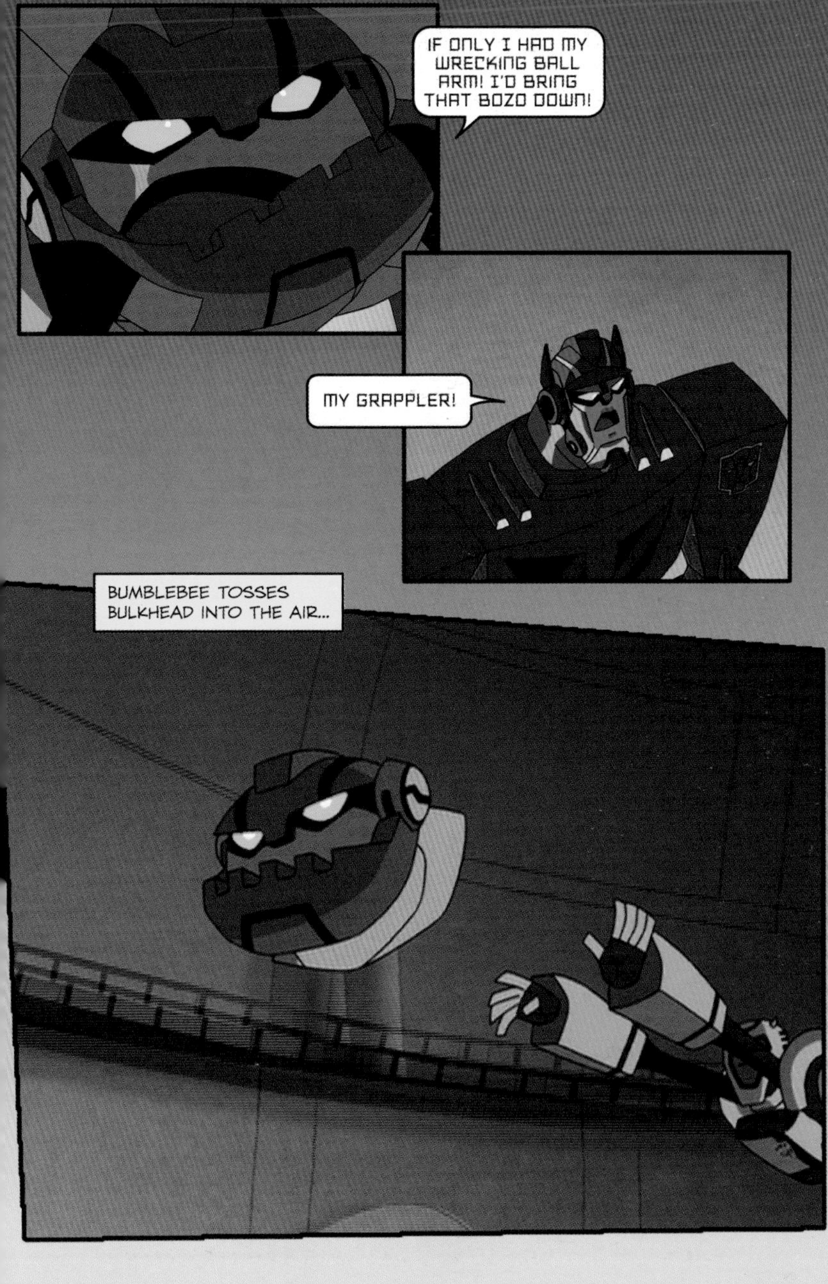
IF ONLY I HAD MY WRECKING BALL ARM! I'D BRING THAT BOZO DOWN!
MY GRAPPLER!
BUMBLEBEE TOSSES BULKHEAD INTO THE AIR...

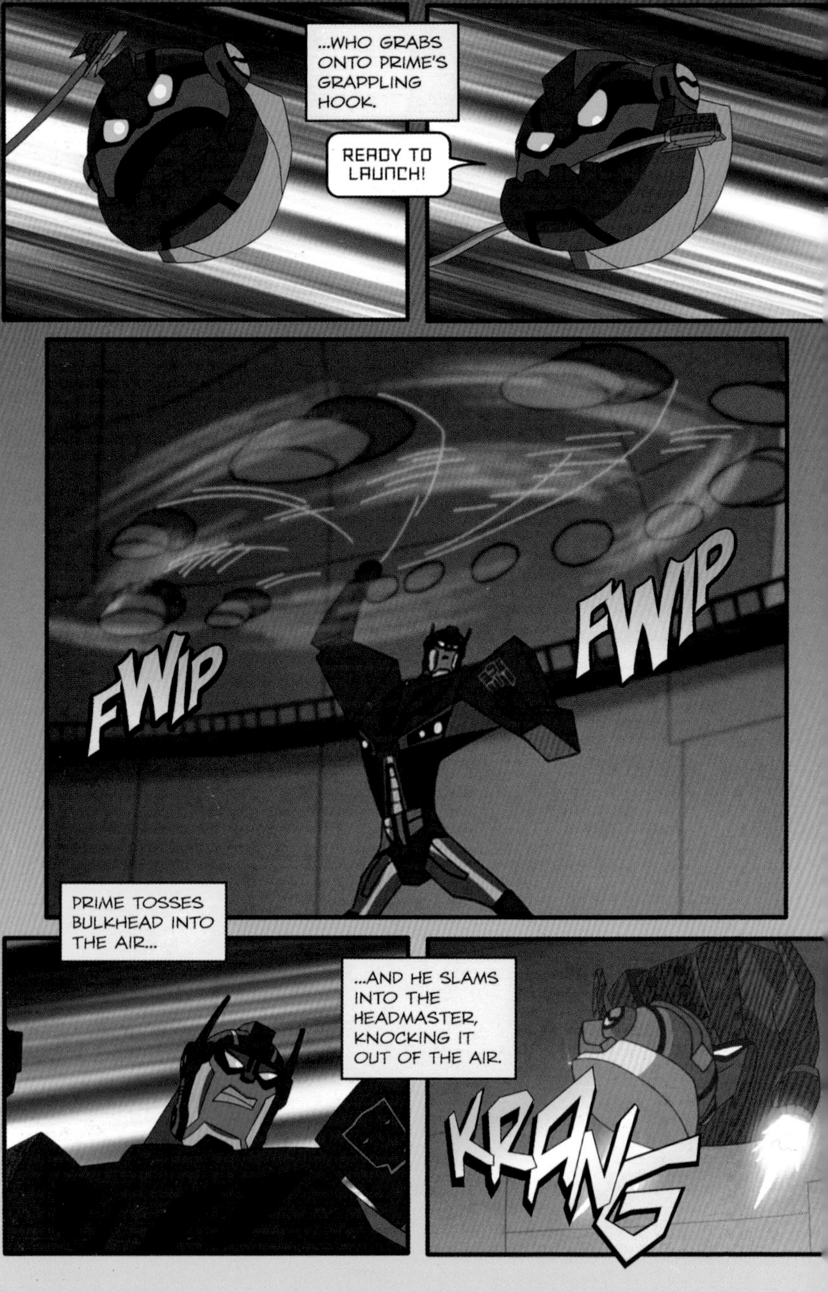
...WHO GRABS ONTO PRIME'S GRAPPLING HOOK.
READY TO LAUNCH!
FWIP
FWIP
PRIME TOSSES BULKHEAD INTO THE AIR...
...AND HE SLAMS INTO THE HEADMASTER, KNOCKING IT OUT OF THE AIR.
KRANG

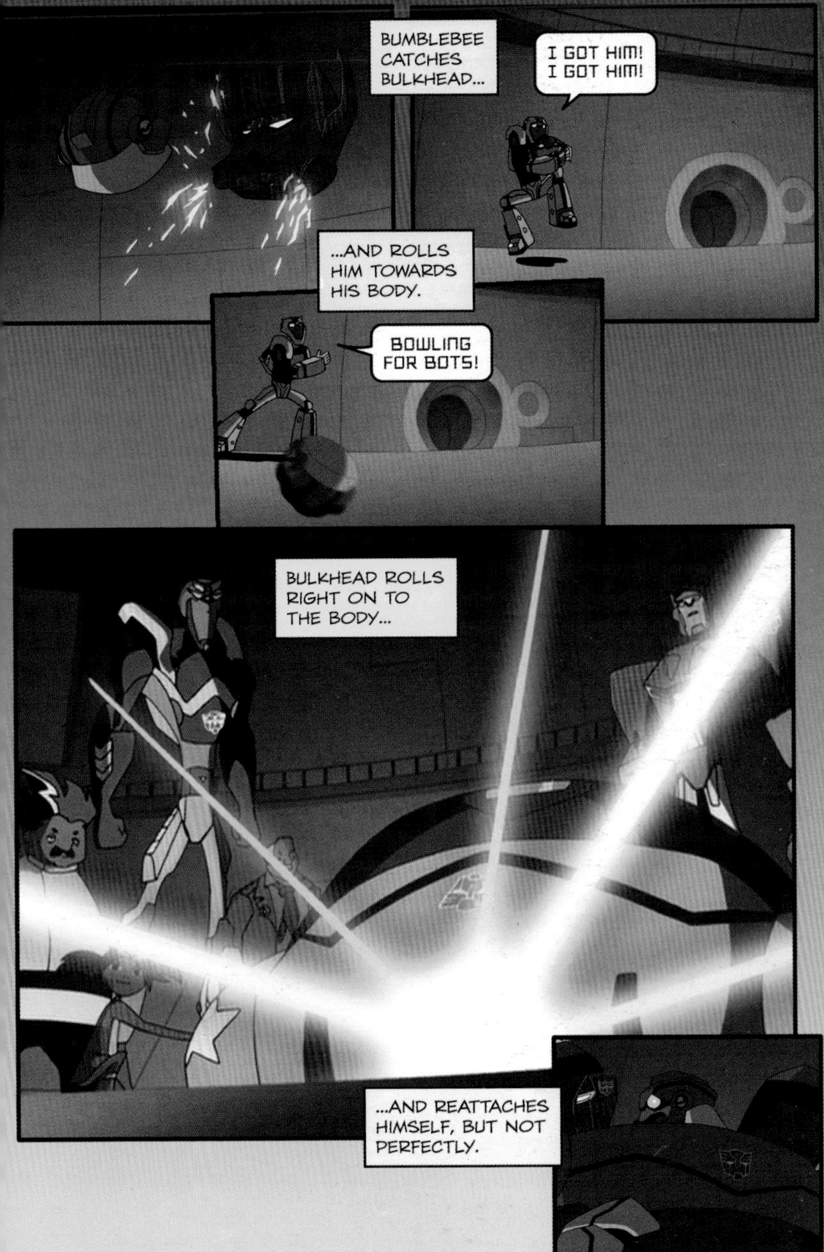
BUMBLEBEE CATCHES BULKHEAD...
I GOT HIM! I GOT HIM!
...AND ROLLS HIM TOWARDS HIS BODY.
BOWLING FOR BOTS!
BULKHEAD ROLLS RIGHT ON TO THE BODY...
...AND REATTACHES HIMSELF, BUT NOT PERFECTLY.

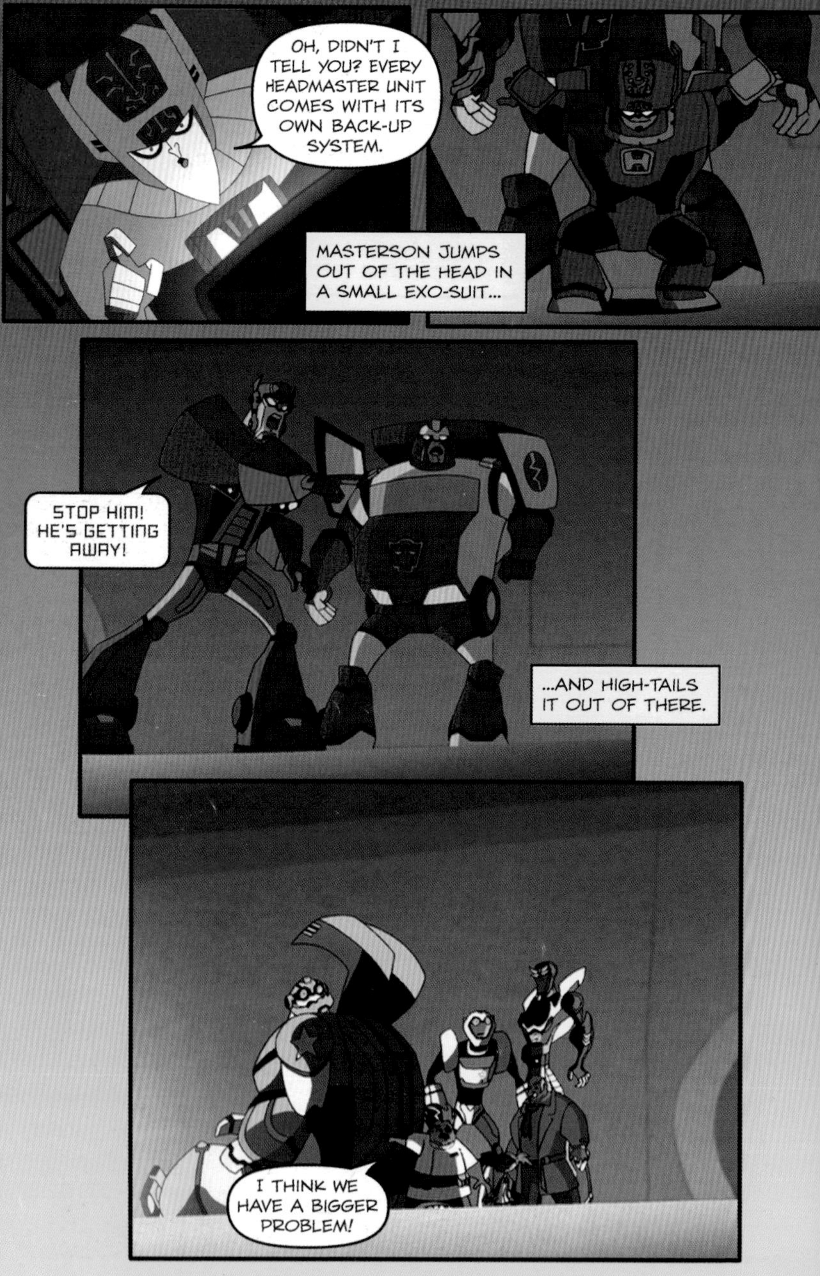
OH, DIDN'T I TELL YOU? EVERY HEADMASTER UNIT COMES WITH ITS OWN BACK-UP SYSTEM.
MASTERSON JUMPS OUT OF THE HEAD IN A SMALL EXO-SUIT...
STOP HIM! HE'S GETTING AWAY!
...AND HIGH-TAILS IT OUT OF THERE.
I THINK WE HAVE A BIGGER PROBLEM!

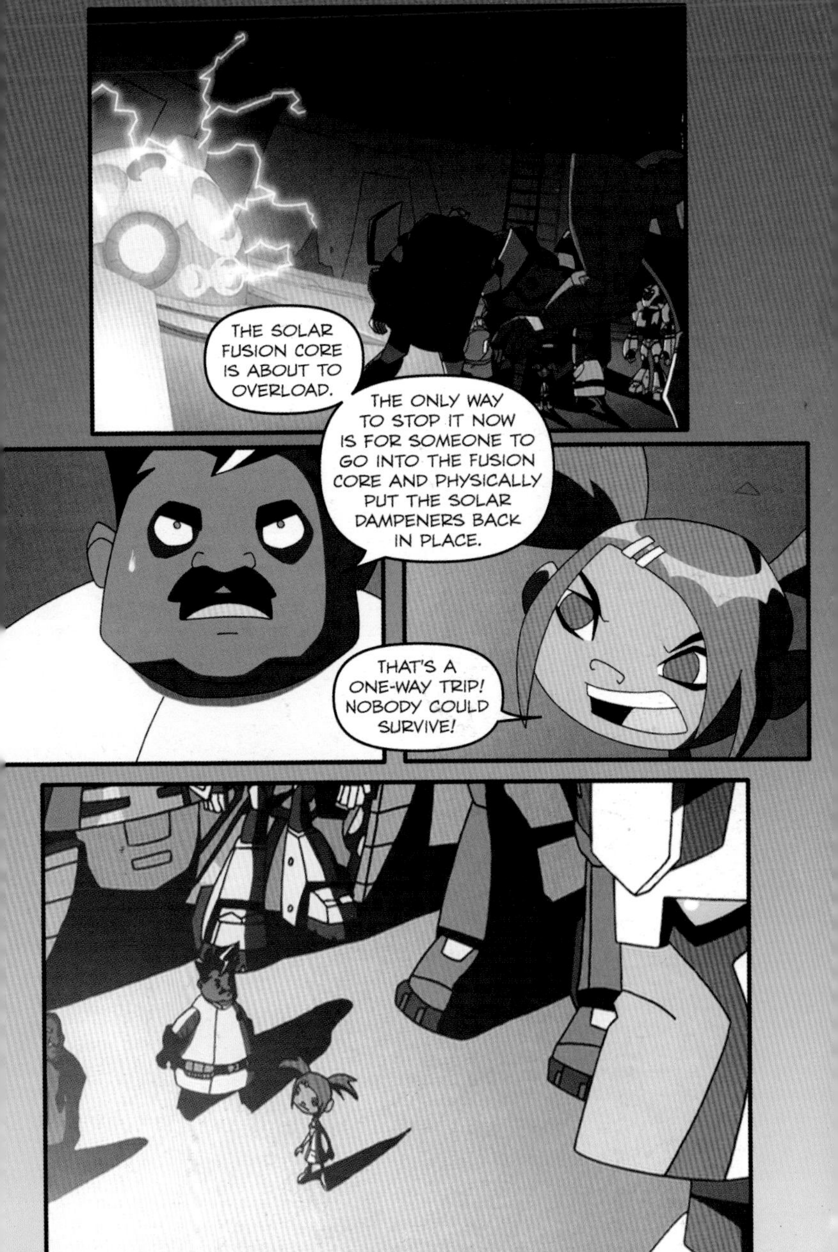
THE SOLAR FUSION CORE IS ABOUT TO OVERLOAD.
THE ONLY WAY TO STOP IT NOW IS FOR SOMEONE TO GO INTO THE FUSION CORE AND PHYSICALLY PUT THE SOLAR DAMPENERS BACK IN PLACE.
THAT'S A ONE-WAY TRIP! NOBODY COULD SURVIVE!

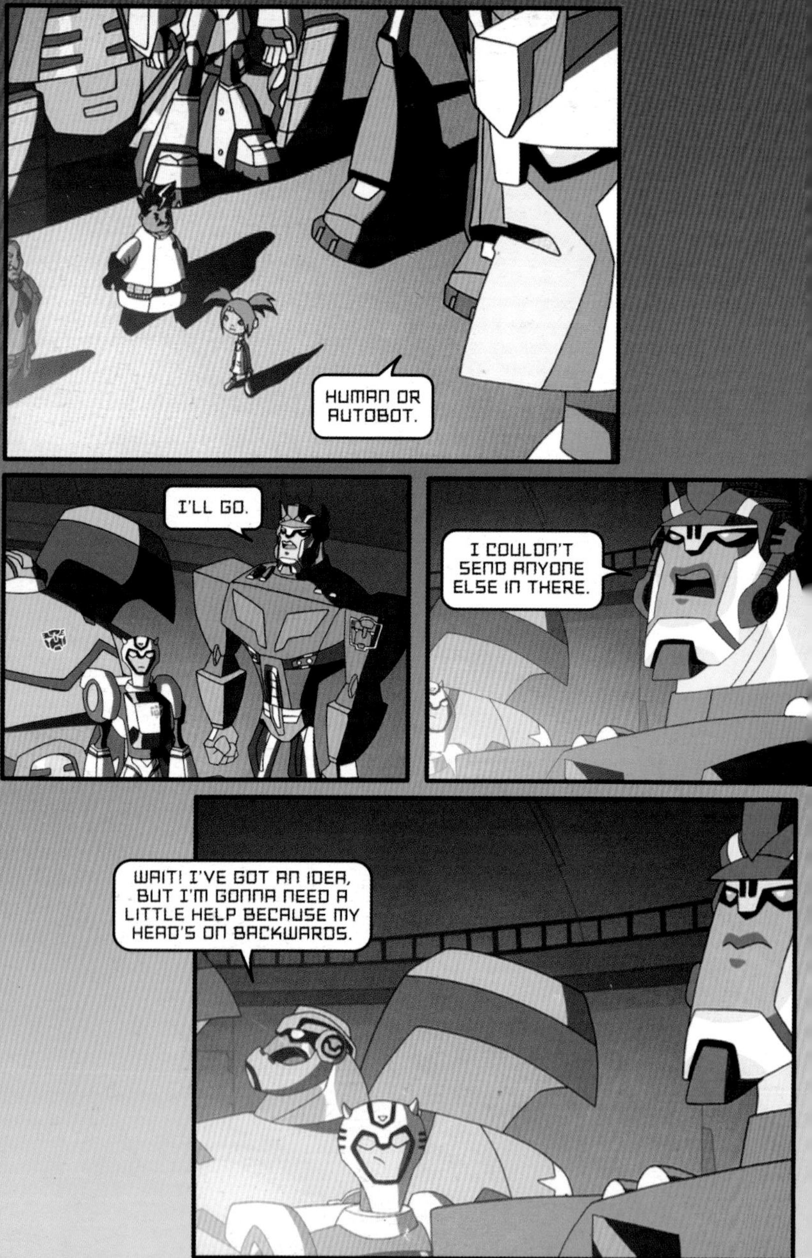
HUMAN OR AUTOBOT.
I'LL GO.
I COULDN'T SEND ANYONE ELSE IN THERE.
WAIT! I'VE GOT AN IDEA, BUT I'M GONNA NEED A LITTLE HELP BECAUSE MY HEAD'S ON BACKWARDS.

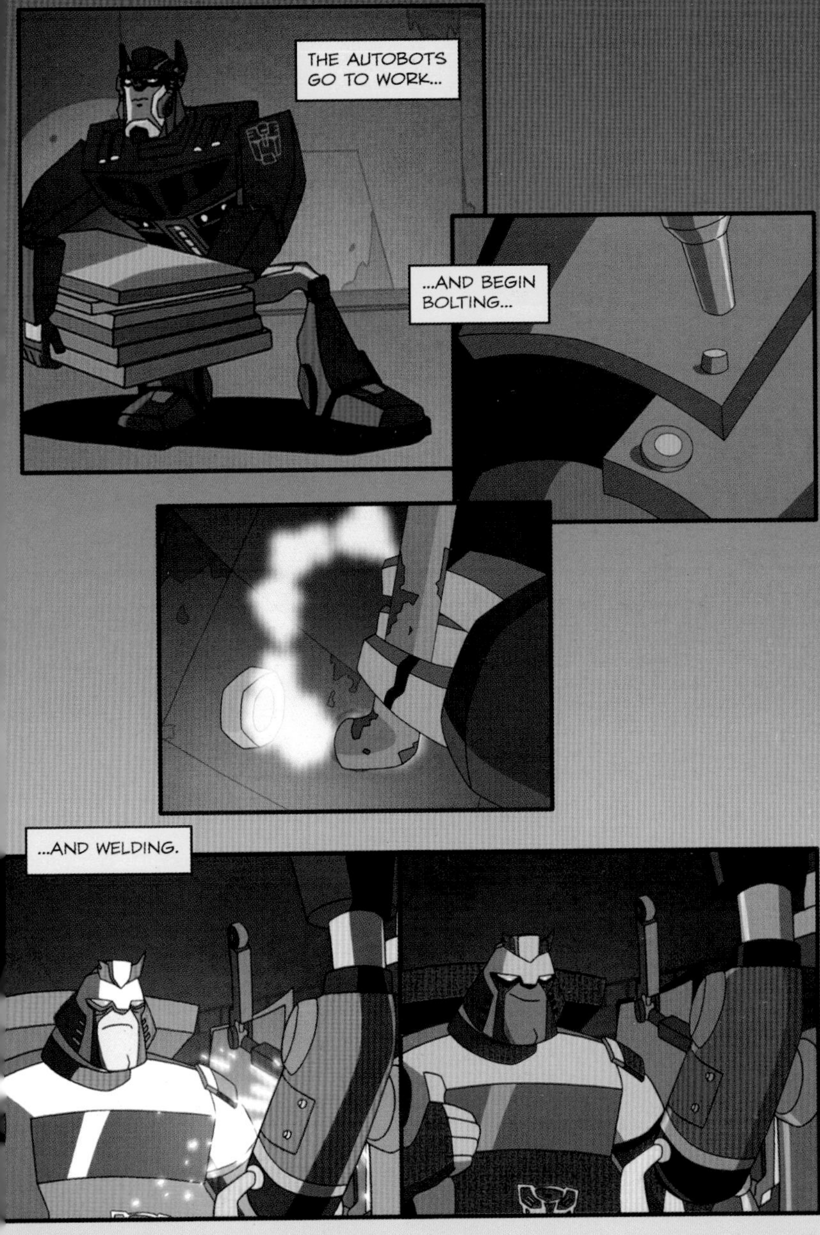
THE AUTOBOTS GO TO WORK...
...AND BEGIN BOLTING...
...AND WELDING.

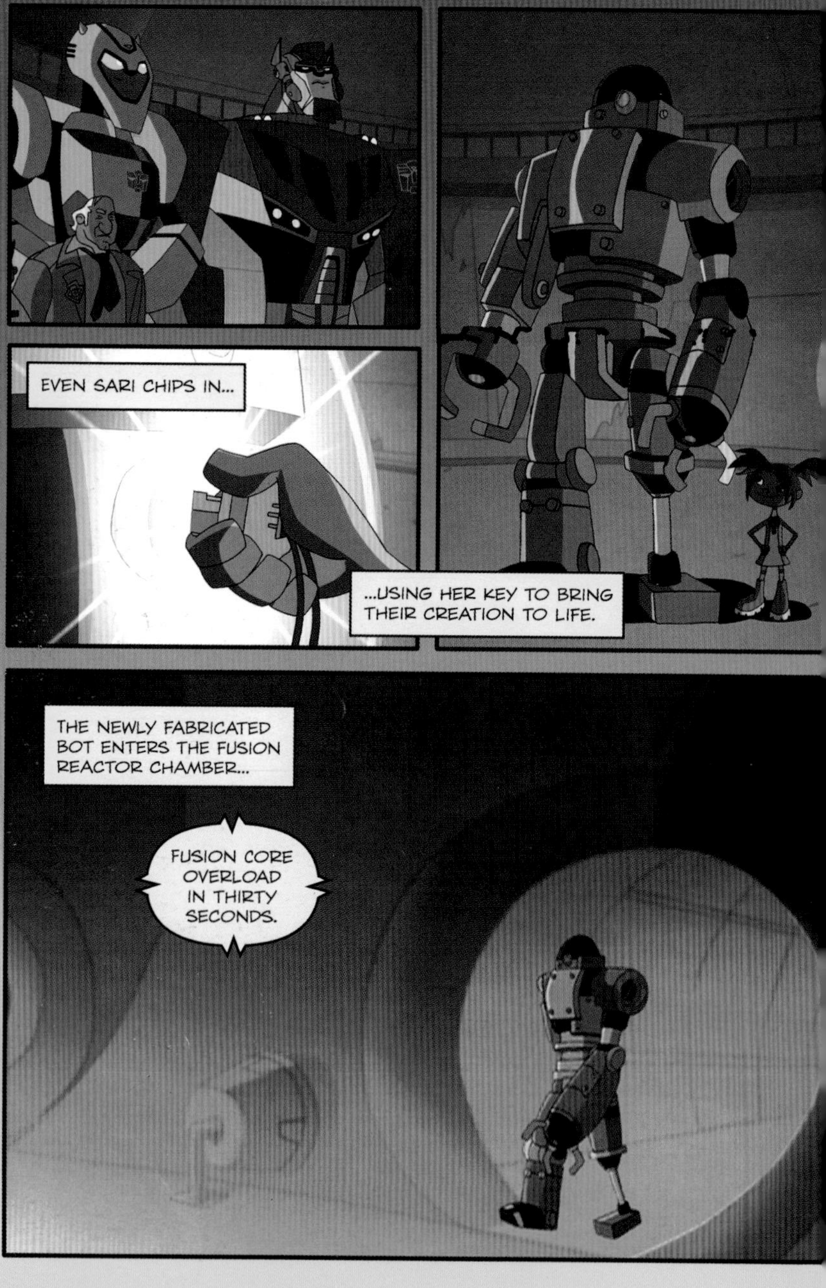
EVEN SARI CHIPS IN...
...USING HER KEY TO BRING THEIR CREATION TO LIFE.
THE NEWLY FABRICATED BOT ENTERS THE FUSION REACTOR CHAMBER...
FUSION CORE OVERLOAD IN THIRTY SECONDS.

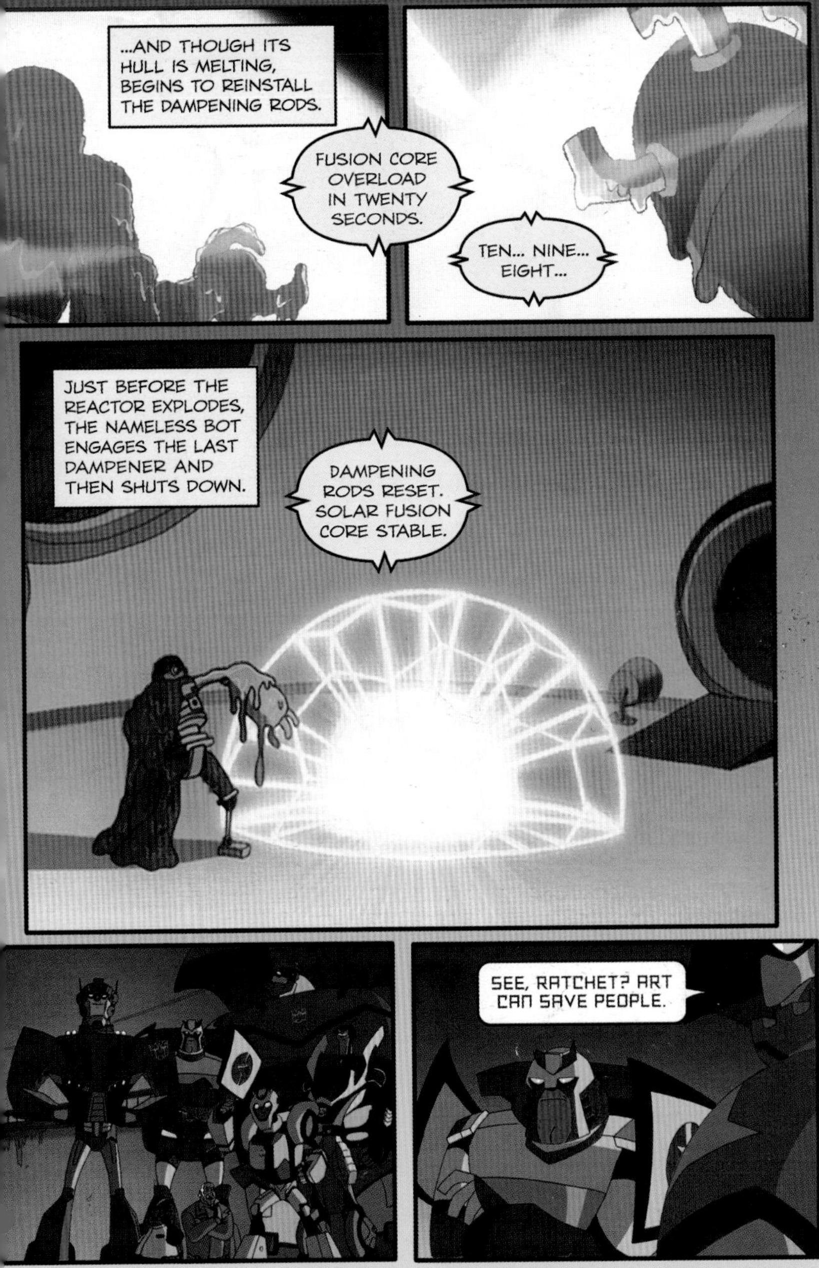
...AND THOUGH ITS HULL IS MELTING, BEGINS TO REINSTALL THE DAMPENING RODS.
FUSION CORE OVERLOAD IN TWENTY SECONDS.
TEN... NINE... EIGHT...
JUST BEFORE THE REACTOR EXPLODES, THE NAMELESS BOT ENGAGES THE LAST DAMPENER AND THEN SHUTS DOWN.
DAMPENING RODS RESET. SOLAR FUSION CORE STABLE.
SEE, RATCHET? ART CAN SAVE PEOPLE.

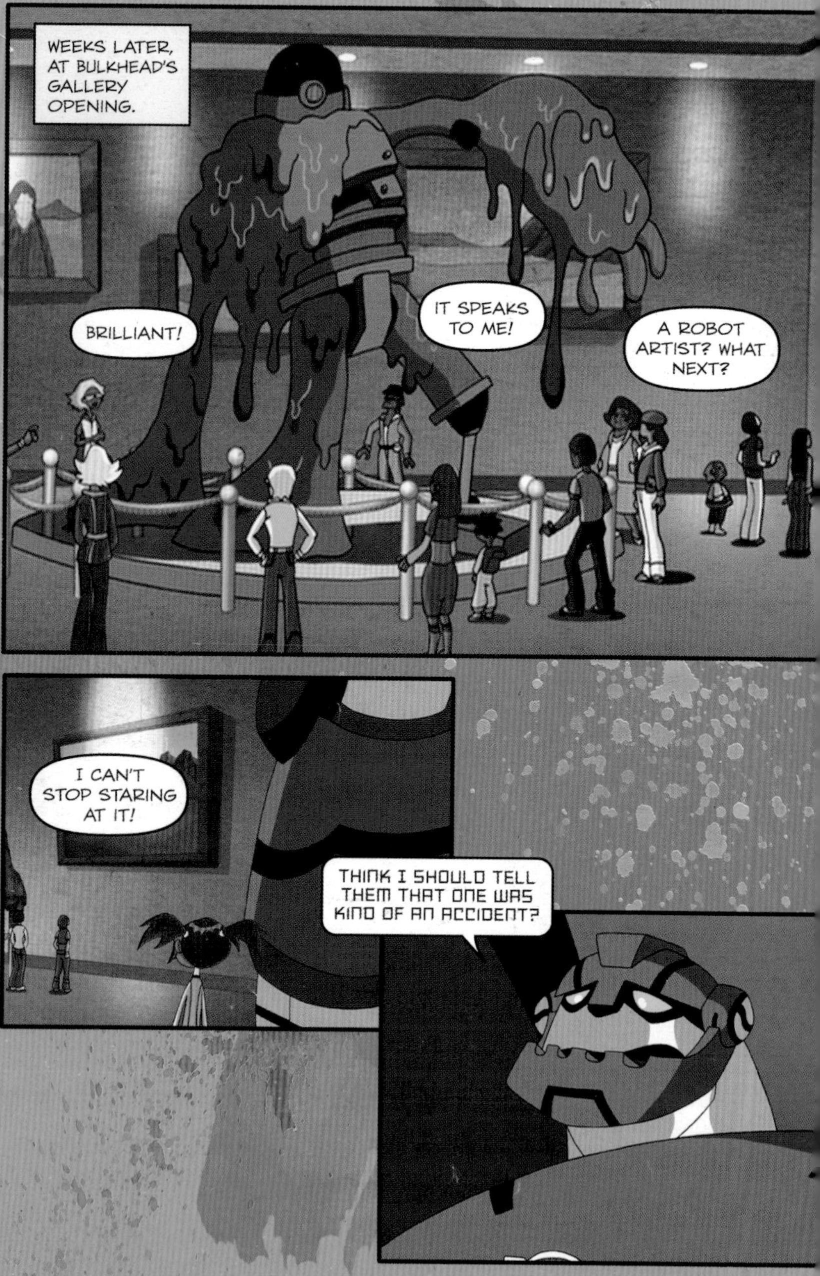
WEEKS LATER, AT BULKHEAD'S GALLERY OPENING.
BRILLIANT!
IT SPEAKS TO ME!
A ROBOT ARTIST? WHAT NEXT?
I CAN'T STOP STARING AT IT!
THINK I SHOULD TELL THEM THAT ONE WAS KIND OF AN ACCIDENT?

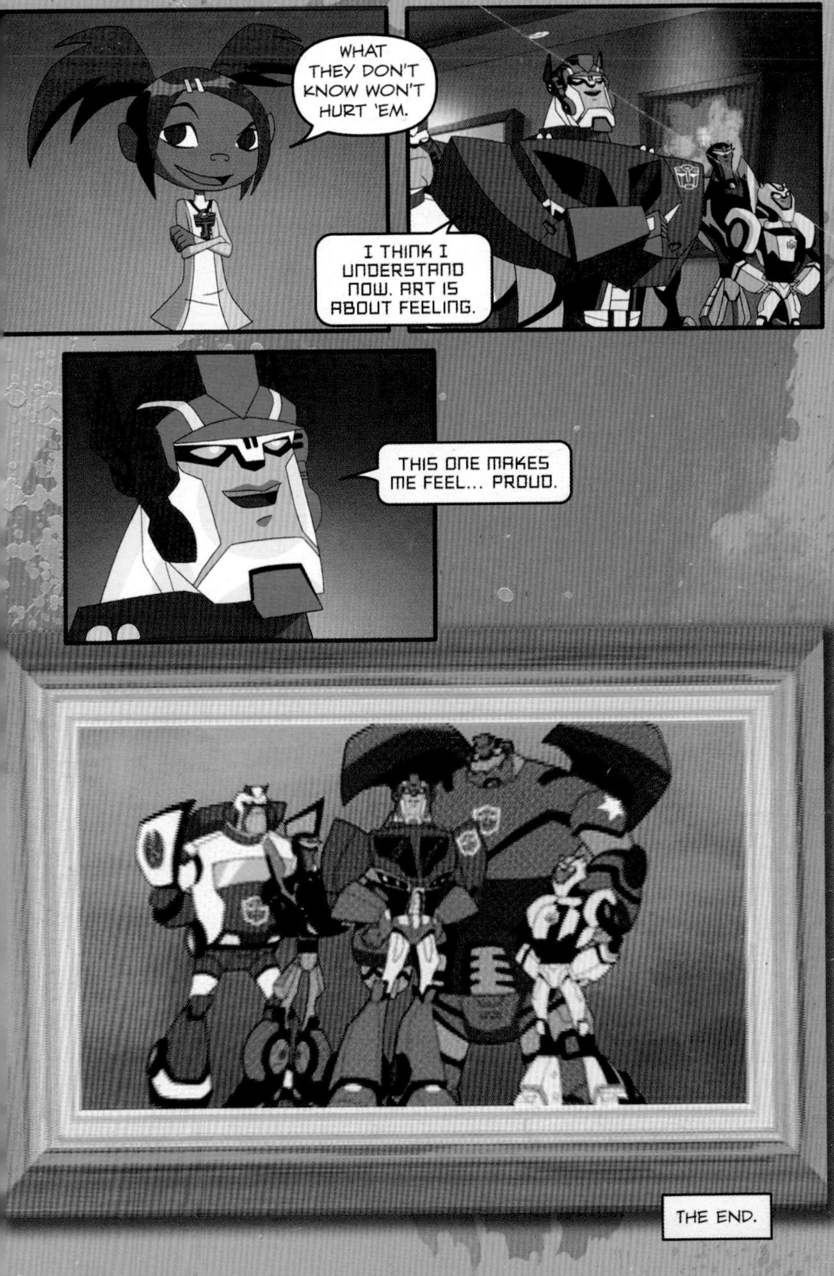
WHAT THEY DON'T KNOW WON'T HURT 'EM.
I THINK I UNDERSTAND NOW. ART IS ABOUT FEELING.
THIS ONE MAKES ME FEEL... PROUD.
THE END.

NATURE CALLS

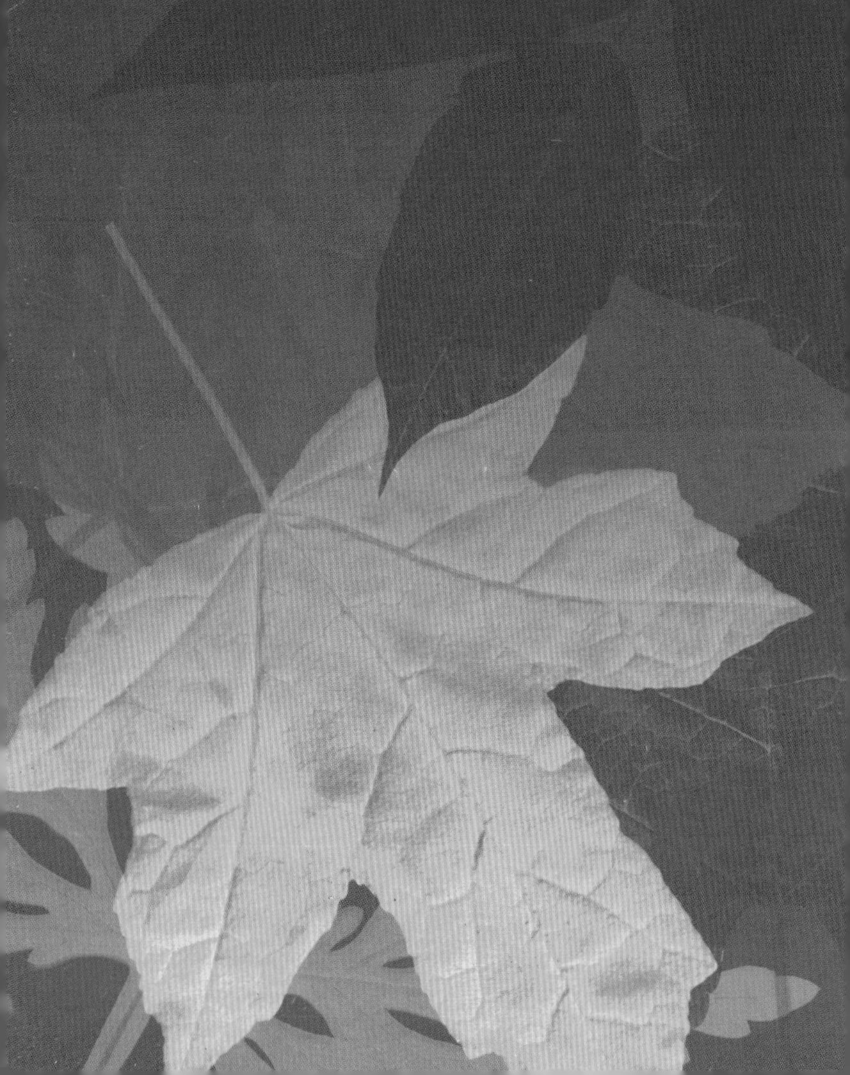

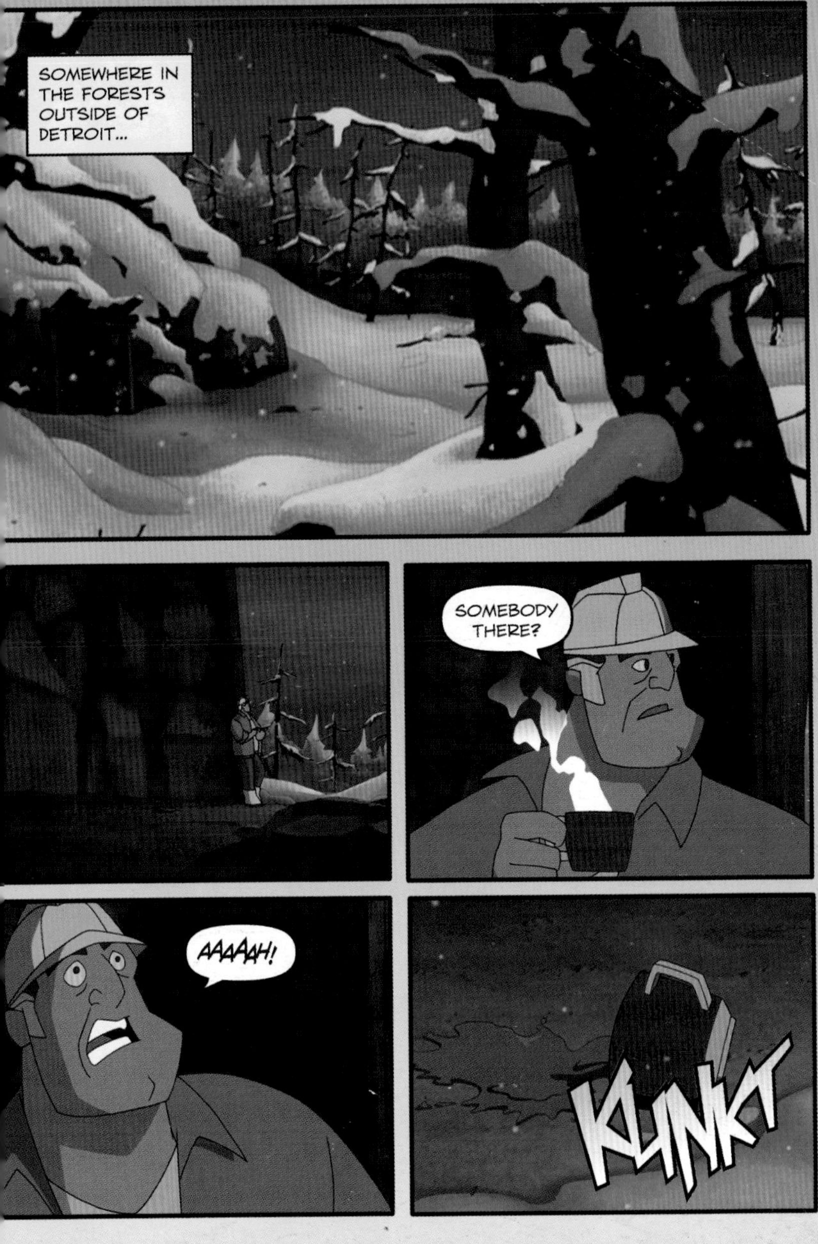
SOMEWHERE IN THE FORESTS OUTSIDE OF DETROIT...
SOMEBODY THERE?
AAAAAH!
KLUNKT

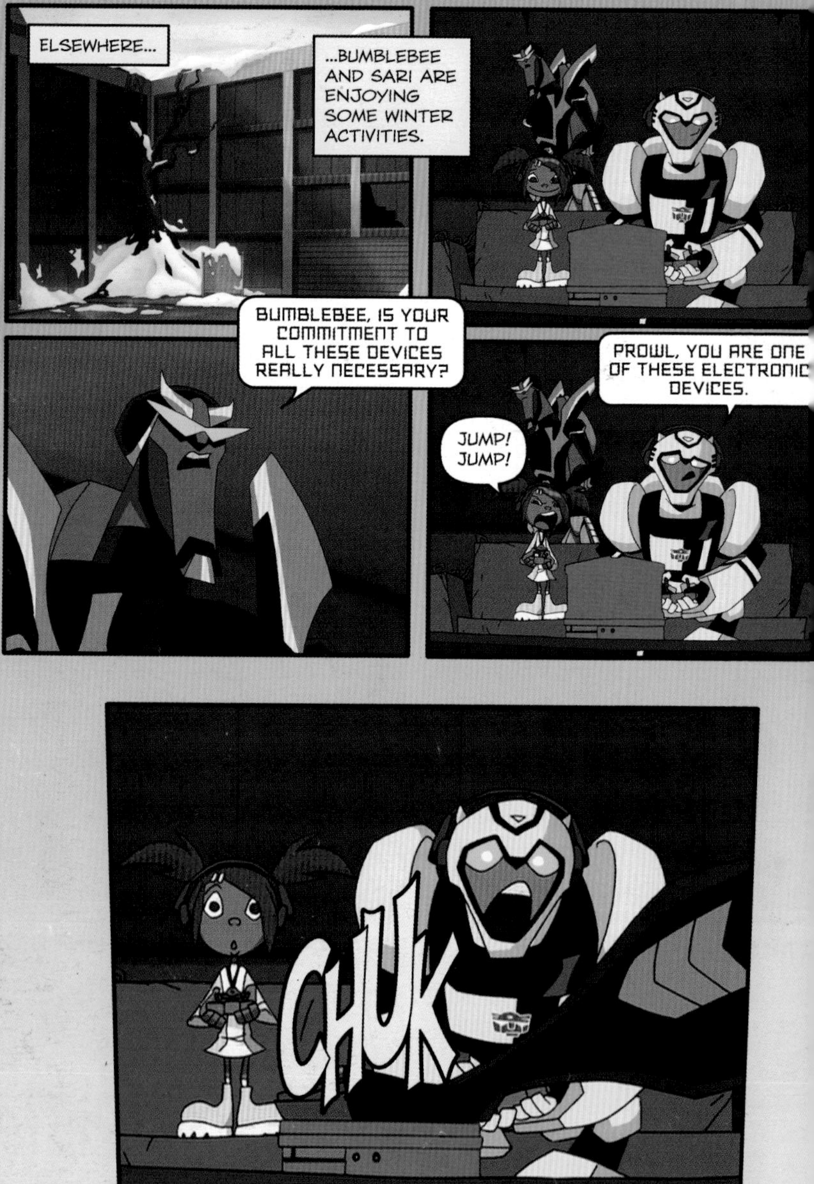
ELSEWHERE...
...BUMBLEBEE AND SARI ARE ENJOYING SOME WINTER ACTIVITIES.
BUMBLEBEE, IS YOUR COMMITMENT TO ALL THESE DEVICES REALLY NECESSARY?
PROWL, YOU ARE ONE OF THESE ELECTRONIC DEVICES.
JUMP! JUMP!
CHUK

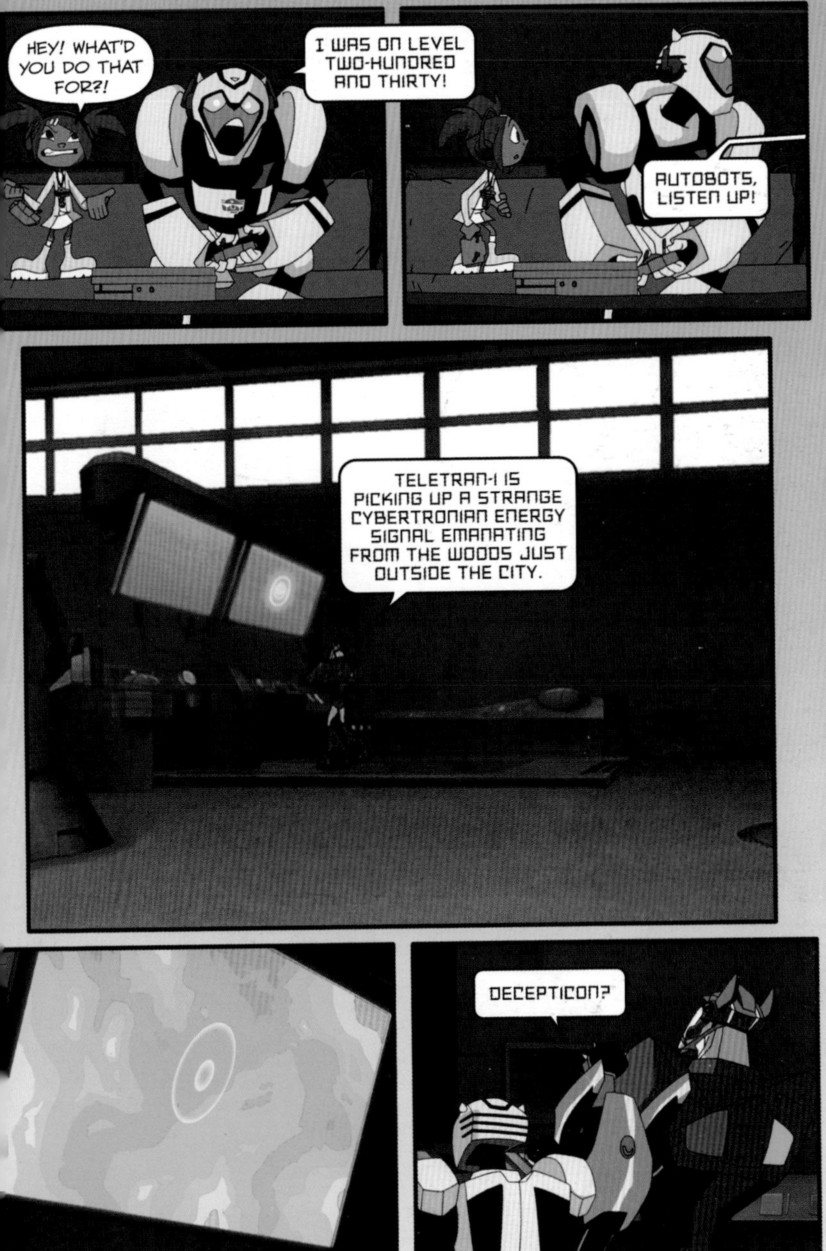
HEY! WHAT'D YOU DO THAT FOR?!
I WAS ON LEVEL TWO-HUNDRED AND THIRTY!
AUTOBOTS, LISTEN UP!
TELETRAN-1 IS PICKING UP A STRANGE CYBERTRONIAN ENERGY SIGNAL EMANATING FROM THE WOODS JUST OUTSIDE THE CITY.
DECEPTICON?

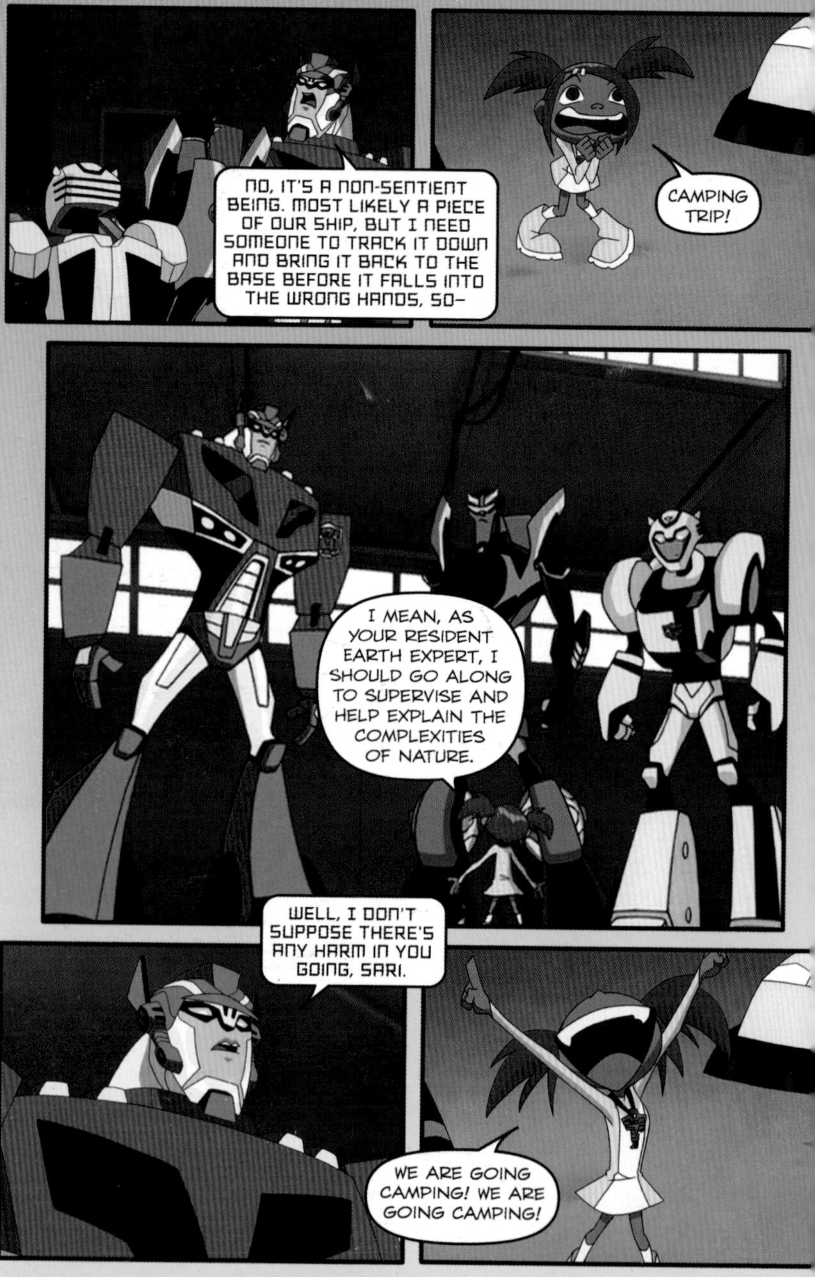
NO, IT'S A NON-SENTIENT BEING. MOST LIKELY A PIECE OF OUR SHIP, BUT I NEED SOMEONE TO TRACK IT DOWN AND BRING IT BACK TO THE BASE BEFORE IT FALLS INTO THE WRONG HANDS, SO–
CAMPING TRIP!
I MEAN, AS YOUR RESIDENT EARTH EXPERT, I SHOULD GO ALONG TO SUPERVISE AND HELP EXPLAIN THE COMPLEXITIES OF NATURE.
WELL, I DON'T SUPPOSE THERE'S ANY HARM IN YOU GOING, SARI.
WE ARE GOING CAMPING! WE ARE GOING CAMPING!

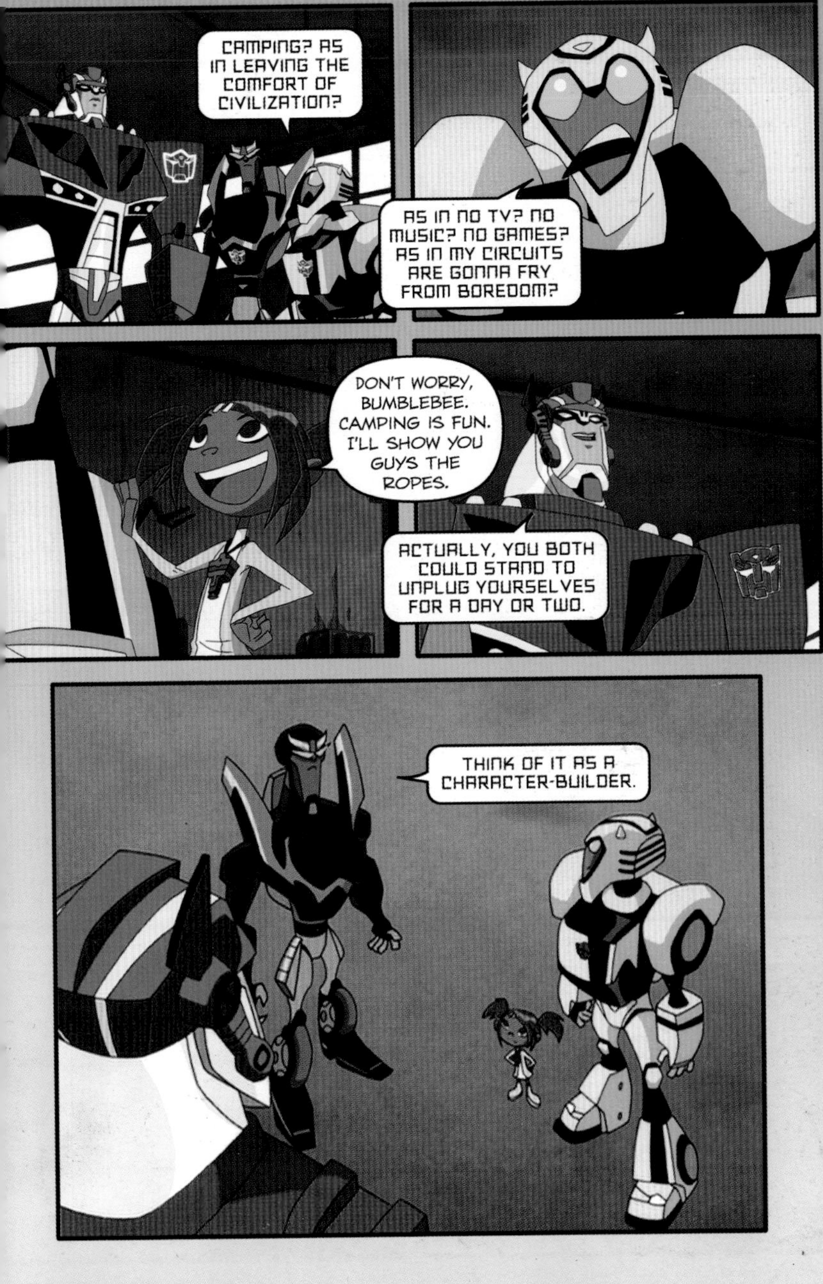
CAMPING? AS IN LEAVING THE COMFORT OF CIVILIZATION?
AS IN NO TV? NO MUSIC? NO GAMES? AS IN MY CIRCUITS ARE GONNA FRY FROM BOREDOM?
DON'T WORRY, BUMBLEBEE. CAMPING IS FUN. I'LL SHOW YOU GUYS THE ROPES.
ACTUALLY, YOU BOTH COULD STAND TO UNPLUG YOURSELVES FOR A DAY OR TWO.
THINK OF IT AS A CHARACTER-BUILDER.

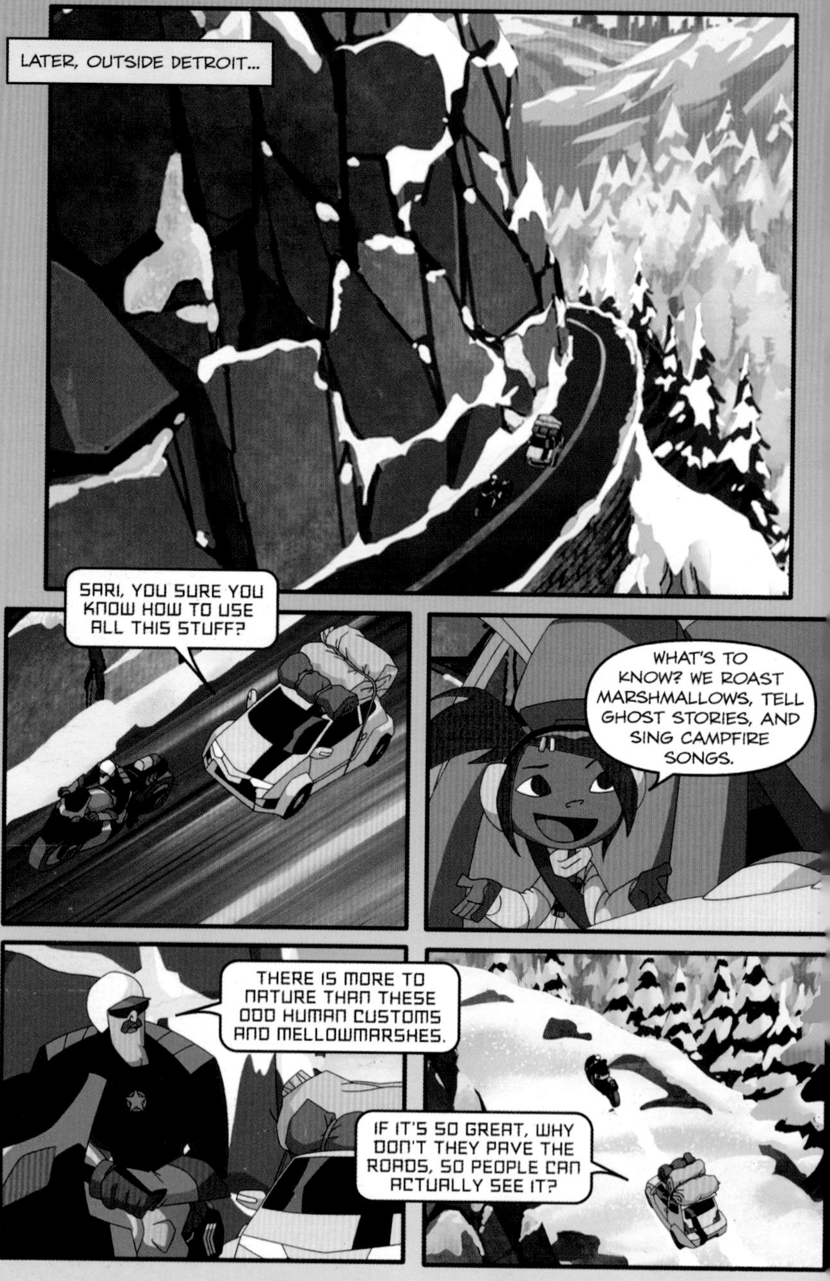
LATER, OUTSIDE DETROIT...
SARI, YOU SURE YOU KNOW HOW TO USE ALL THIS STUFF?
WHAT'S TO KNOW? WE ROAST MARSHMALLOWS, TELL GHOST STORIES, AND SING CAMPFIRE SONGS.
THERE IS MORE TO NATURE THAN THESE ODD HUMAN CUSTOMS AND MELLOWMARSHES.
IF IT'S SO GREAT, WHY DON'T THEY PAVE THE ROADS, SO PEOPLE CAN ACTUALLY SEE IT?

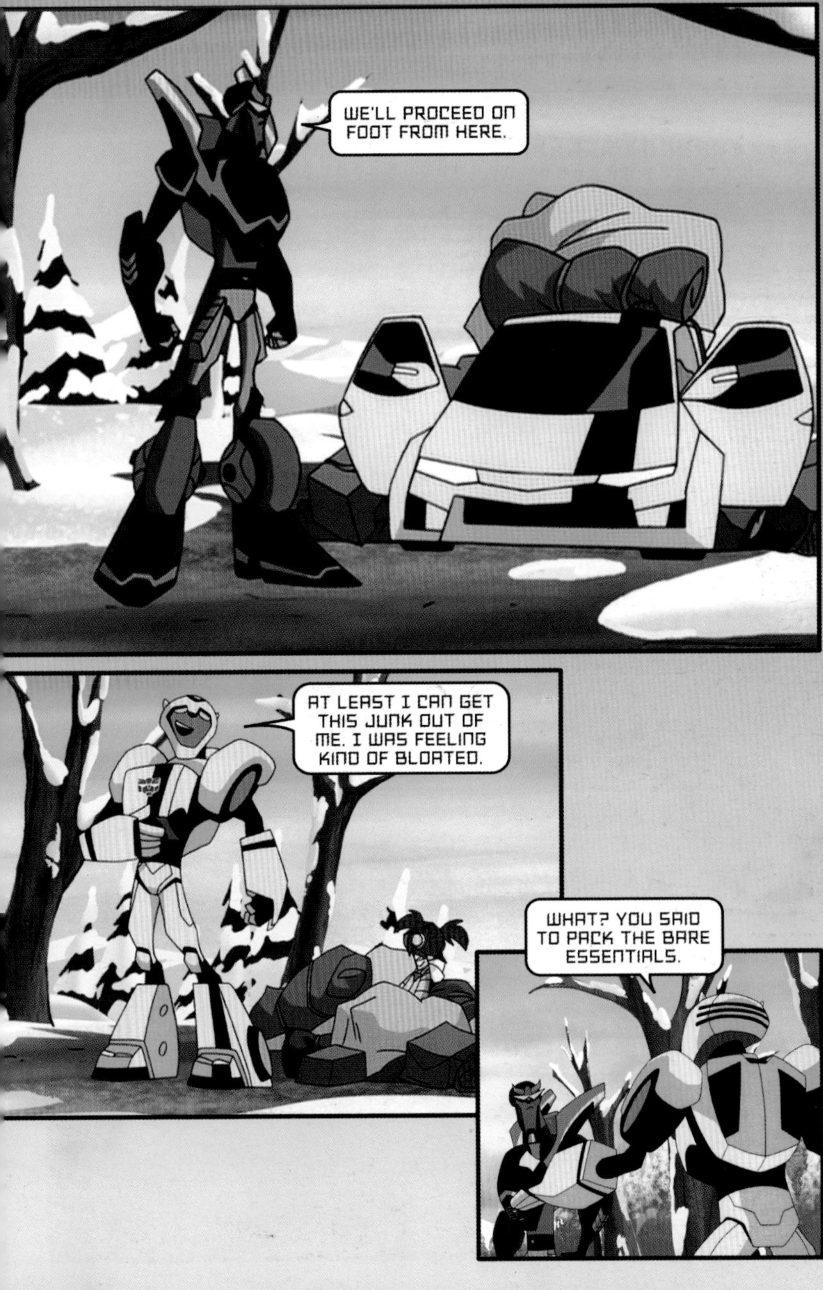
WE'LL PROCEED ON FOOT FROM HERE.
AT LEAST I CAN GET THIS JUNK OUT OF ME. I WAS FEELING KIND OF BLOATED.
WHAT? YOU SAID TO PACK THE BARE ESSENTIALS.

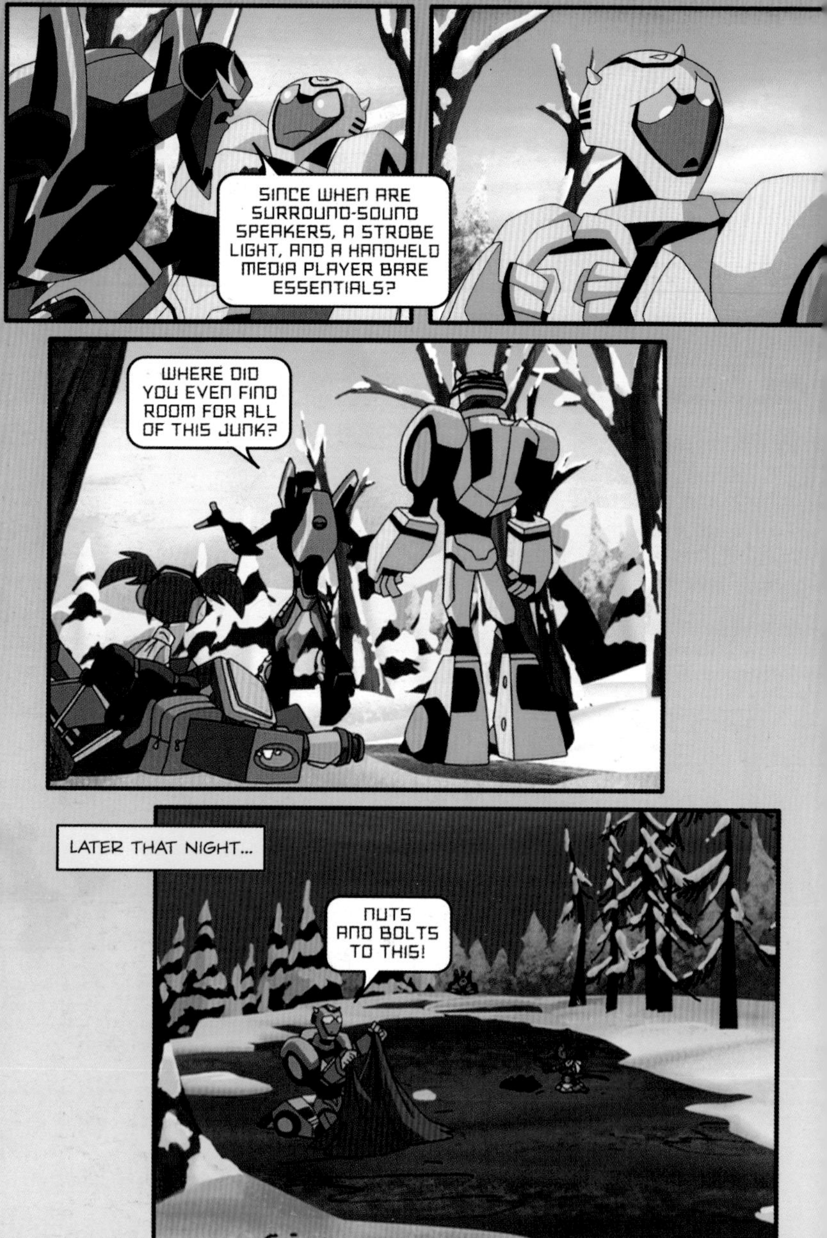
SINCE WHEN ARE SURROUND-SOUND SPEAKERS, A STROBE LIGHT, AND A HANDHELD MEDIA PLAYER BARE ESSENTIALS?
WHERE DID YOU EVEN FIND ROOM FOR ALL OF THIS JUNK?
LATER THAT NIGHT...
NUTS AND BOLTS TO THIS!

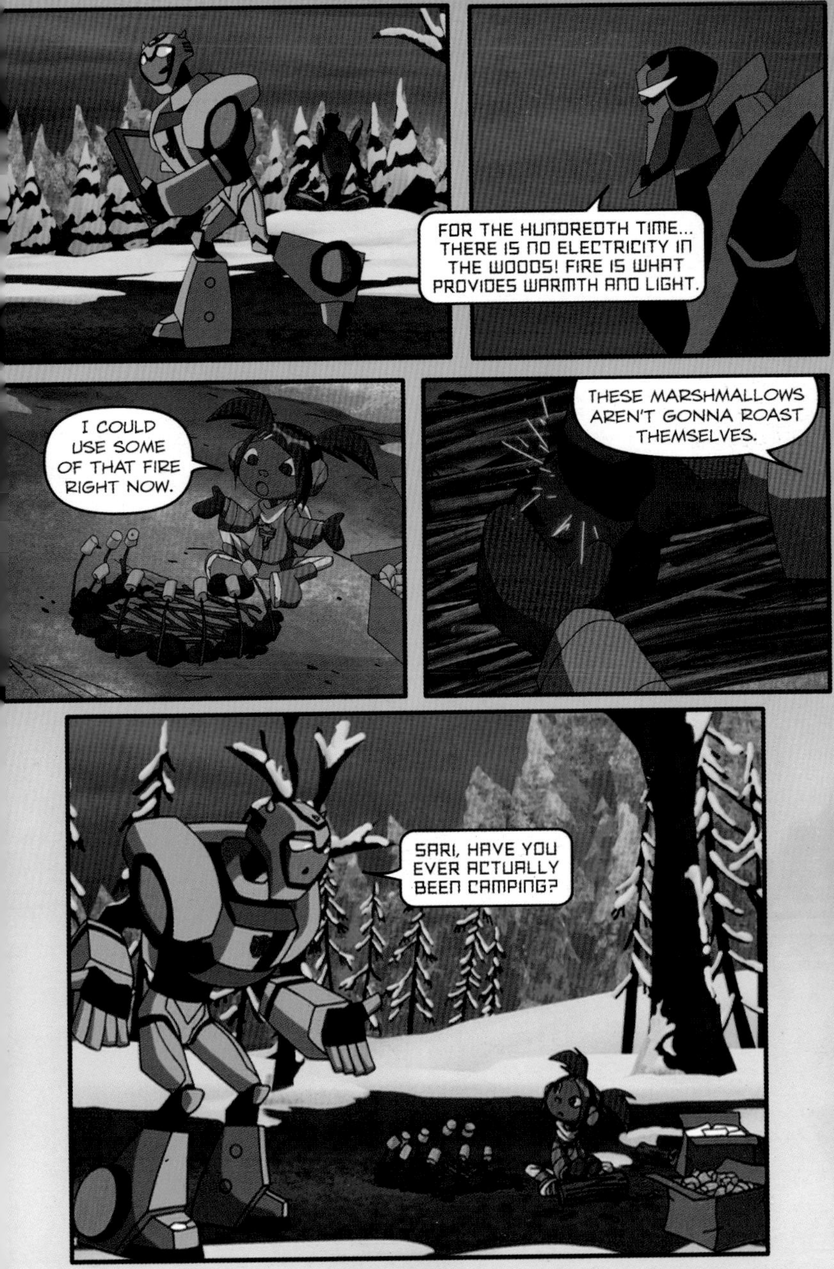
FOR THE HUNDREDTH TIME... THERE IS NO ELECTRICITY IN THE WOODS! FIRE IS WHAT PROVIDES WARMTH AND LIGHT.
I COULD USE SOME OF THAT FIRE RIGHT NOW.
THESE MARSHMALLOWS AREN'T GONNA ROAST THEMSELVES.
SARI, HAVE YOU EVER ACTUALLY BEEN CAMPING?

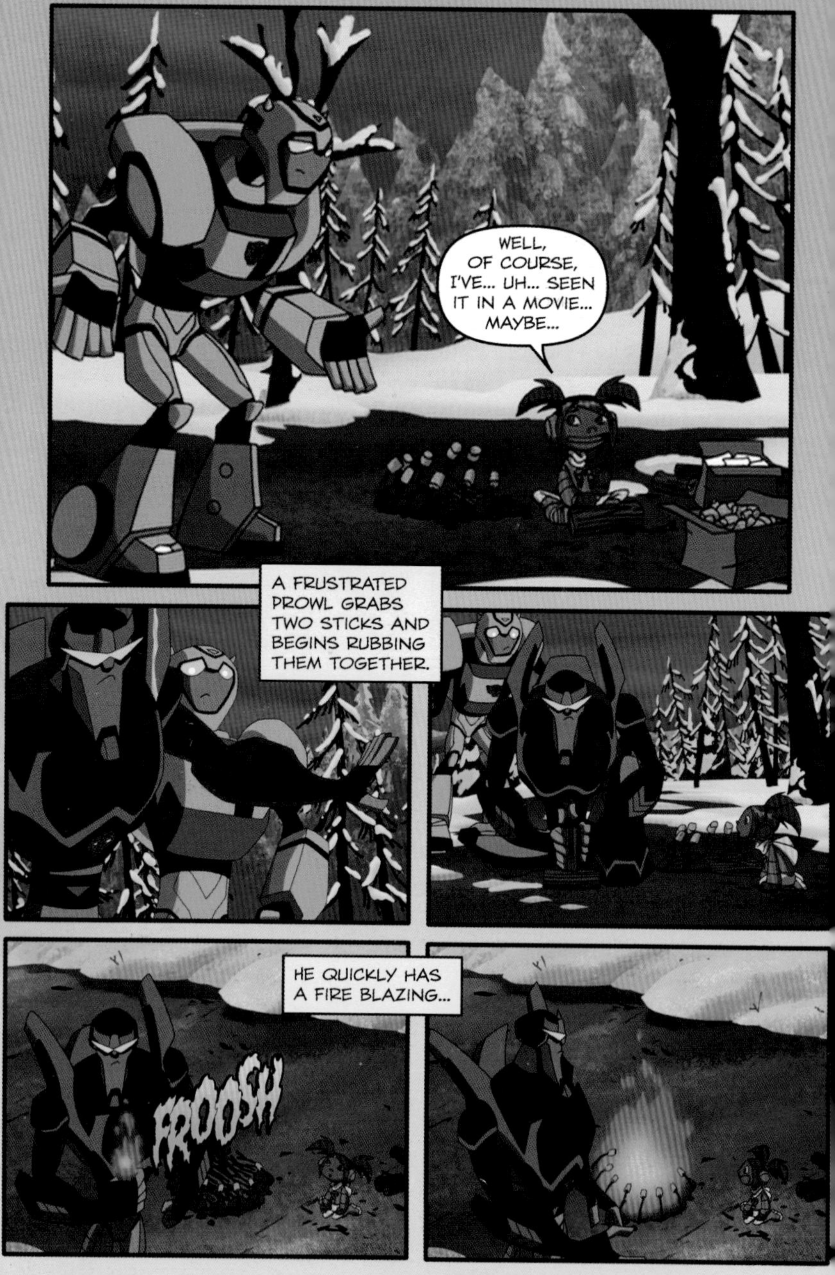
WELL, OF COURSE, I'VE... UH... SEEN IT IN A MOVIE... MAYBE...
A FRUSTRATED PROWL GRABS TWO STICKS AND BEGINS RUBBING THEM TOGETHER.
FROOSH
HE QUICKLY HAS A FIRE BLAZING...

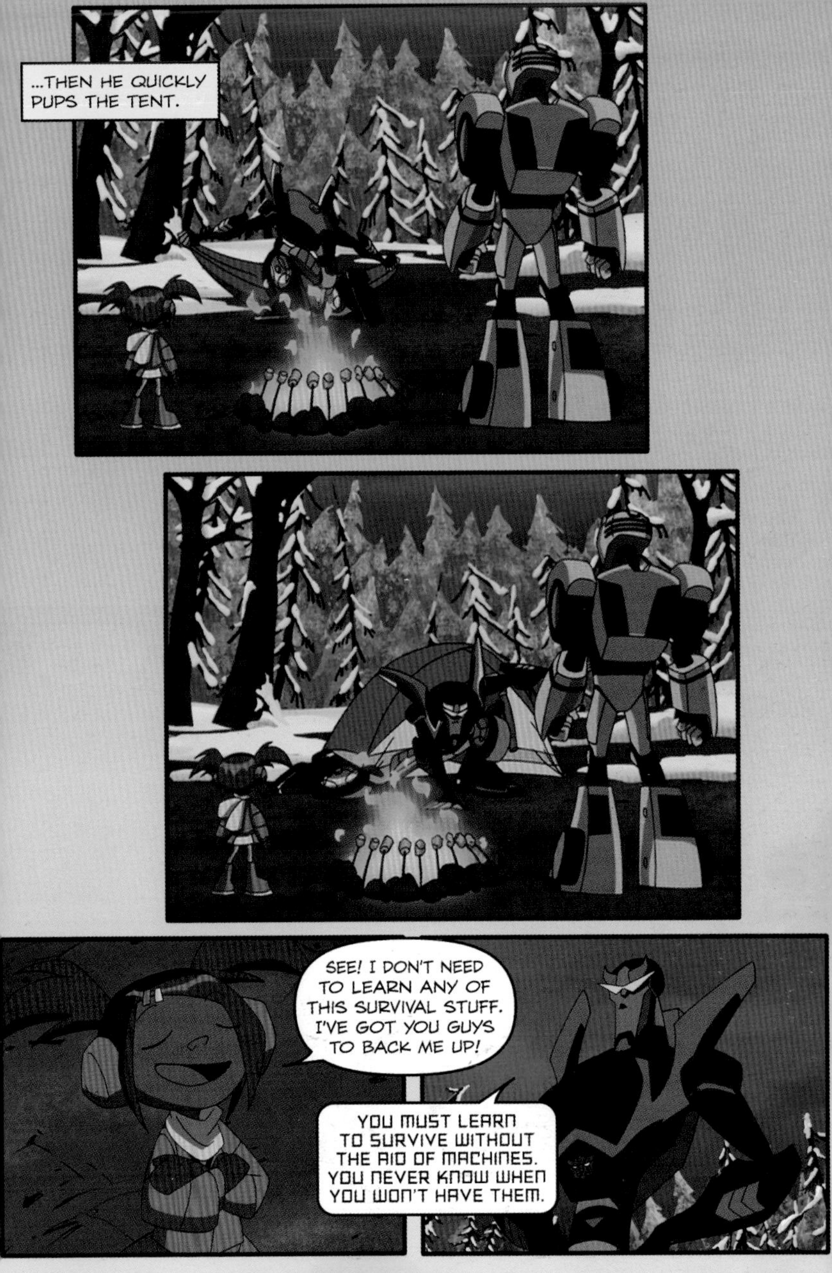
...THEN HE QUICKLY PUPS THE TENT.
SEE! I DON'T NEED TO LEARN ANY OF THIS SURVIVAL STUFF. I'VE GOT YOU GUYS TO BACK ME UP!
YOU MUST LEARN TO SURVIVE WITHOUT THE AID OF MACHINES. YOU NEVER KNOW WHEN YOU WON'T HAVE THEM.

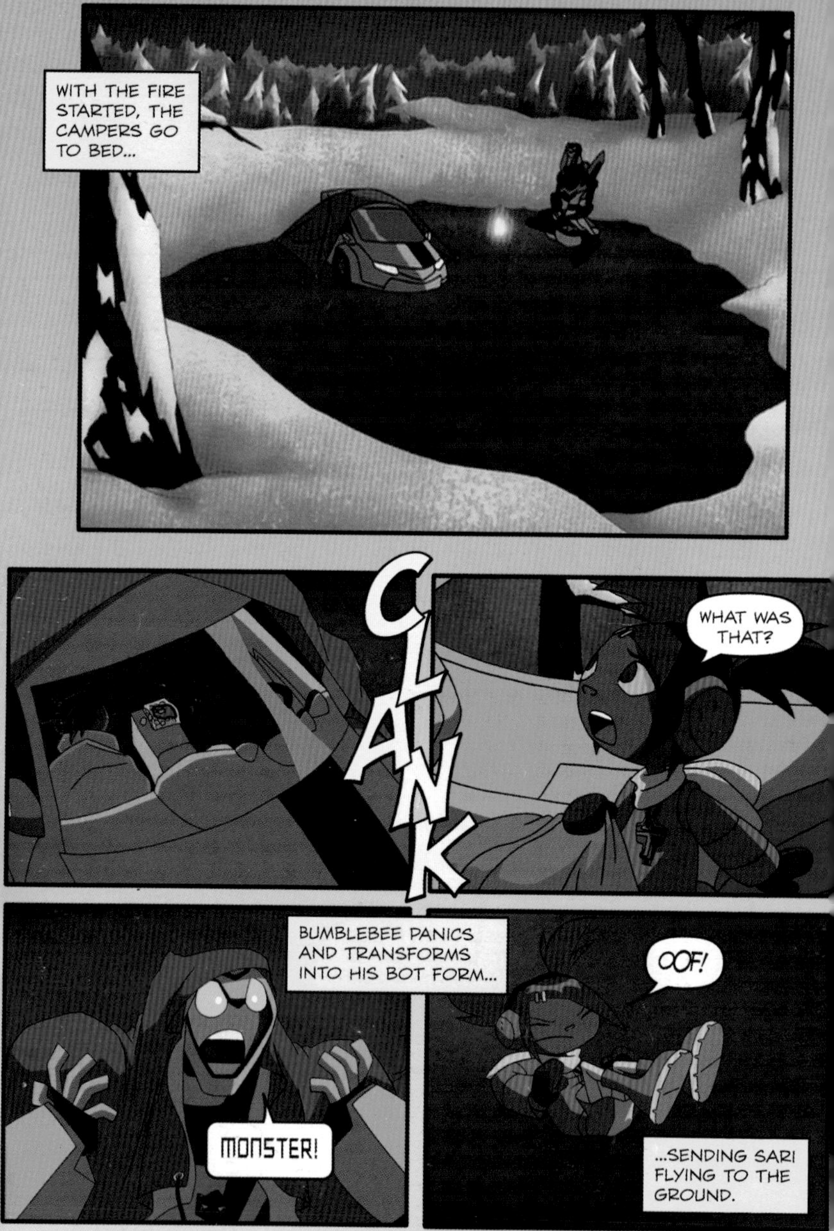
WITH THE FIRE STARTED, THE CAMPERS GO TO BED...
CLANK
WHAT WAS THAT?
BUMBLEBEE PANICS AND TRANSFORMS INTO HIS BOT FORM...
MONSTER!
OOF!
...SENDING SARI FLYING TO THE GROUND.

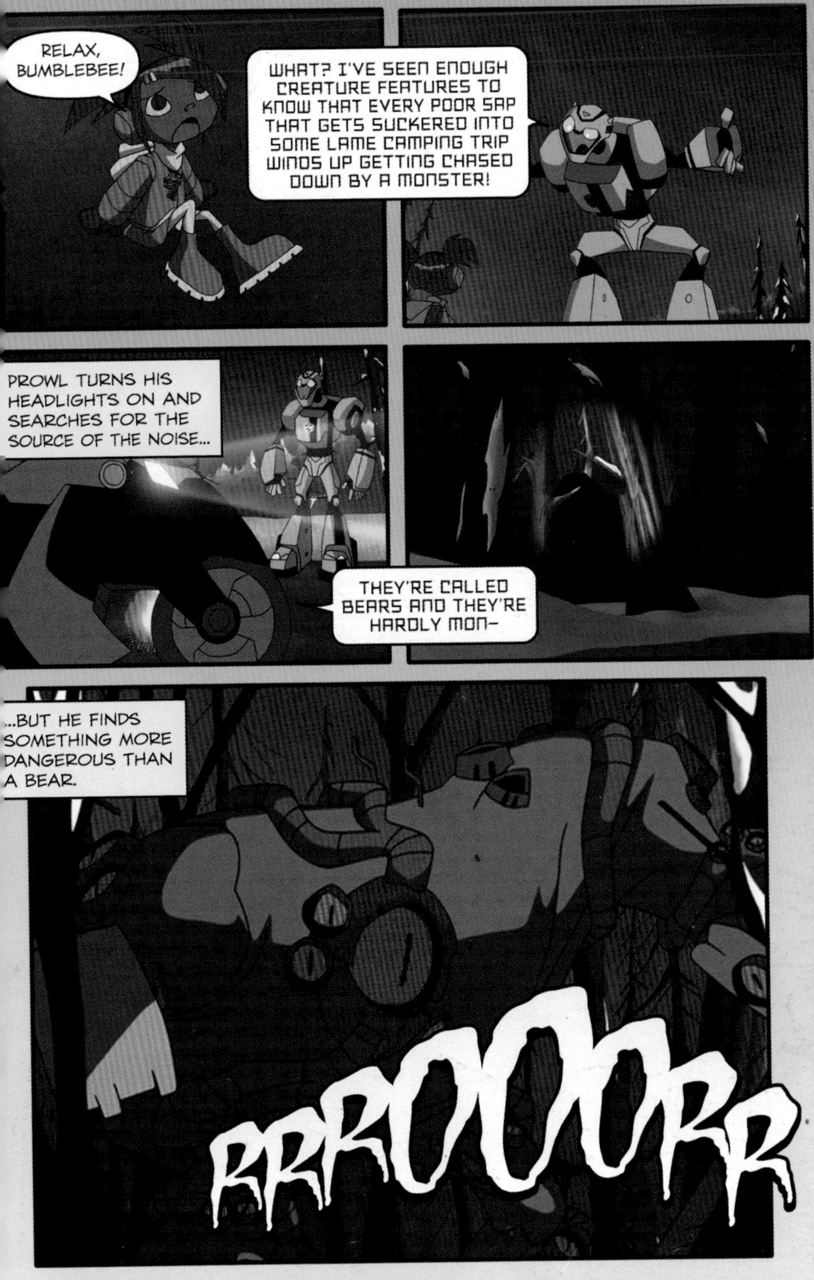

RELAX, BUMBLEBEE!
WHAT? I'VE SEEN ENOUGH CREATURE FEATURES TO KNOW THAT EVERY POOR SAP THAT GETS SUCKERED INTO SOME LAME CAMPING TRIP WINDS UP GETTING CHASED DOWN BY A MONSTER!
PROWL TURNS HIS HEADLIGHTS ON AND SEARCHES FOR THE SOURCE OF THE NOISE...
THEY'RE CALLED BEARS AND THEY'RE HARDLY MON–
...BUT HE FINDS SOMETHING MORE DANGEROUS THAN A BEAR.
RRROOORR

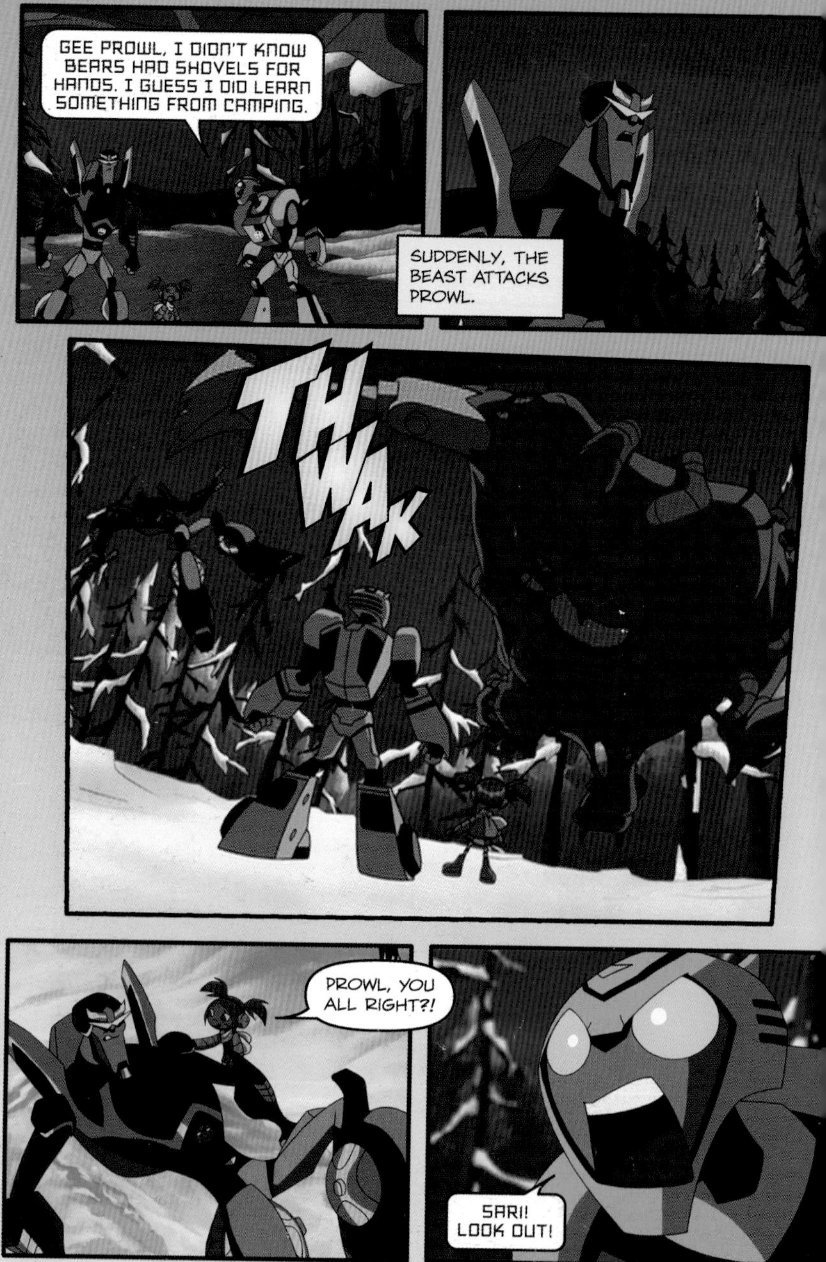
GEE PROWL, I DIDN'T KNOW BEARS HAD SHOVELS FOR HANDS. I GUESS I DID LEARN SOMETHING FROM CAMPING.
SUDDENLY, THE BEAST ATTACKS PROWL.
THWAK
PROWL, YOU ALL RIGHT?!
SARI! LOOK OUT!

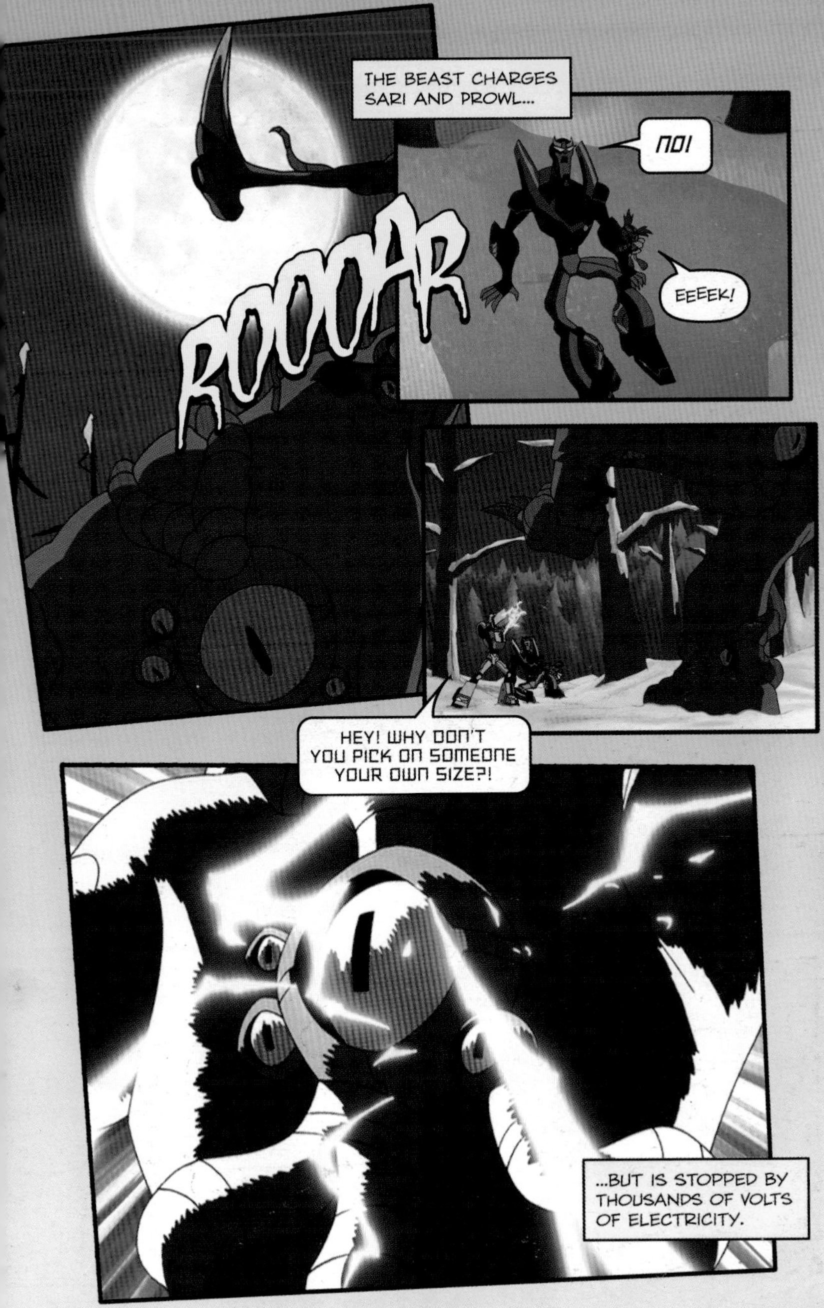
THE BEAST CHARGES SARI AND PROWL...
NO!
ROOOAR
EEEEK!
HEY! WHY DON'T YOU PICK ON SOMEONE YOUR OWN SIZE?!
...BUT IS STOPPED BY THOUSANDS OF VOLTS OF ELECTRICITY.

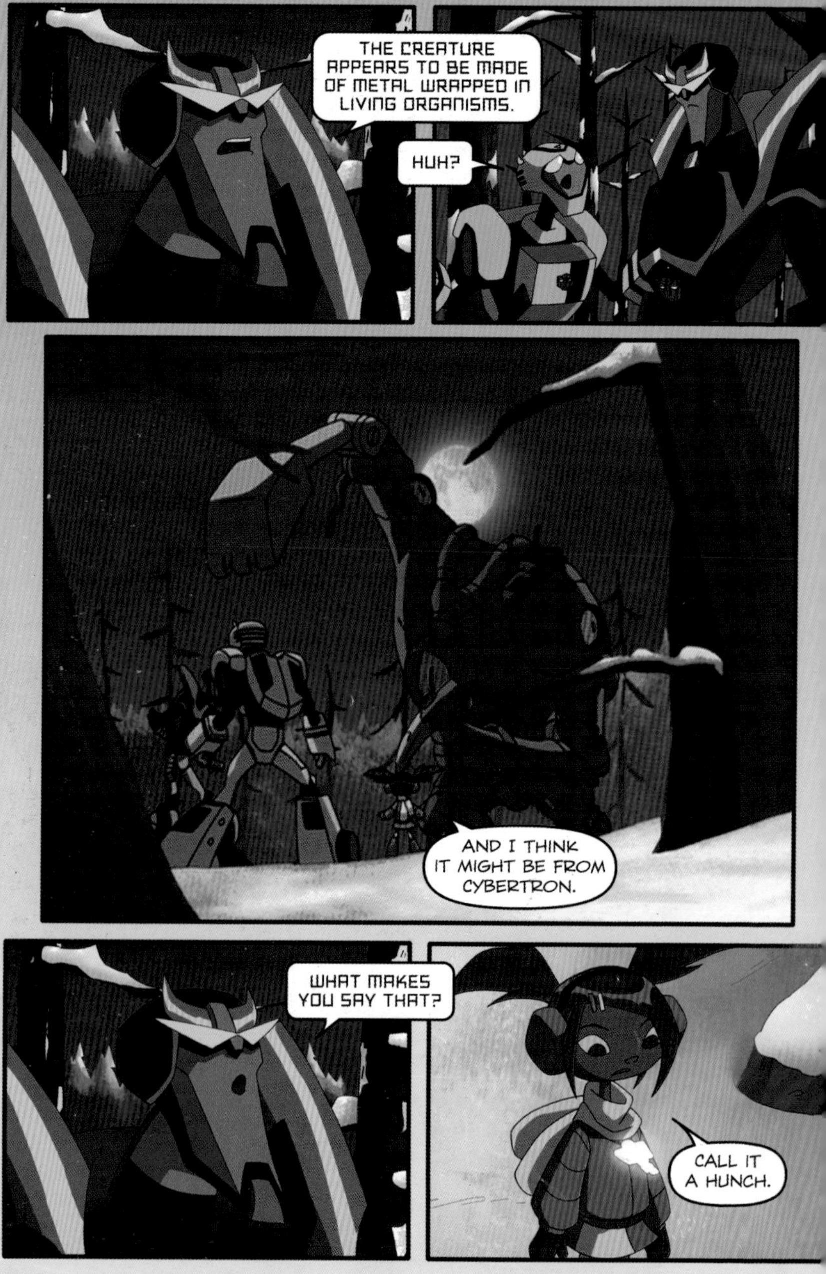
THE CREATURE APPEARS TO BE MADE OF METAL WRAPPED IN LIVING ORGANISMS.
HUH?
AND I THINK IT MIGHT BE FROM CYBERTRON.
WHAT MAKES YOU SAY THAT?
CALL IT A HUNCH.

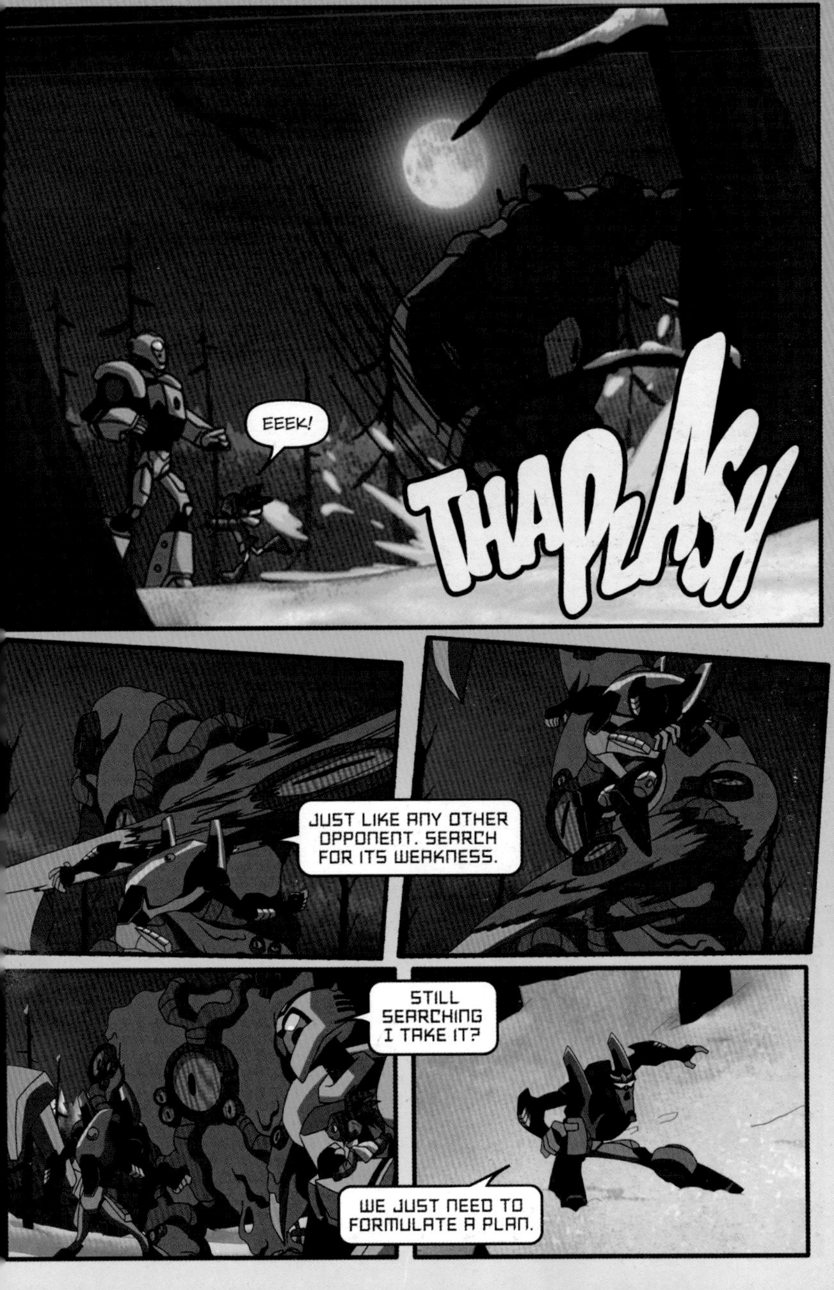
EEEK!
THAPLASH
JUST LIKE ANY OTHER OPPONENT. SEARCH FOR ITS WEAKNESS.
STILL SEARCHING I TAKE IT?
WE JUST NEED TO FORMULATE A PLAN.

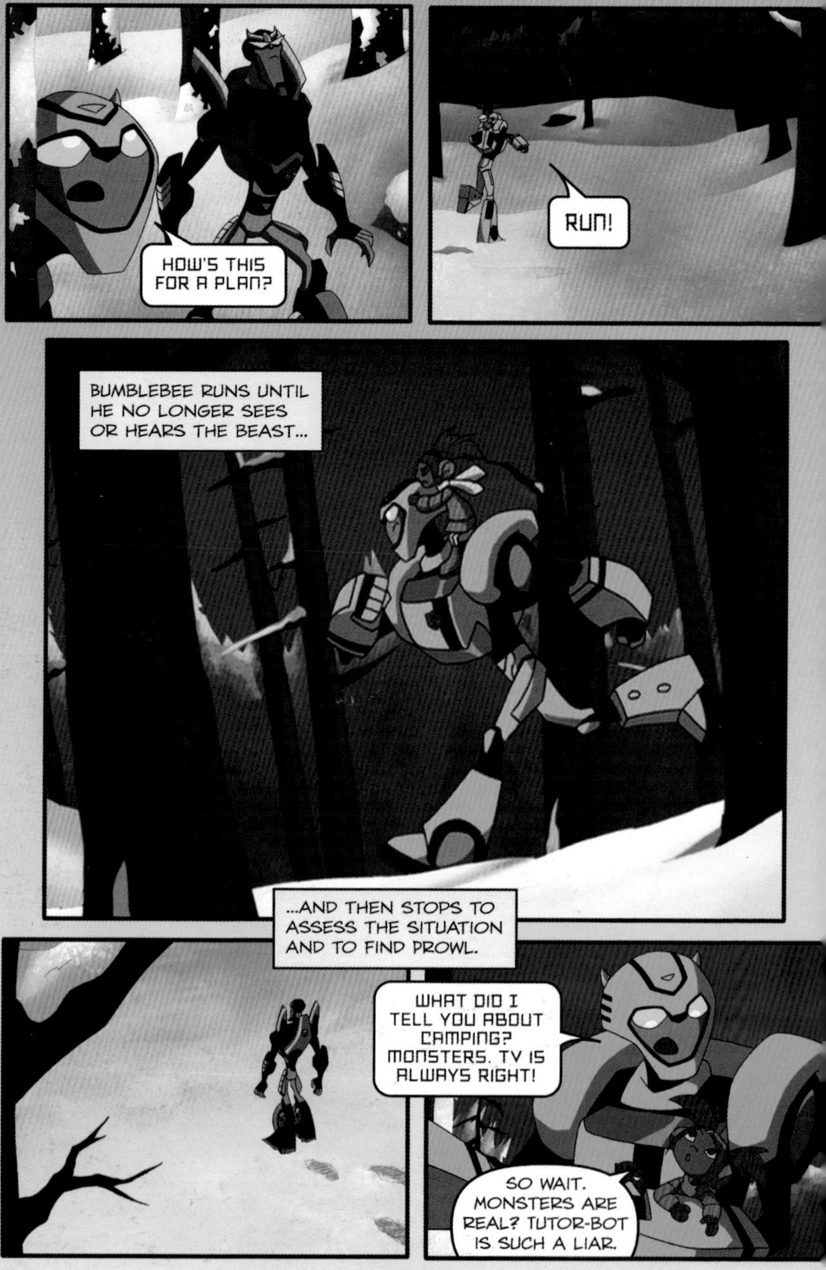
HOW'S THIS FOR A PLAN?
RUN!
BUMBLEBEE RUNS UNTIL HE NO LONGER SEES OR HEARS THE BEAST...
...AND THEN STOPS TO ASSESS THE SITUATION AND TO FIND PROWL.
WHAT DID I TELL YOU ABOUT CAMPING? MONSTERS. TV IS ALWAYS RIGHT!
SO WAIT. MONSTERS ARE REAL? TUTOR-BOT IS SUCH A LIAR.

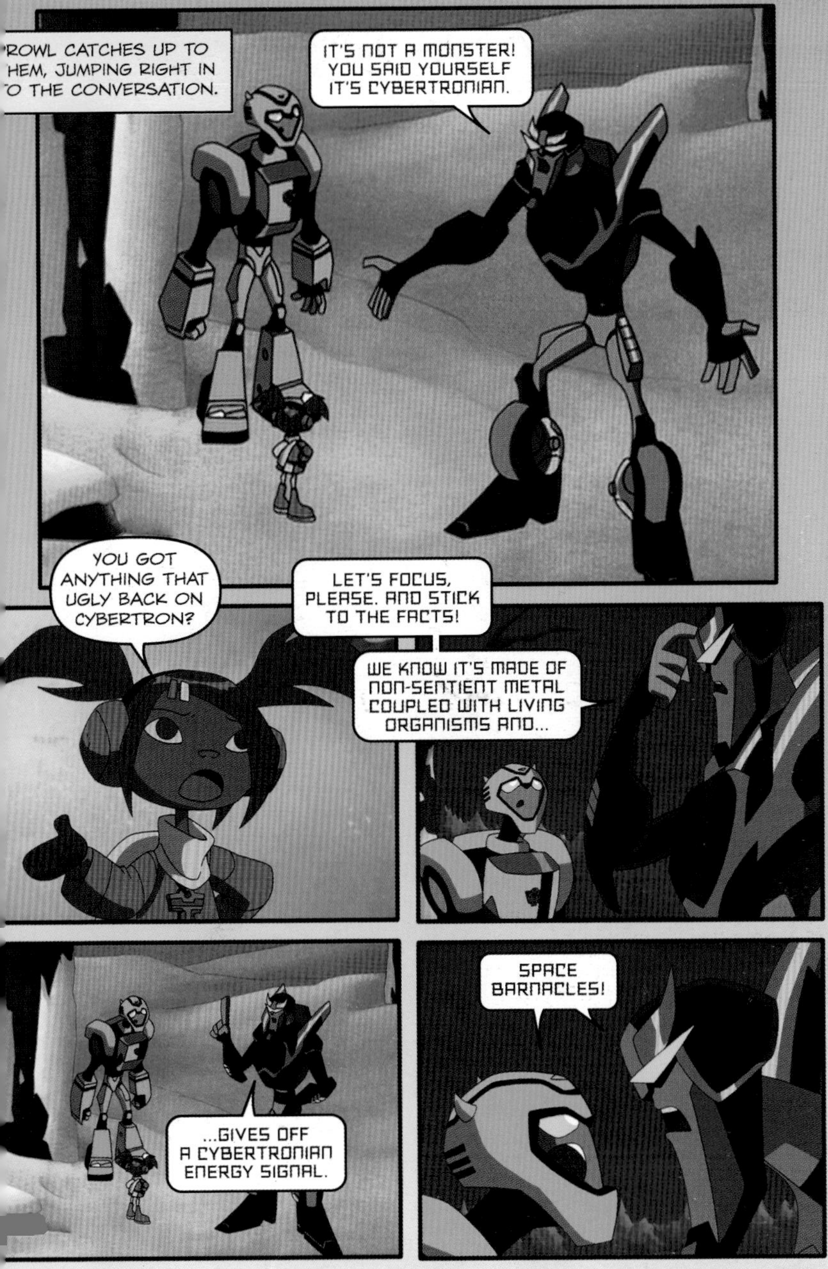

'ROWL CATCHES UP TO HEM, JUMPING RIGHT IN O THE CONVERSATION.
IT'S NOT A MONSTER! YOU SAID YOURSELF IT'S CYBERTRONIAN.
YOU GOT ANYTHING THAT UGLY BACK ON CYBERTRON?
LET'S FOCUS, PLEASE. AND STICK TO THE FACTS!
WE KNOW IT'S MADE OF NON-SENTIENT METAL COUPLED WITH LIVING ORGANISMS AND...
...GIVES OFF A CYBERTRONIAN ENERGY SIGNAL.
SPACE BARNACLES!

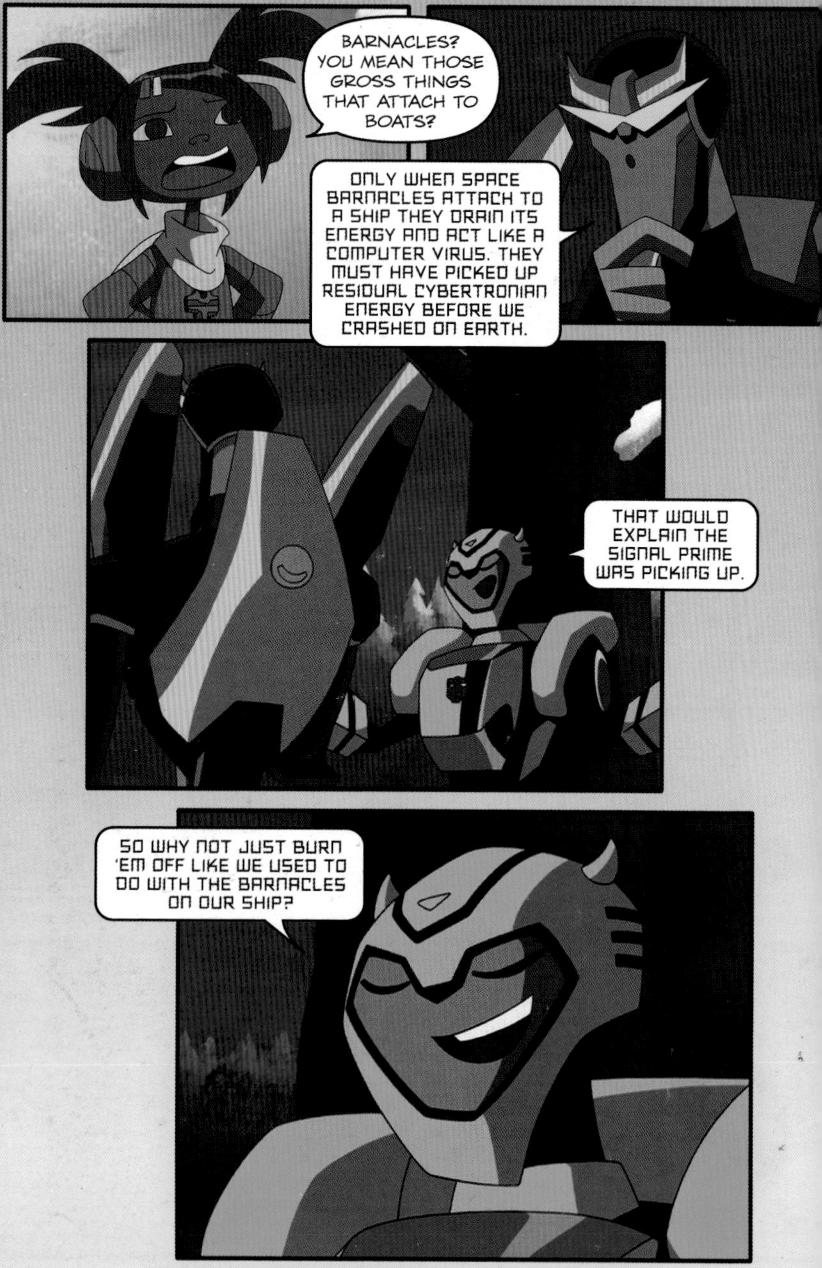
BARNACLES? YOU MEAN THOSE GROSS THINGS THAT ATTACH TO BOATS?
ONLY WHEN SPACE BARNACLES ATTACH TO A SHIP THEY DRAIN ITS ENERGY AND ACT LIKE A COMPUTER VIRUS. THEY MUST HAVE PICKED UP RESIDUAL CYBERTRONIAN ENERGY BEFORE WE CRASHED ON EARTH.
THAT WOULD EXPLAIN THE SIGNAL PRIME WAS PICKING UP.
SO WHY NOT JUST BURN 'EM OFF LIKE WE USED TO DO WITH THE BARNACLES ON OUR SHIP?

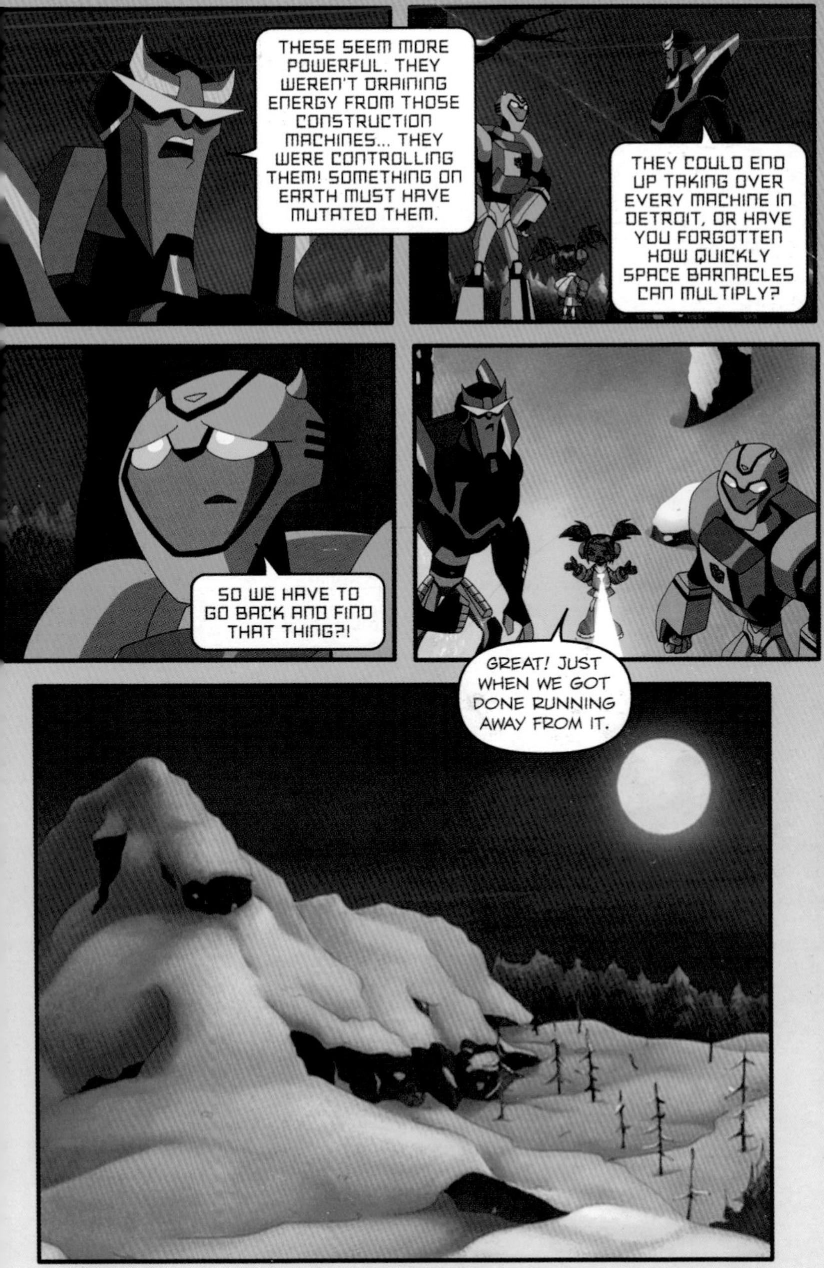

THESE SEEM MORE POWERFUL. THEY WEREN'T DRAINING ENERGY FROM THOSE CONSTRUCTION MACHINES... THEY WERE CONTROLLING THEM! SOMETHING ON EARTH MUST HAVE MUTATED THEM.
THEY COULD END UP TAKING OVER EVERY MACHINE IN DETROIT, OR HAVE YOU FORGOTTEN HOW QUICKLY SPACE BARNACLES CAN MULTIPLY?
SO WE HAVE TO GO BACK AND FIND THAT THING?!
GREAT! JUST WHEN WE GOT DONE RUNNING AWAY FROM IT.

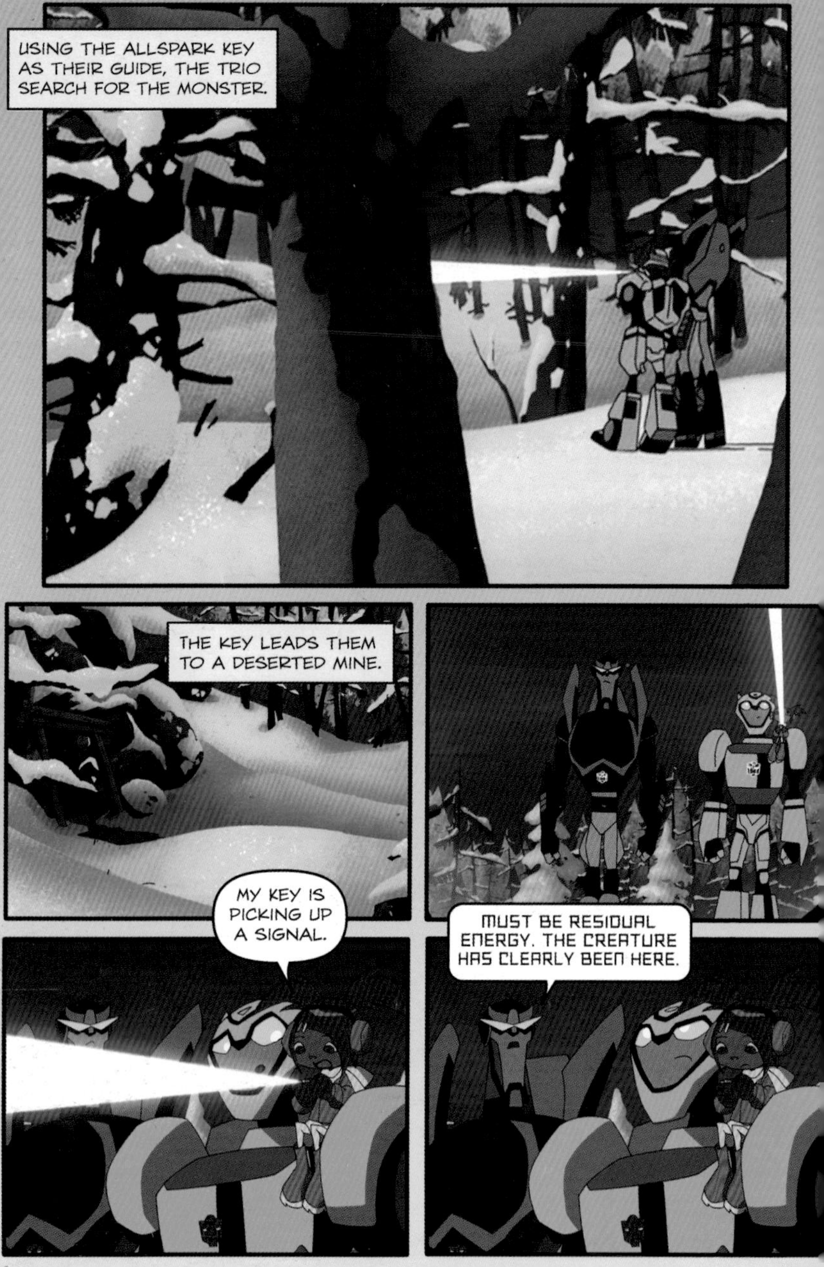
USING THE ALLSPARK KEY AS THEIR GUIDE, THE TRIO SEARCH FOR THE MONSTER.
THE KEY LEADS THEM TO A DESERTED MINE.
MY KEY IS PICKING UP A SIGNAL.
MUST BE RESIDUAL ENERGY. THE CREATURE HAS CLEARLY BEEN HERE.

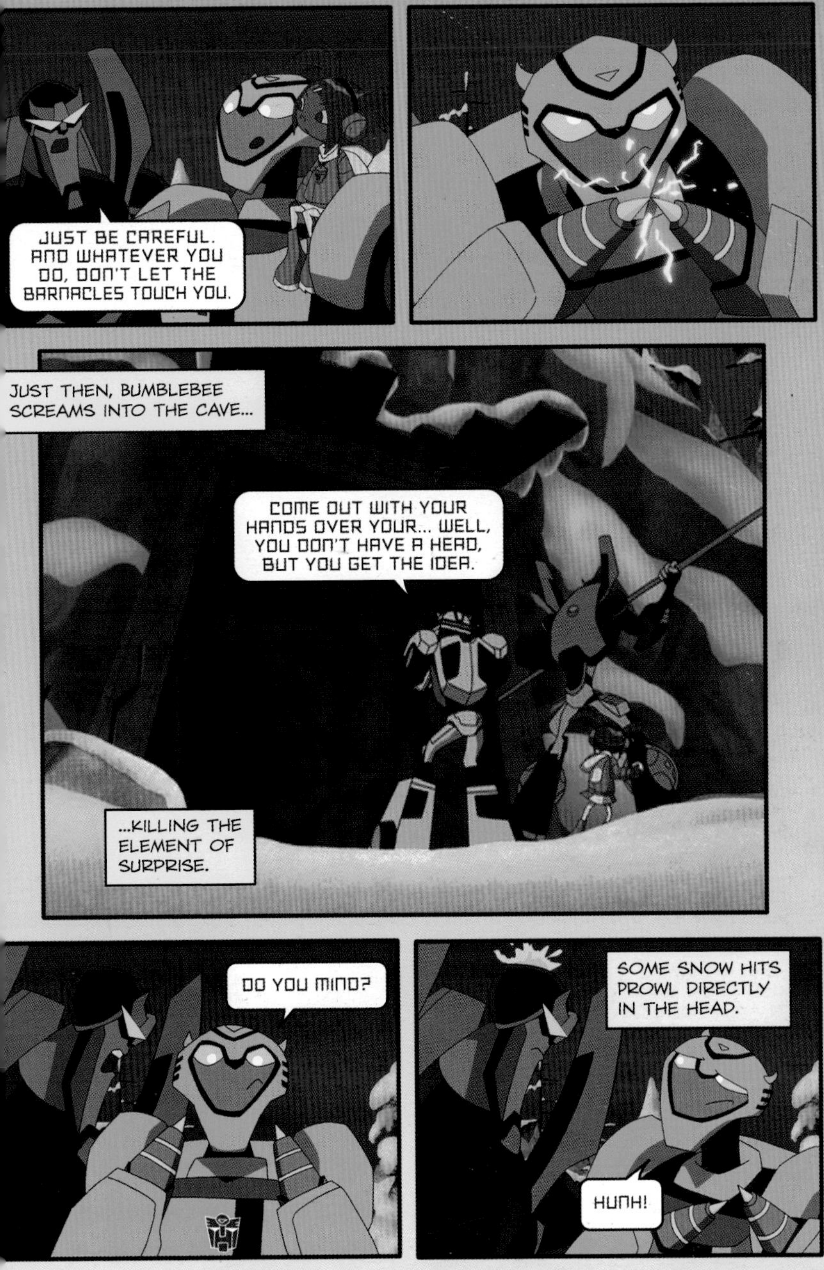
JUST BE CAREFUL. AND WHATEVER YOU DO, DON'T LET THE BARNACLES TOUCH YOU.
JUST THEN, BUMBLEBEE SCREAMS INTO THE CAVE...
COME OUT WITH YOUR HANDS OVER YOUR... WELL, YOU DON'T HAVE A HEAD, BUT YOU GET THE IDEA.
...KILLING THE ELEMENT OF SURPRISE.
DO YOU MIND?
SOME SNOW HITS PROWL DIRECTLY IN THE HEAD.
HUNH!

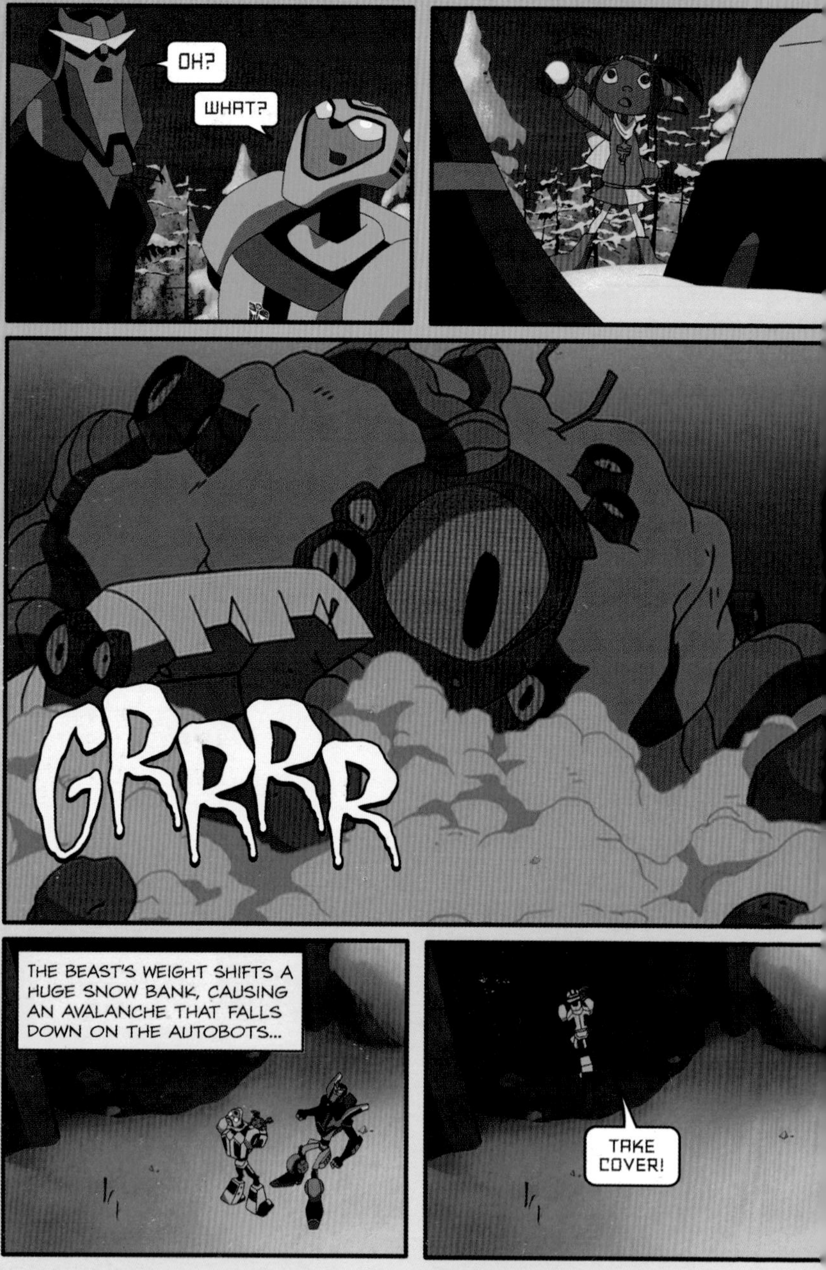
OH?
WHAT?
GRRRR
THE BEAST'S WEIGHT SHIFTS A HUGE SNOW BANK, CAUSING AN AVALANCHE THAT FALLS DOWN ON THE AUTOBOTS...
TAKE COVER!

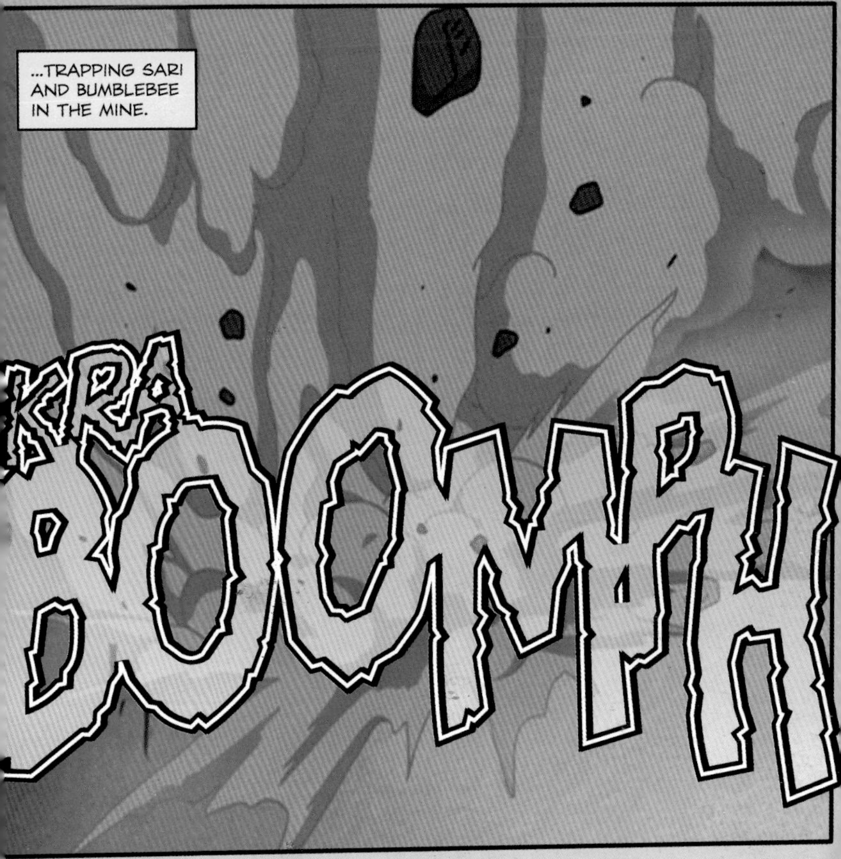
...TRAPPING SARI AND BUMBLEBEE IN THE MINE.
KRA-BOOMPH

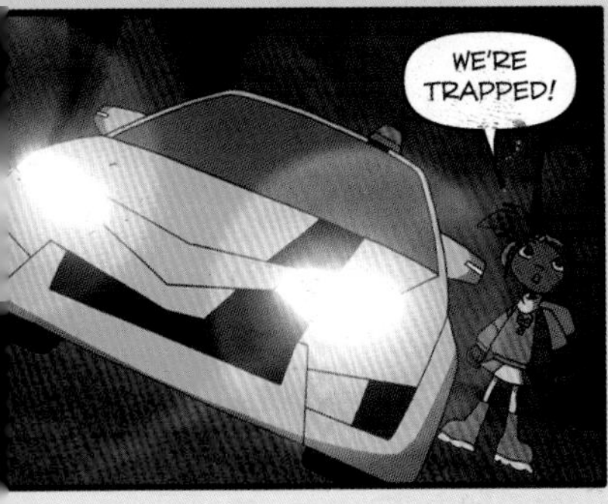
WE'RE TRAPPED!

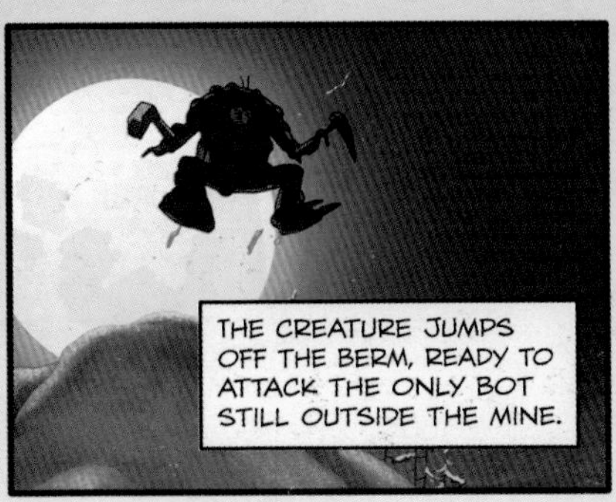
THE CREATURE JUMPS OFF THE BERM, READY TO ATTACK THE ONLY BOT STILL OUTSIDE THE MINE.

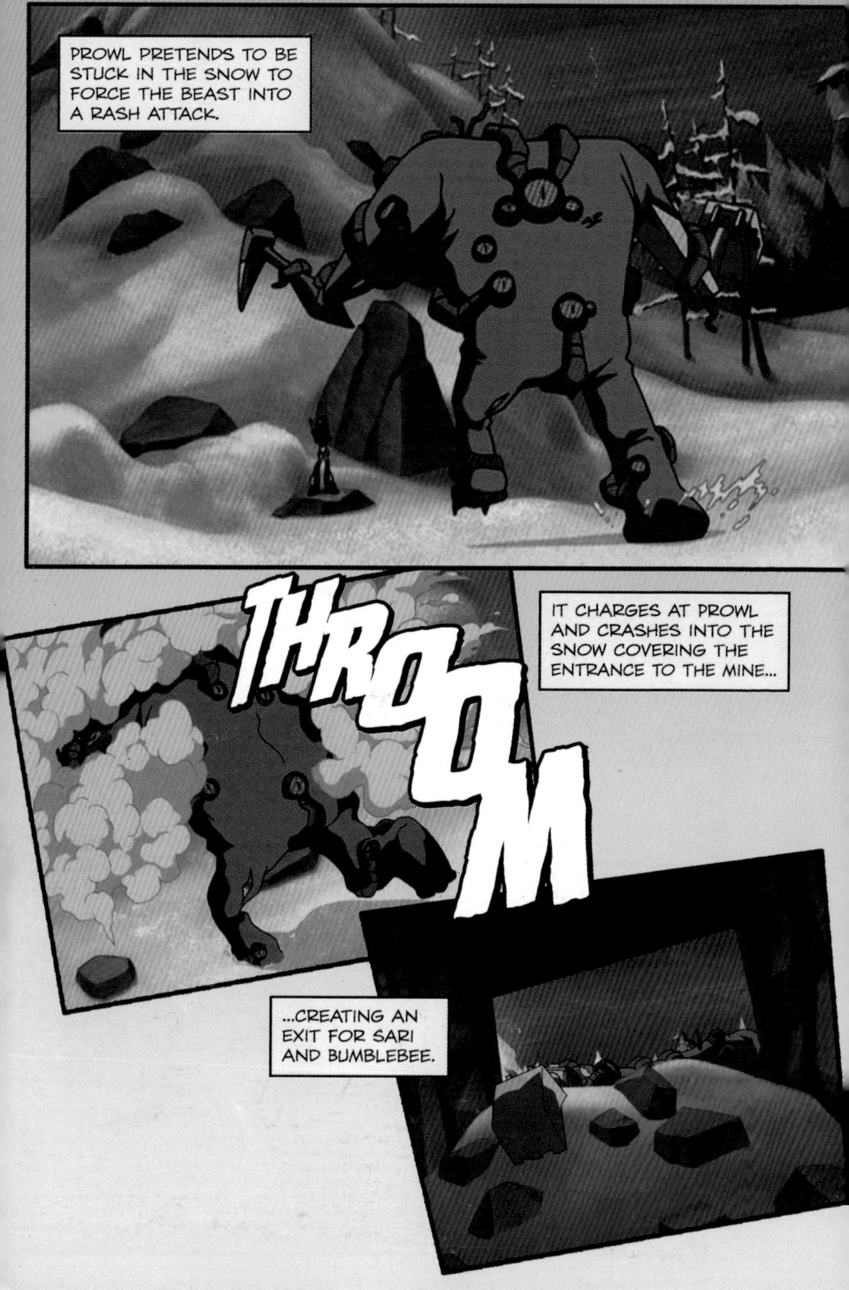
PROWL PRETENDS TO BE STUCK IN THE SNOW TO FORCE THE BEAST INTO A RASH ATTACK.
THROOM
IT CHARGES AT PROWL AND CRASHES INTO THE SNOW COVERING THE ENTRANCE TO THE MINE...
...CREATING AN EXIT FOR SARI AND BUMBLEBEE.

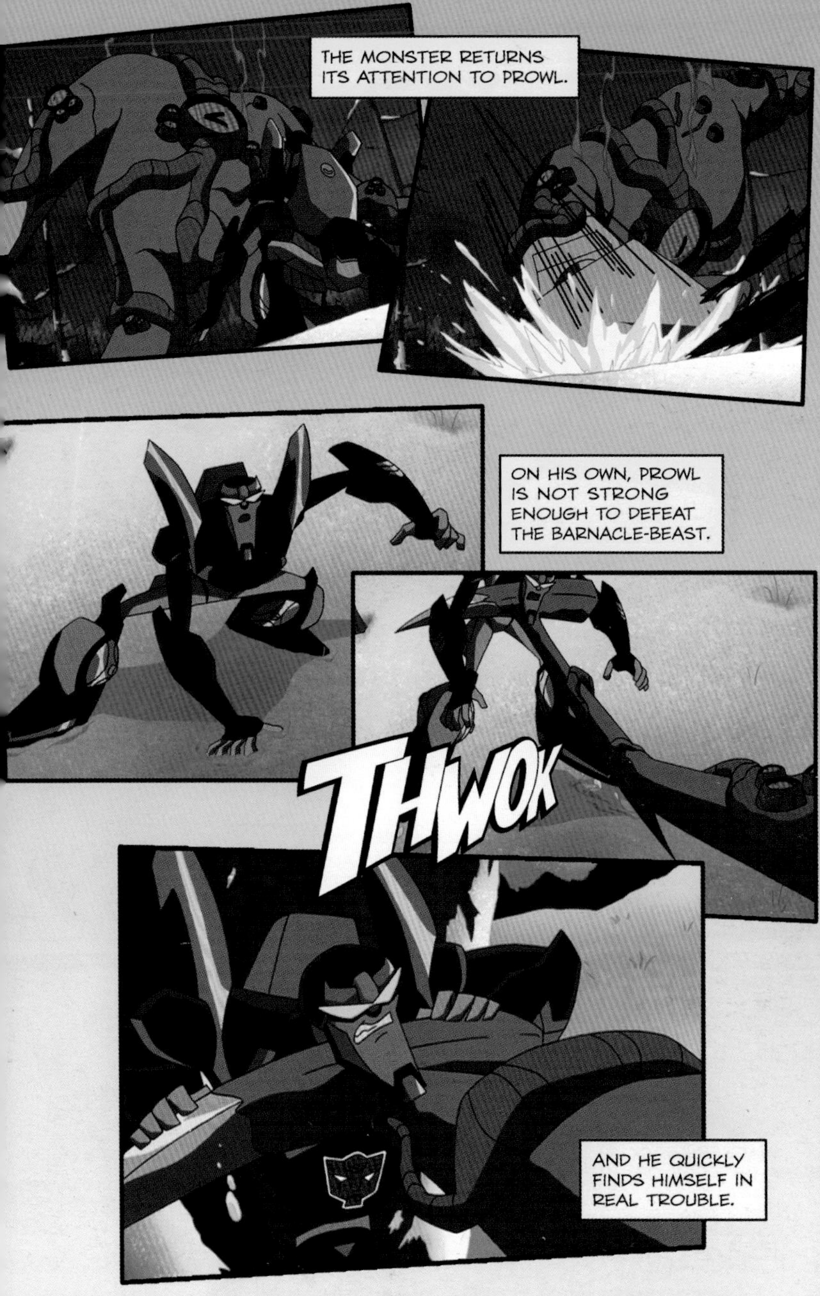
THE MONSTER RETURNS ITS ATTENTION TO PROWL.
ON HIS OWN, PROWL IS NOT STRONG ENOUGH TO DEFEAT THE BARNACLE-BEAST.
THWOK
AND HE QUICKLY FINDS HIMSELF IN REAL TROUBLE.

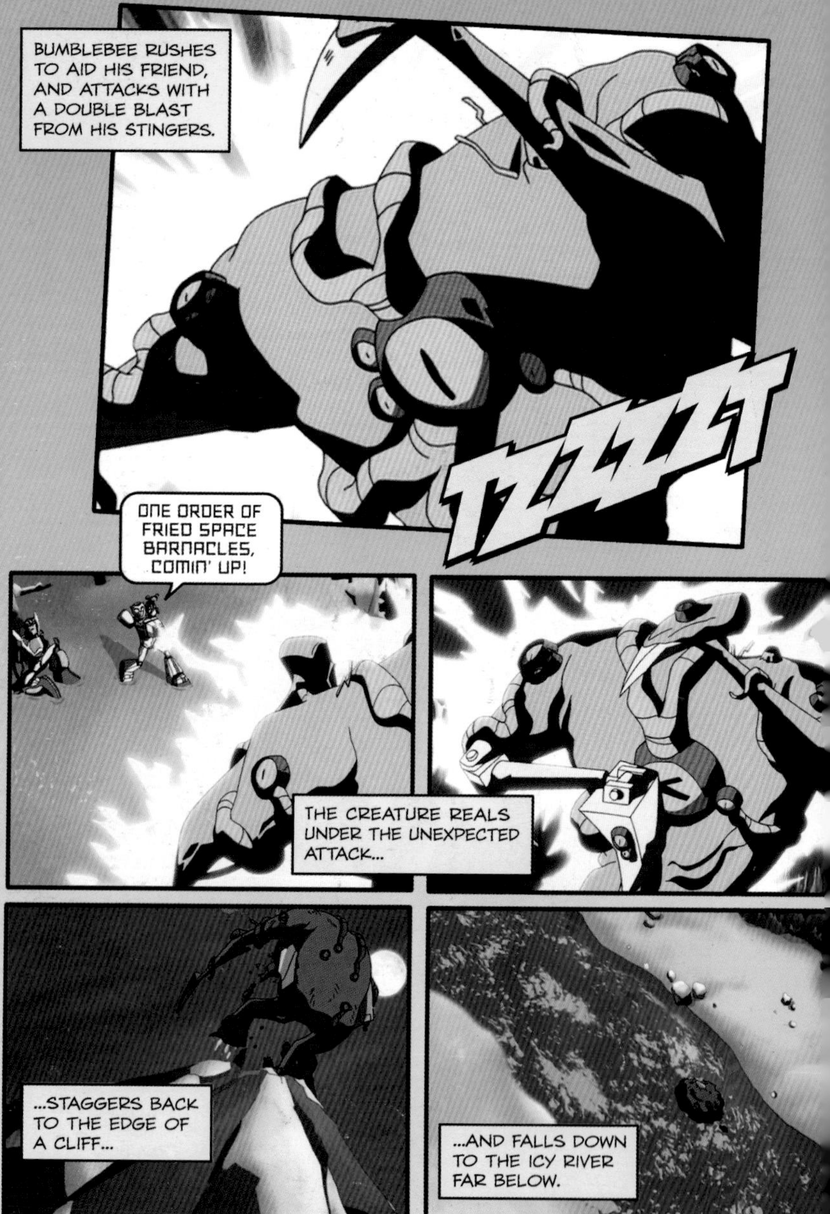
BUMBLEBEE RUSHES TO AID HIS FRIEND, AND ATTACKS WITH A DOUBLE BLAST FROM HIS STINGERS.
TZZZT
ONE ORDER OF FRIED SPACE BARNACLES, COMIN' UP!
THE CREATURE REALS UNDER THE UNEXPECTED ATTACK...
...STAGGERS BACK TO THE EDGE OF A CLIFF...
...AND FALLS DOWN TO THE ICY RIVER FAR BELOW.

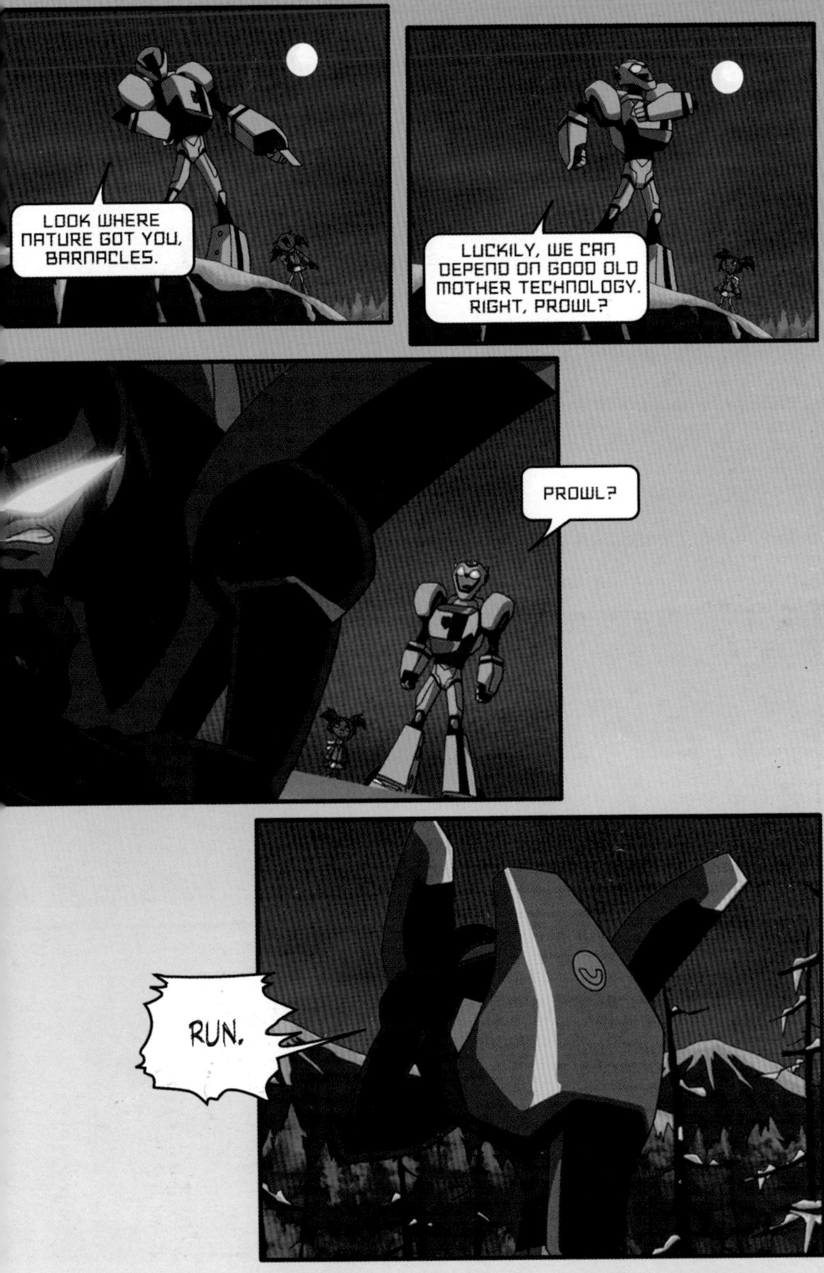
LOOK WHERE NATURE GOT YOU, BARNACLES.
LUCKILY, WE CAN DEPEND ON GOOD OLD MOTHER TECHNOLOGY. RIGHT, PROWL?
PROWL?
RUN.

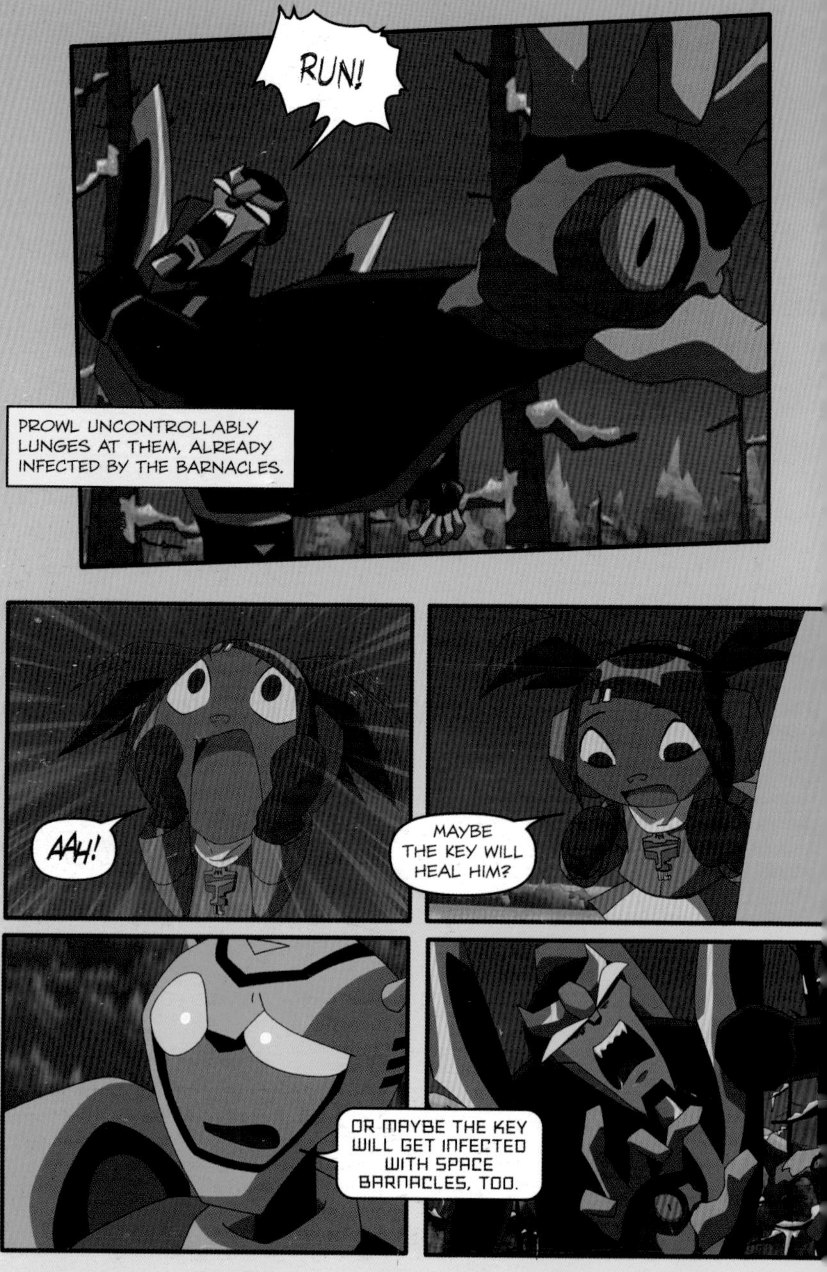
RUN!
PROWL UNCONTROLLABLY LUNGES AT THEM, ALREADY INFECTED BY THE BARNACLES.
AAH!
MAYBE THE KEY WILL HEAL HIM?
OR MAYBE THE KEY WILL GET INFECTED WITH SPACE BARNACLES, TOO.

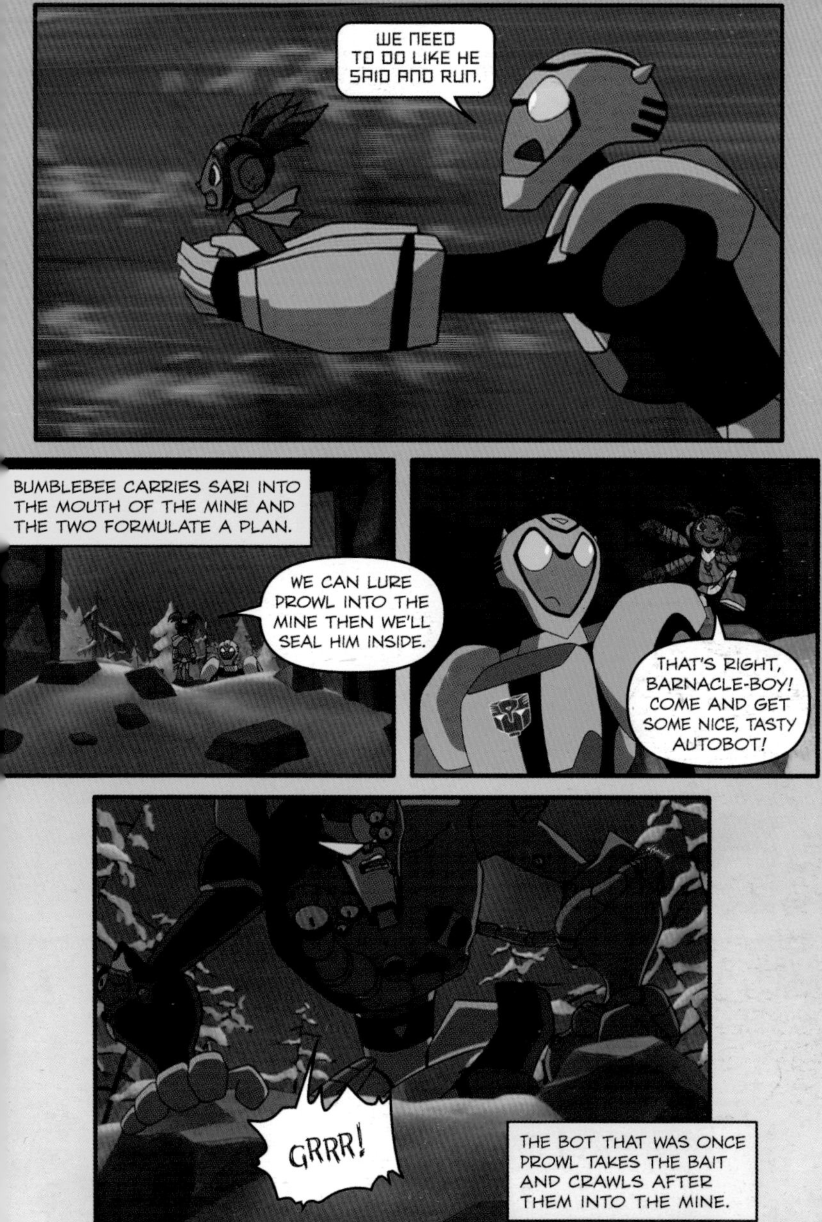
WE NEED TO DO LIKE HE SAID AND RUN.
BUMBLEBEE CARRIES SARI INTO THE MOUTH OF THE MINE AND THE TWO FORMULATE A PLAN.
WE CAN LURE PROWL INTO THE MINE THEN WE'LL SEAL HIM INSIDE.
THAT'S RIGHT, BARNACLE-BOY! COME AND GET SOME NICE, TASTY AUTOBOT!
GRRR!
THE BOT THAT WAS ONCE PROWL TAKES THE BAIT AND CRAWLS AFTER THEM INTO THE MINE.

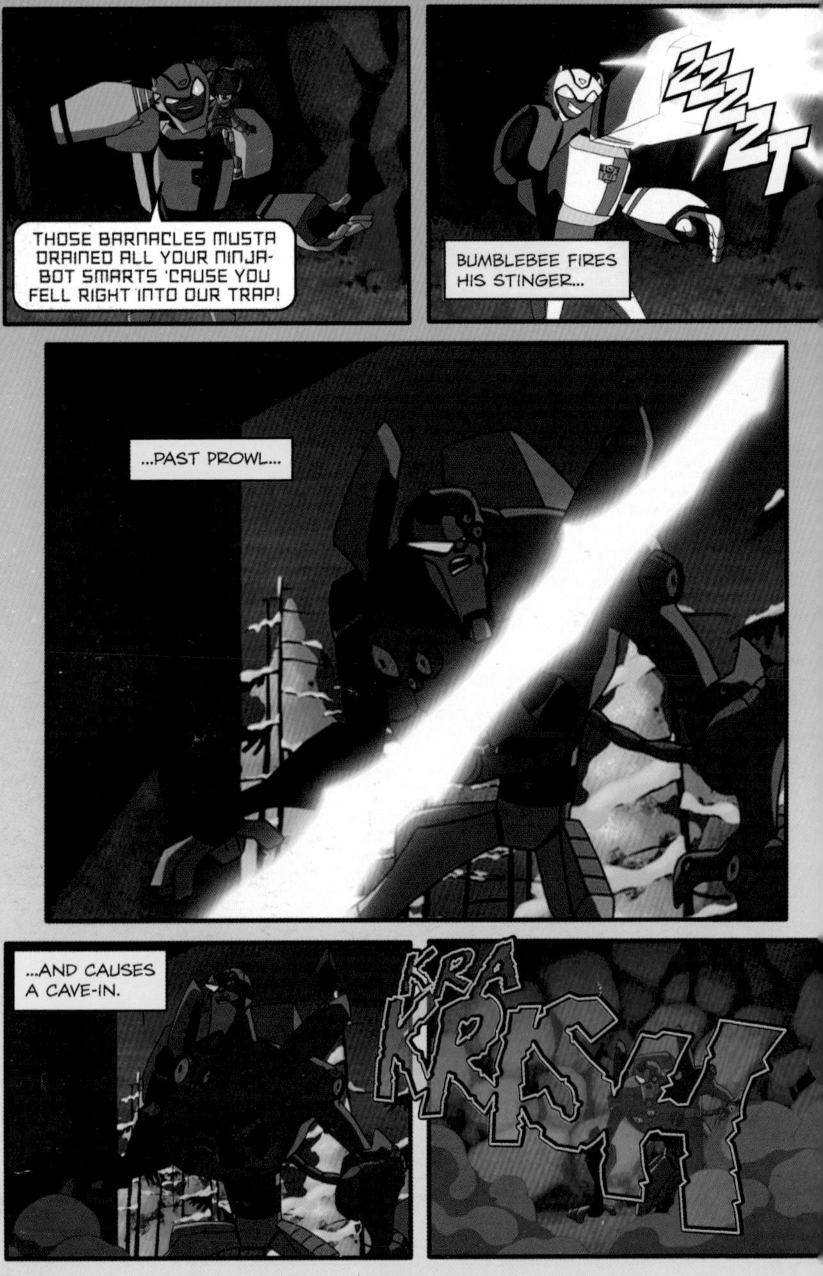
THOSE BARNACLES MUSTA DRAINED ALL YOUR NINJA-BOT SMARTS 'CAUSE YOU FELL RIGHT INTO OUR TRAP!
BUMBLEBEE FIRES HIS STINGER...
ZZZZT
...PAST PROWL...
...AND CAUSES A CAVE-IN.
KRA KRSH

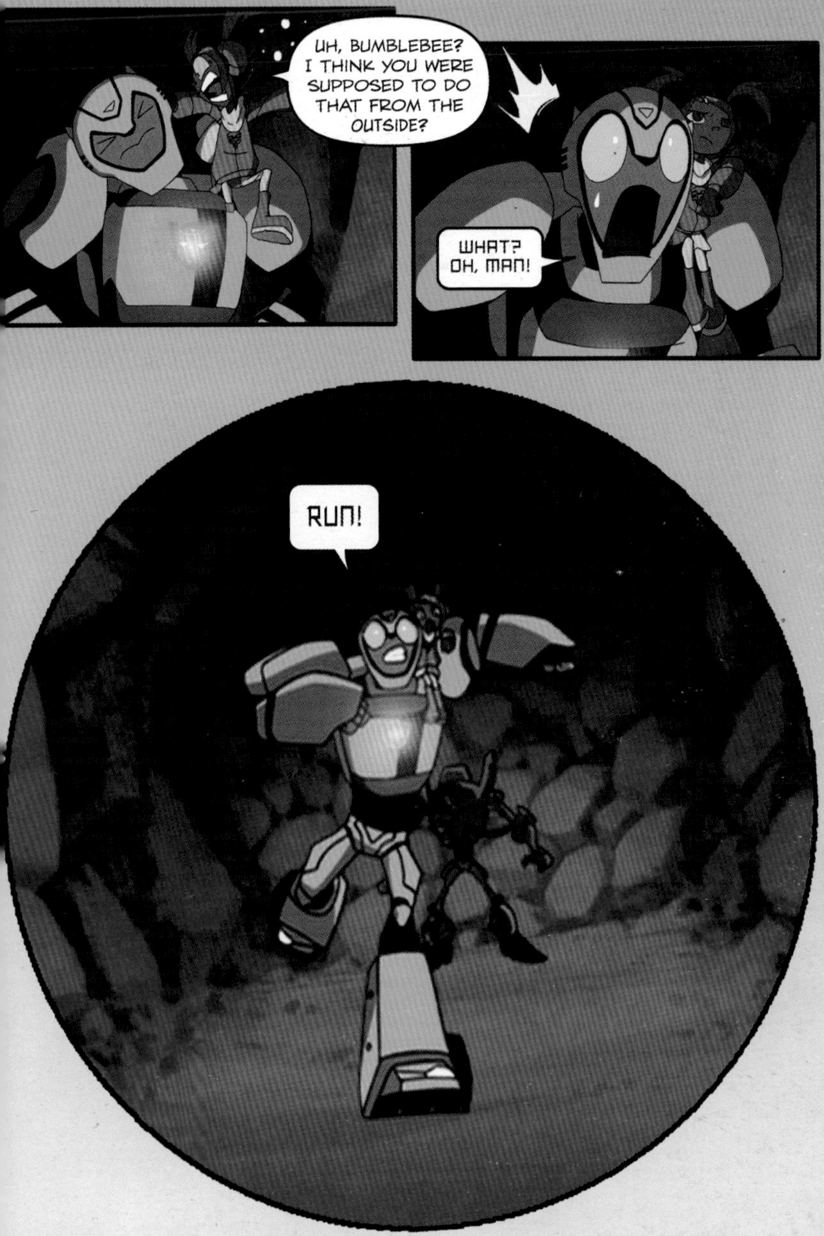
UH, BUMBLEBEE? I THINK YOU WERE SUPPOSED TO DO THAT FROM THE OUTSIDE?
WHAT? OH, MAN!
RUN!

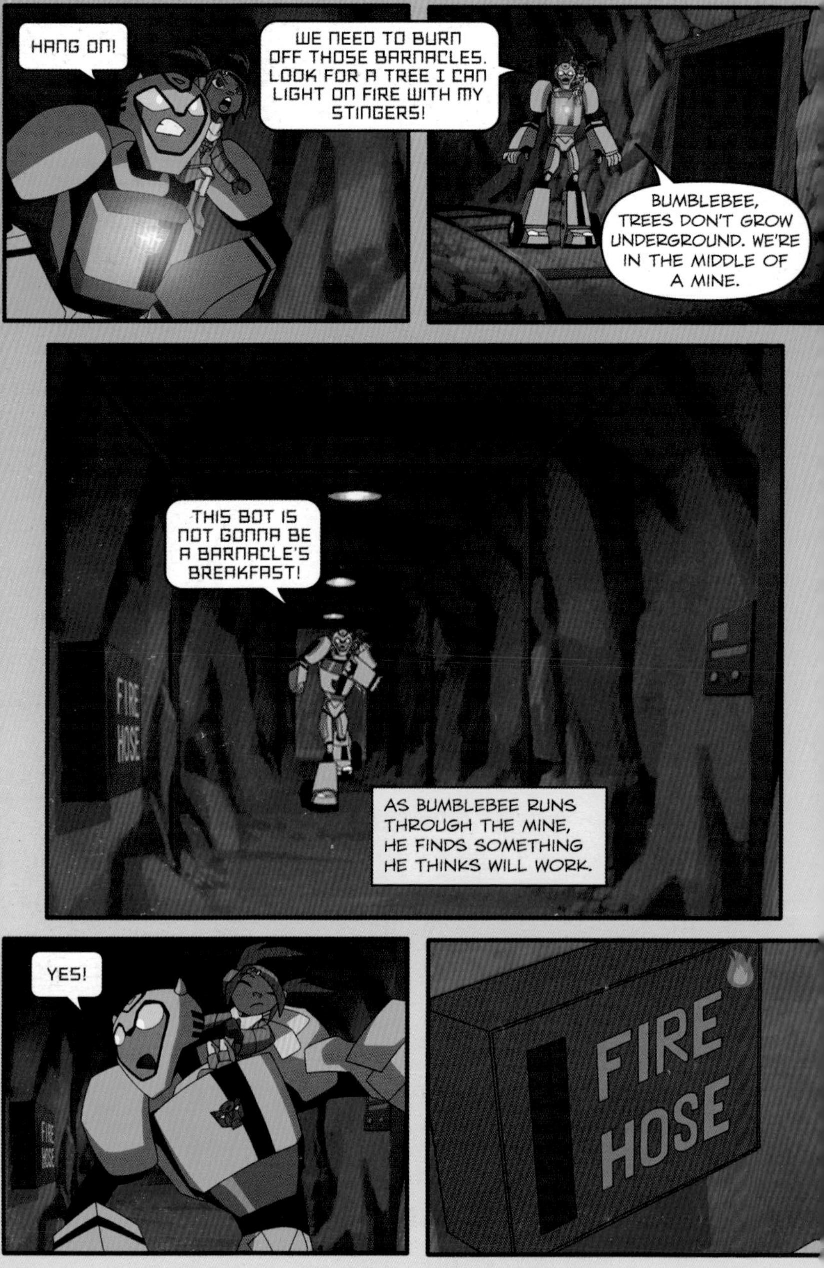
HANG ON!
WE NEED TO BURN OFF THOSE BARNACLES. LOOK FOR A TREE I CAN LIGHT ON FIRE WITH MY STINGERS!
BUMBLEBEE, TREES DON'T GROW UNDERGROUND. WE'RE IN THE MIDDLE OF A MINE.
THIS BOT IS NOT GONNA BE A BARNACLE'S BREAKFAST!
FIRE HOSE
AS BUMBLEBEE RUNS THROUGH THE MINE, HE FINDS SOMETHING HE THINKS WILL WORK.
YES!
FIRE HOSE

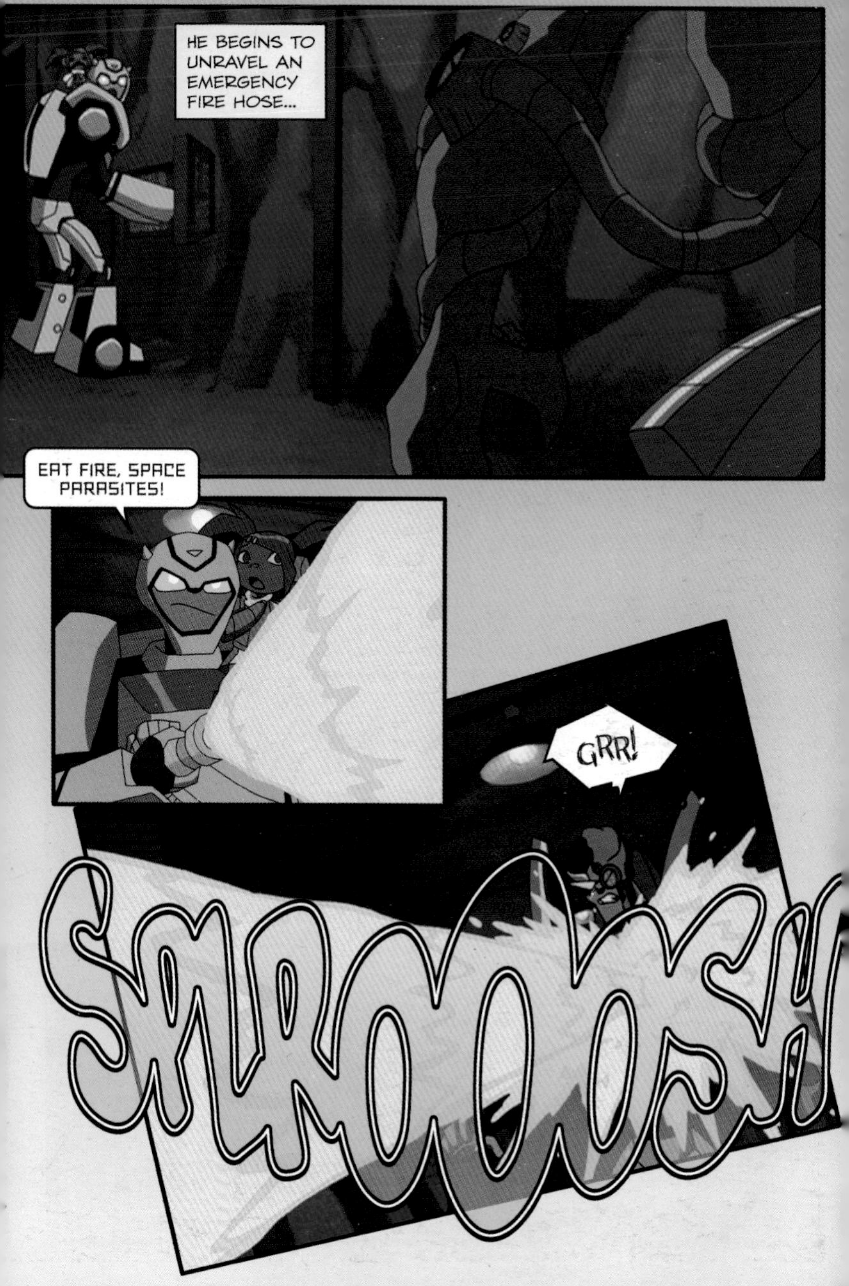
HE BEGINS TO UNRAVEL AN EMERGENCY FIRE HOSE...
EAT FIRE, SPACE PARASITES!
GRR!
SPROOOOSH!

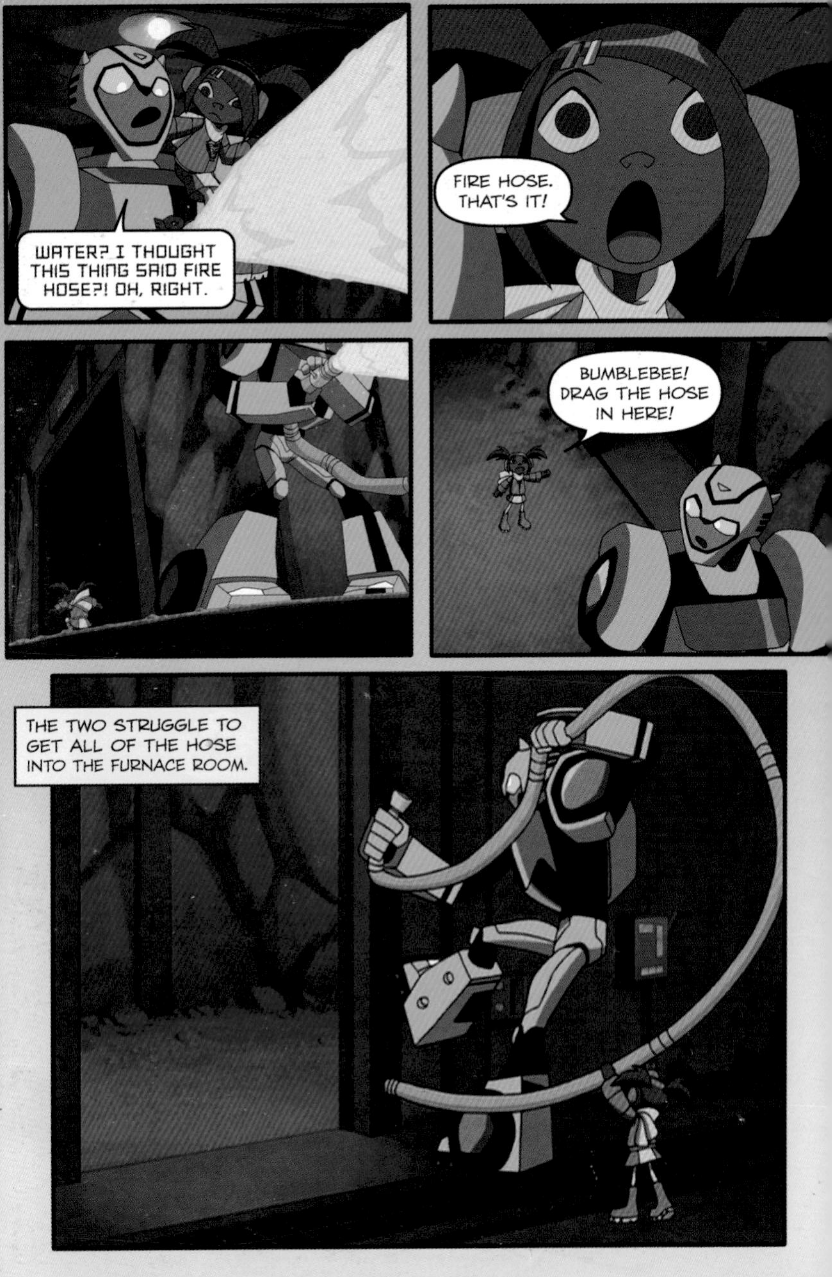
WATER? I THOUGHT THIS THING SAID FIRE HOSE?! OH, RIGHT.
FIRE HOSE. THAT'S IT!
BUMBLEBEE! DRAG THE HOSE IN HERE!
THE TWO STRUGGLE TO GET ALL OF THE HOSE INTO THE FURNACE ROOM.

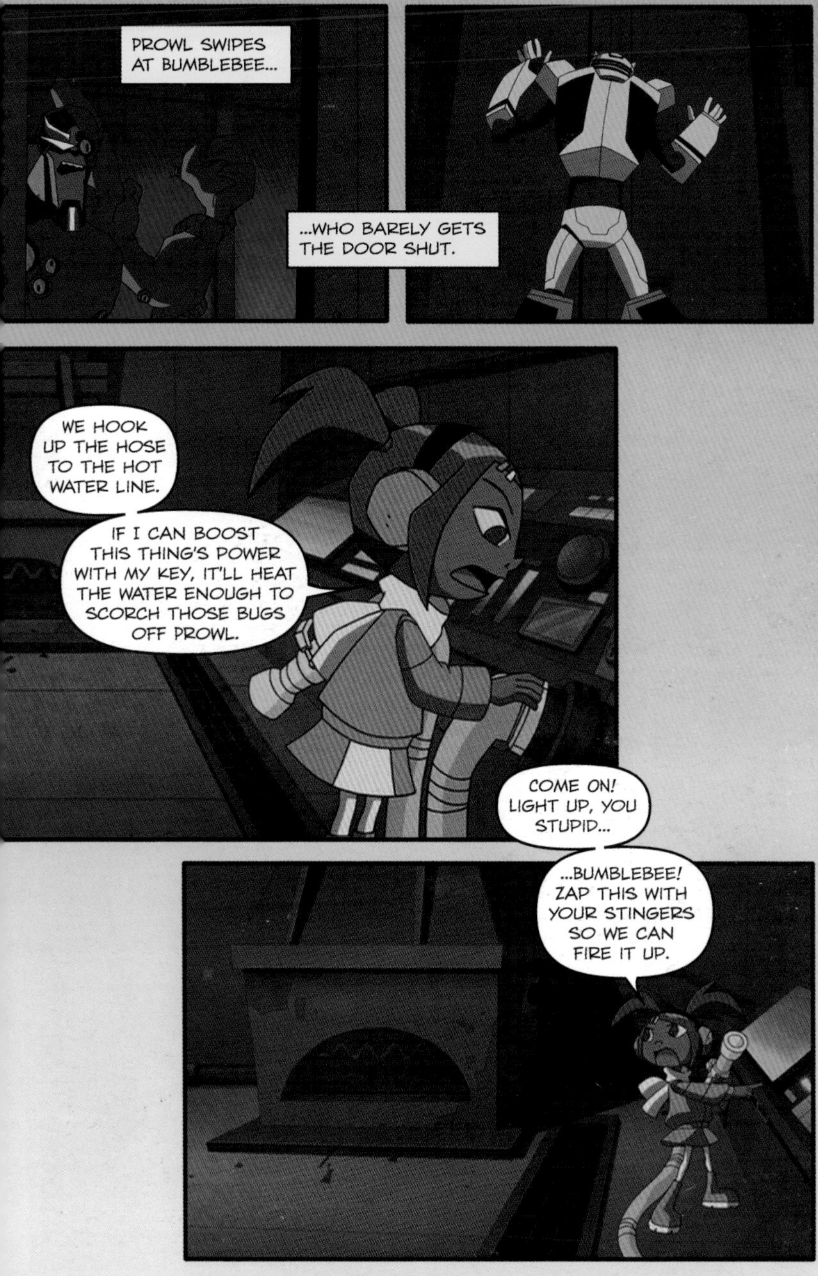
PROWL SWIPES AT BUMBLEBEE...
...WHO BARELY GETS THE DOOR SHUT.
WE HOOK UP THE HOSE TO THE HOT WATER LINE.
IF I CAN BOOST THIS THING'S POWER WITH MY KEY, IT'LL HEAT THE WATER ENOUGH TO SCORCH THOSE BUGS OFF PROWL.
COME ON! LIGHT UP, YOU STUPID...
...BUMBLEBEE! ZAP THIS WITH YOUR STINGERS SO WE CAN FIRE IT UP.

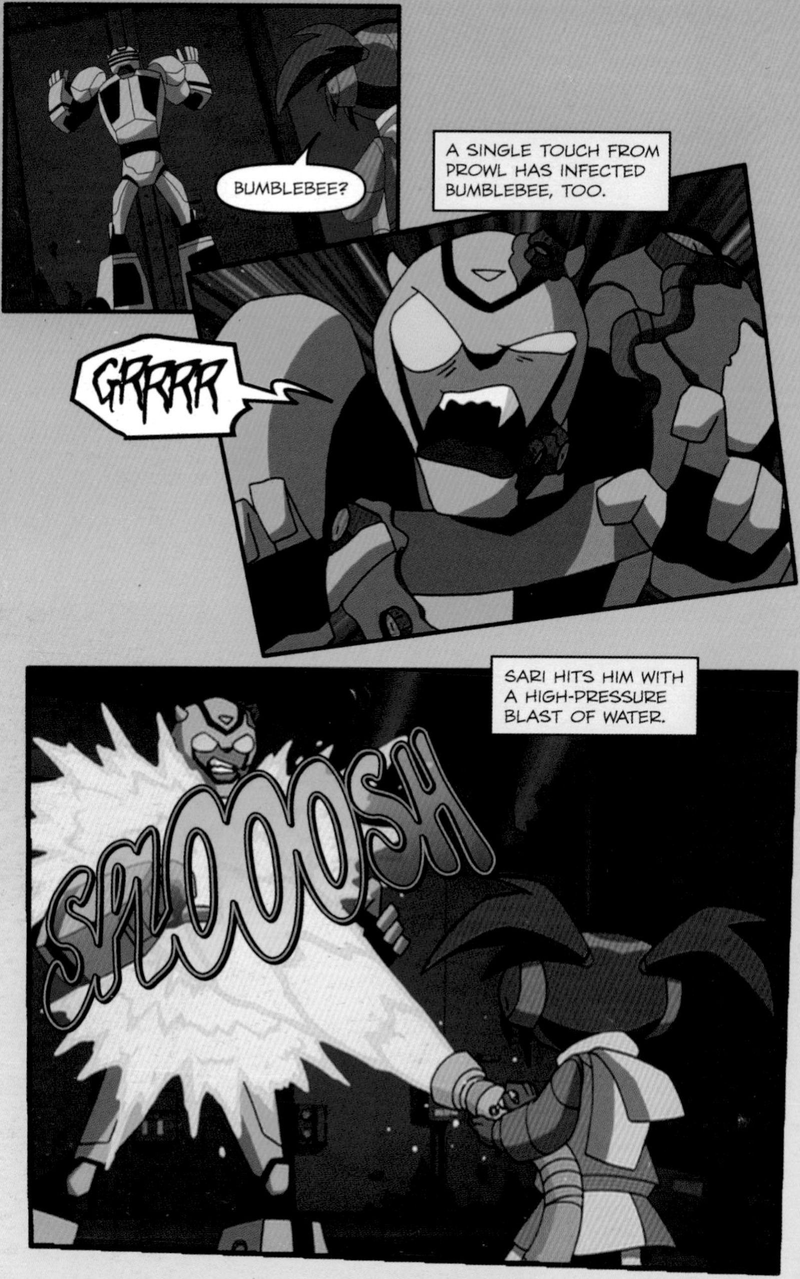
BUMBLEBEE?
A SINGLE TOUCH FROM PROWL HAS INFECTED BUMBLEBEE, TOO.
GRRRR
SARI HITS HIM WITH A HIGH-PRESSURE BLAST OF WATER.
SPLOOOSH

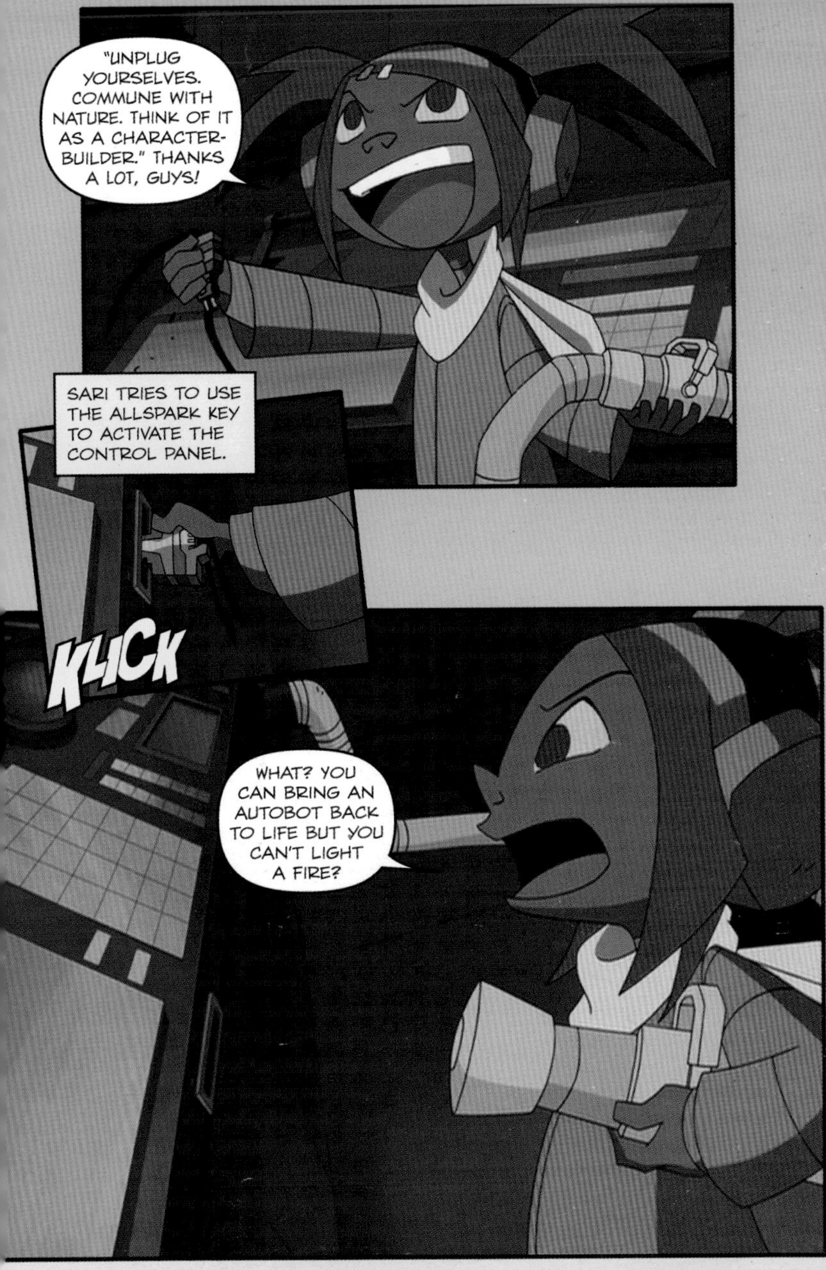
"UNPLUG YOURSELVES. COMMUNE WITH NATURE. THINK OF IT AS A CHARACTER-BUILDER." THANKS A LOT, GUYS!
SARI TRIES TO USE THE ALLSPARK KEY TO ACTIVATE THE CONTROL PANEL.
KLICK
WHAT? YOU CAN BRING AN AUTOBOT BACK TO LIFE BUT YOU CAN'T LIGHT A FIRE?

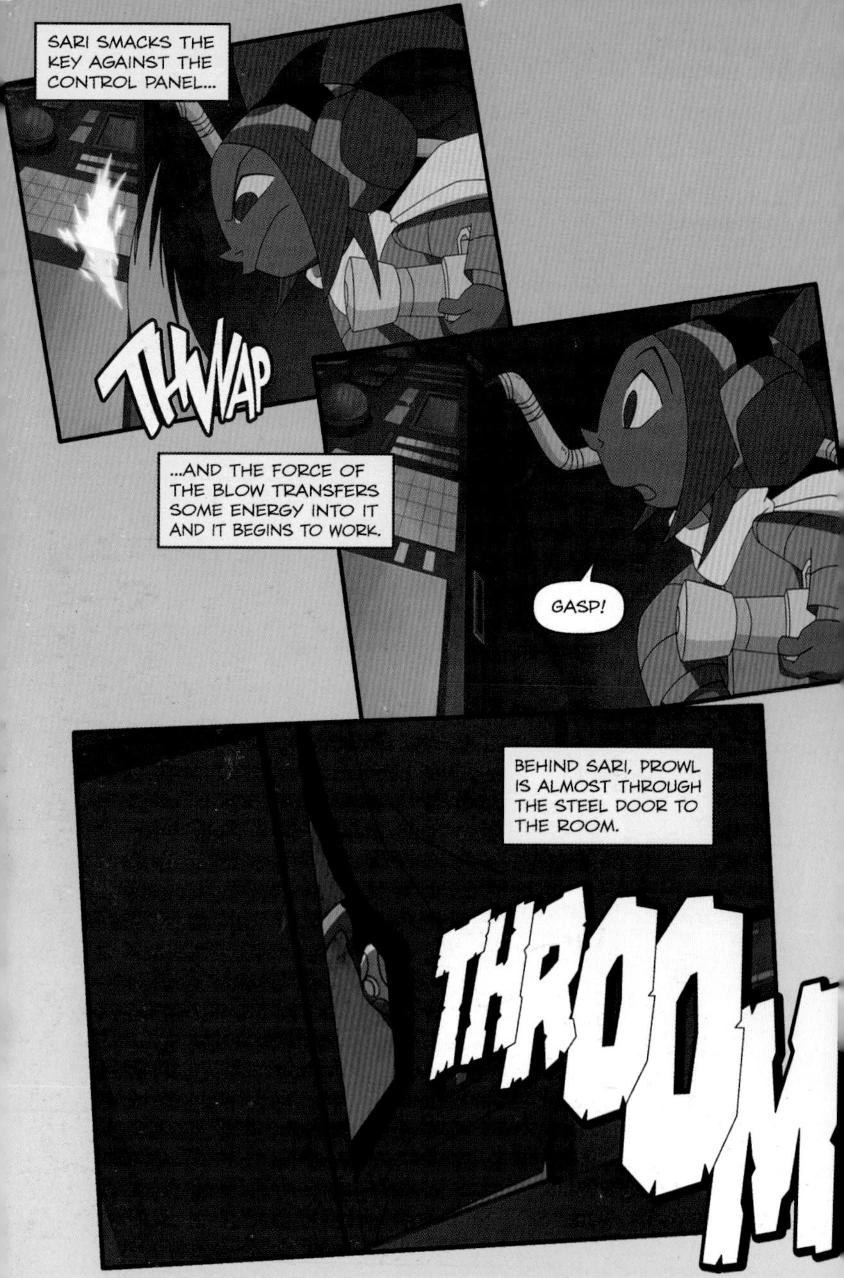
SARI SMACKS THE KEY AGAINST THE CONTROL PANEL...
THWAP
...AND THE FORCE OF THE BLOW TRANSFERS SOME ENERGY INTO IT AND IT BEGINS TO WORK.
GASP!
BEHIND SARI, PROWL IS ALMOST THROUGH THE STEEL DOOR TO THE ROOM.
THROOM

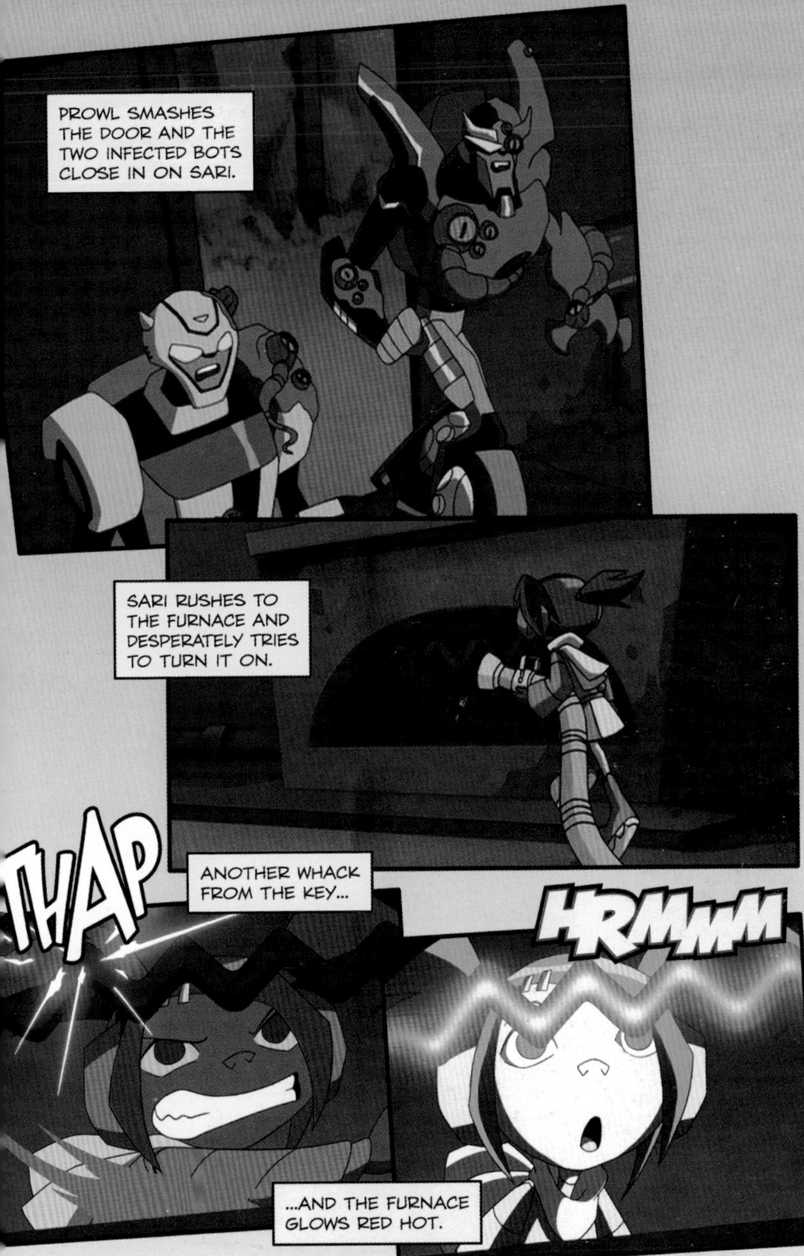
PROWL SMASHES THE DOOR AND THE TWO INFECTED BOTS CLOSE IN ON SARI.
SARI RUSHES TO THE FURNACE AND DESPERATELY TRIES TO TURN IT ON.
THAP
ANOTHER WHACK FROM THE KEY...
HRMMMM
...AND THE FURNACE GLOWS RED HOT.

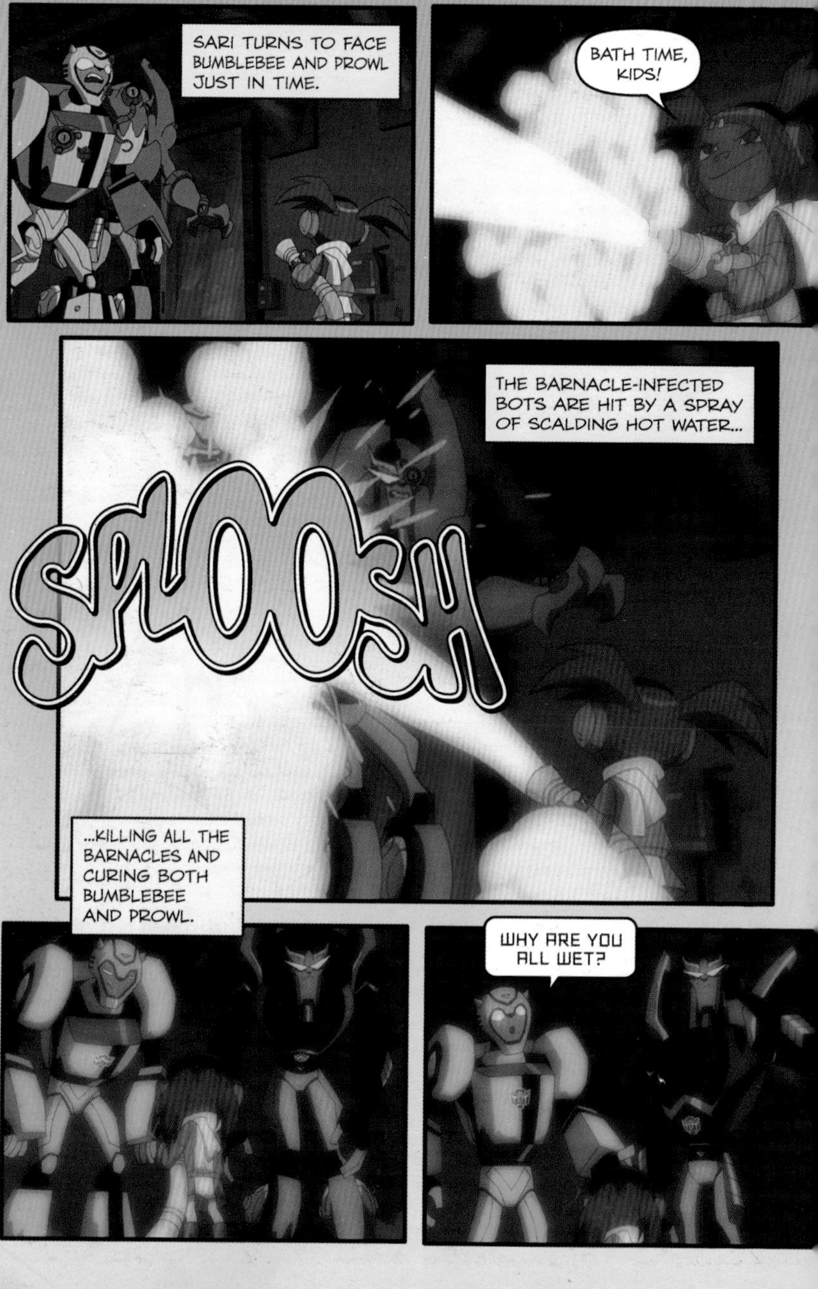
SARI TURNS TO FACE BUMBLEBEE AND PROWL JUST IN TIME.
BATH TIME, KIDS!
THE BARNACLE-INFECTED BOTS ARE HIT BY A SPRAY OF SCALDING HOT WATER...
SPLOOSH
...KILLING ALL THE BARNACLES AND CURING BOTH BUMBLEBEE AND PROWL.
WHY ARE YOU ALL WET?

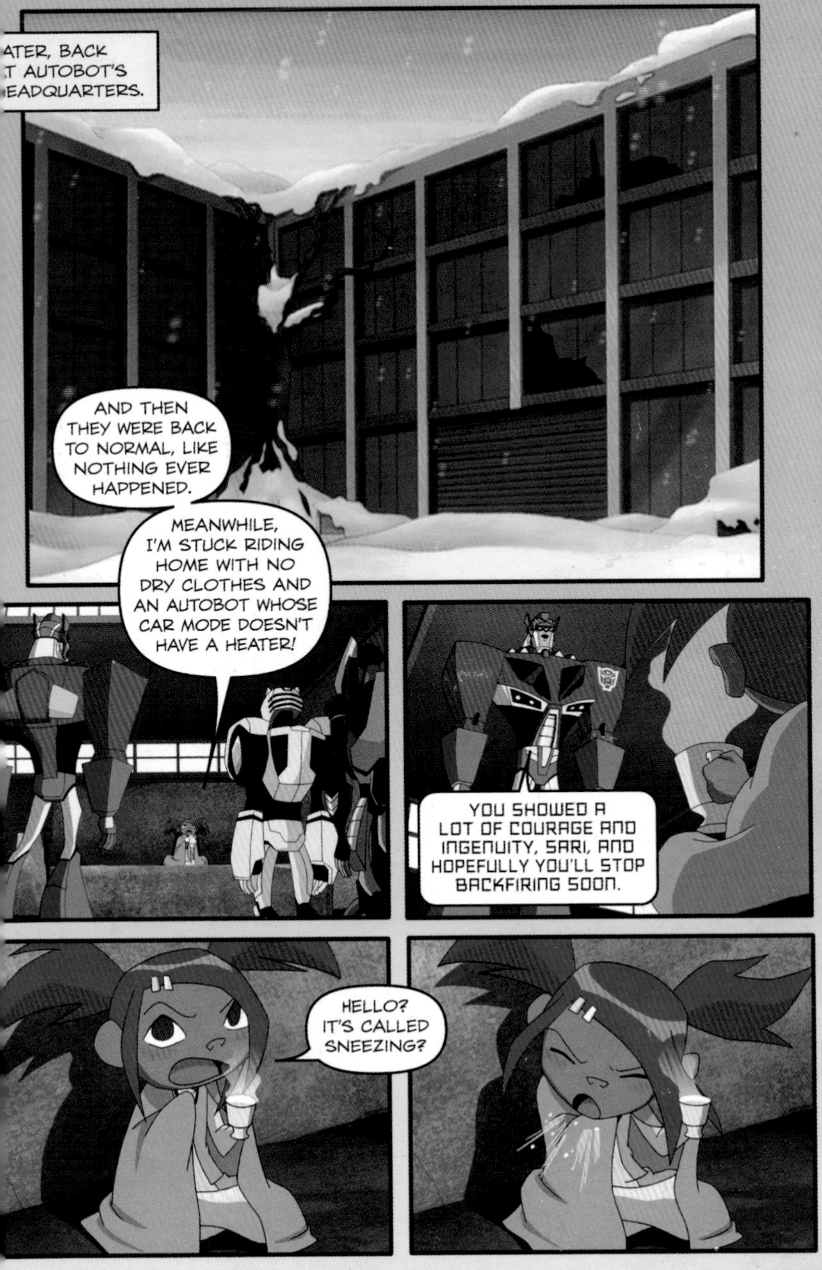
ATER, BACK
T AUTOBOT'S
EADQUARTERS.
AND THEN THEY WERE BACK TO NORMAL, LIKE NOTHING EVER HAPPENED.
MEANWHILE, I'M STUCK RIDING HOME WITH NO DRY CLOTHES AND AN AUTOBOT WHOSE CAR MODE DOESN'T HAVE A HEATER!
YOU SHOWED A LOT OF COURAGE AND INGENUITY, SARI, AND HOPEFULLY YOU'LL STOP BACKFIRING SOON.
HELLO? IT'S CALLED SNEEZING?

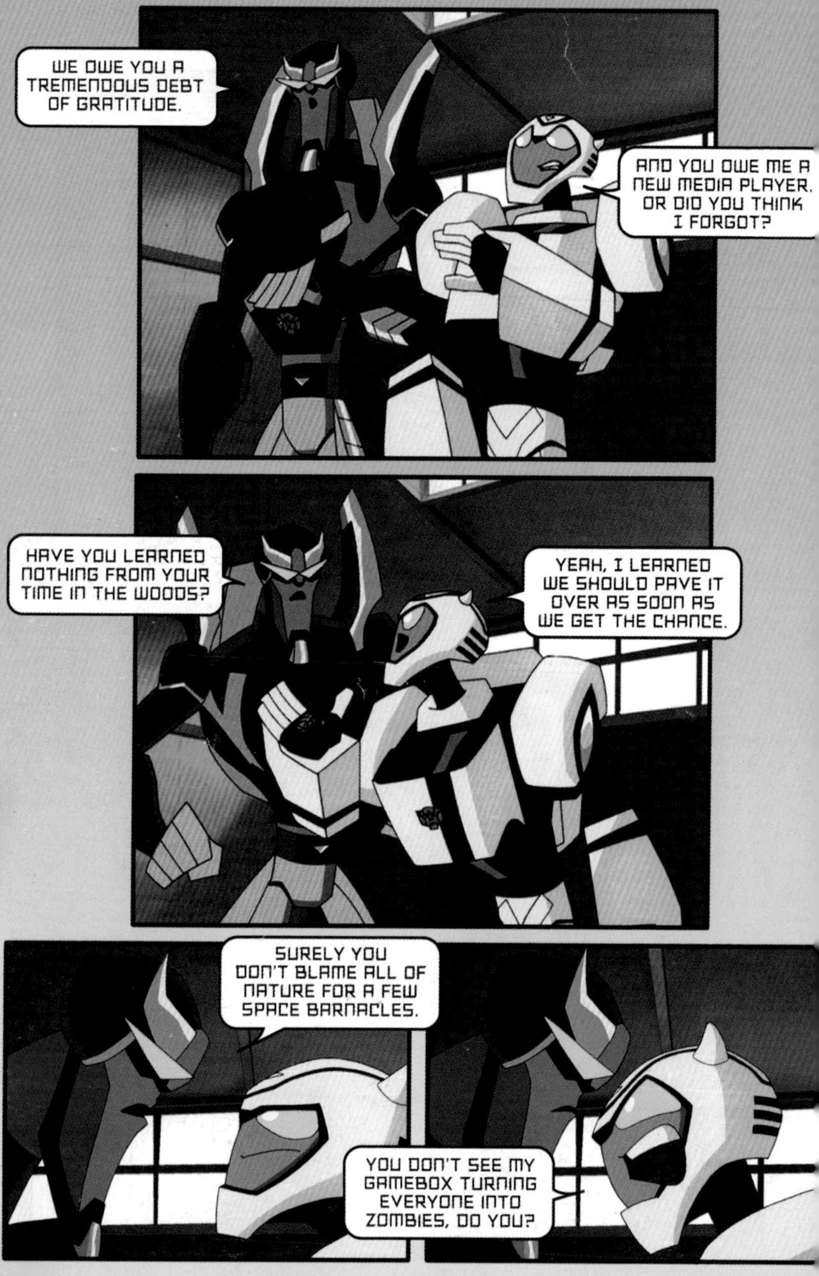
WE OWE YOU A TREMENDOUS DEBT OF GRATITUDE.
AND YOU OWE ME A NEW MEDIA PLAYER. OR DID YOU THINK I FORGOT?
HAVE YOU LEARNED NOTHING FROM YOUR TIME IN THE WOODS?
YEAH, I LEARNED WE SHOULD PAVE IT OVER AS SOON AS WE GET THE CHANCE.
SURELY YOU DON'T BLAME ALL OF NATURE FOR A FEW SPACE BARNACLES.
YOU DON'T SEE MY GAMEBOX TURNING EVERYONE INTO ZOMBIES, DO YOU?

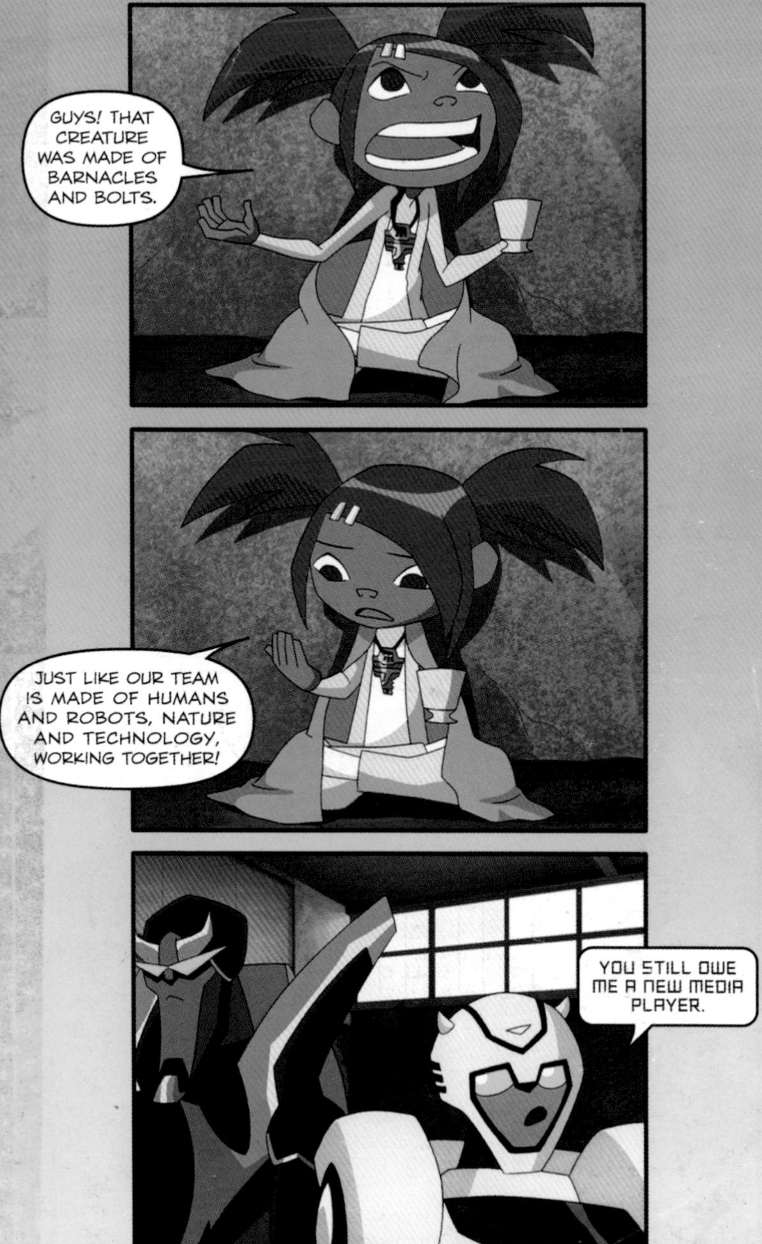
GUYS! THAT CREATURE WAS MADE OF BARNACLES AND BOLTS.
JUST LIKE OUR TEAM IS MADE OF HUMANS AND ROBOTS, NATURE AND TECHNOLOGY, WORKING TOGETHER!
YOU STILL OWE ME A NEW MEDIA PLAYER.

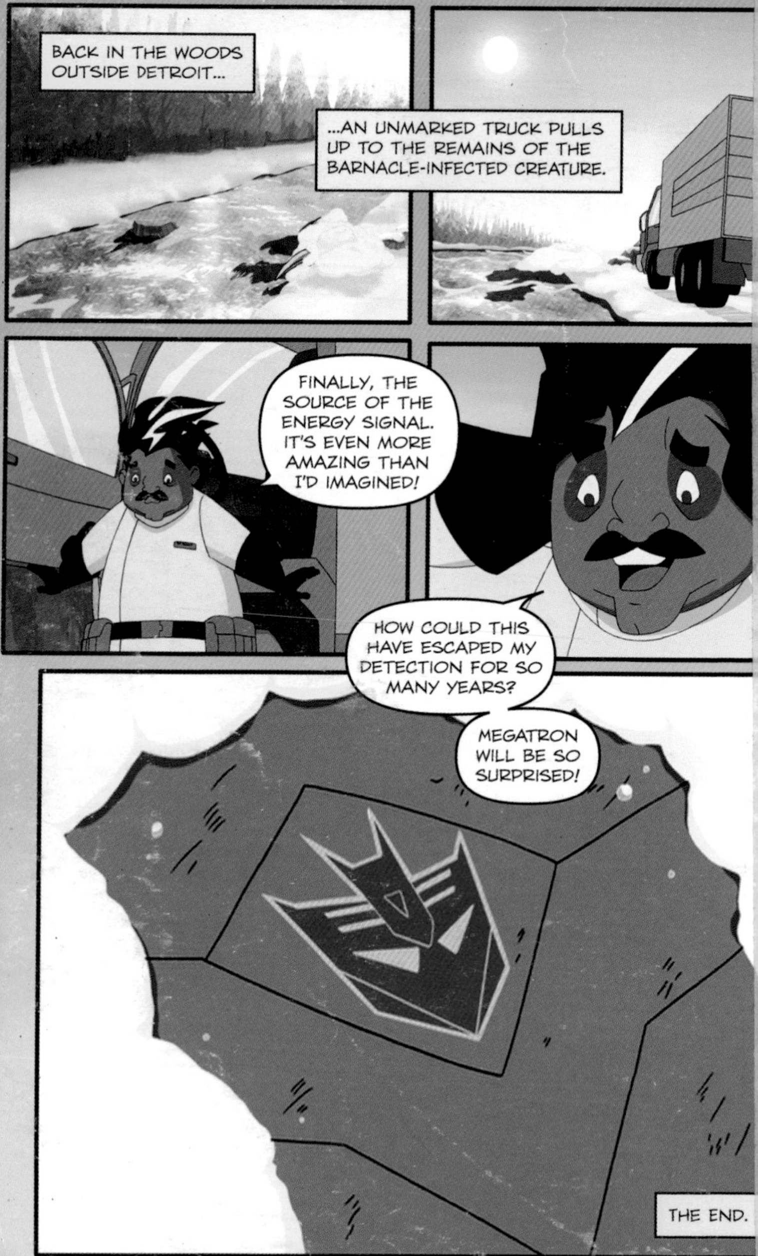
BACK IN THE WOODS OUTSIDE DETROIT...
...AN UNMARKED TRUCK PULLS UP TO THE REMAINS OF THE BARNACLE-INFECTED CREATURE.
FINALLY, THE SOURCE OF THE ENERGY SIGNAL. IT'S EVEN MORE AMAZING THAN I'D IMAGINED!
HOW COULD THIS HAVE ESCAPED MY DETECTION FOR SO MANY YEARS?
MEGATRON WILL BE SO SURPRISED!
THE END.